Tales frc

The Nigel Logan Stories #3
Dark Days of Judgment

Kirk S. Jockell

ISBN-13: 978-1546583738
ISBN-10: 1546583734

KIRK S. JOCKELL

The *Tales from Stool 17* series is a work of fiction. Names, characters, places, and incidents, except where indicated, are either products of the author's imagination or are used fictitiously. Any resemblance to actual events or locales or persons, living or dead, is strictly coincidental. Reproduction in whole or part of this publication without express written consent is strictly prohibited.

DEDICATION

This book is dedicated to author Randy Wayne White.

Randy Wayne White is one of my favorite authors, and I'm a huge fan of the Doc Ford series. I'm not ashamed to admit my groupie status and have attended a few book signings. I have never once heard him speak that he didn't encourage his attendees to write their own book. He would say, and I'll paraphrase here: *Your enthusiasm and interest in being here today means you are not just an active reader, you are also a writer. You just don't realize it yet. Each of you should write your own book.*

It only took hearing those words like three times, but I give them full credit for sparking the creation of Tales from Stool 17. RWW, if it weren't for you, all this crazy shit would still be bouncing around in my head. More importantly, if you hadn't motivated me to write, I may have never felt the humbling pride that comes with hearing, from a perfect stranger, the words, *I loved your book. When does the next one come out?* Thank you, good sir.

KIRK S. JOCKELL

Loving life on the Forgotten Coast,
Cruising the beach or out on a boat.
Yeah … I'm digging living in Gulf County, FLA.
St. Joe Beach, Cape San Blas, Money Bayou, and Indian Pass,
Ain't life great, on Highway 98.

Brian Bowen, *Ode to Port St. Joe*

ACKNOWLEDGEMENTS

Port St. Joe and The Forgotten Coast are real. Also real is the Leave No Trace ordinance that has been enacted to protect it. The basic idea behind it: Don't bring a bunch of shit to the beach and leave it out there all night. Leave it like you found it, every day. Returning for a third round of punishment is my good friend and guitar-toting troubadour, Brian Bowen. He can be caught playing at numerous locations all around the region, including Bowery Station in Apalachicola. Bowery Station, otherwise known as BS, is owned and operated by Matt and Lisa Gardi. BS is always full of fabulous folks, great music, cold beer, and yes … plenty of BS. And, of course, what would The Forgotten Coast be without tuning into Oyster Radio, WOYS 100.5 on your FM dial or via the TuneIn radio app on your smart device? While all the above are real, they are used fictitiously throughout these stories.

During my journey writing Stool 17, I couldn't have done it without the support of so many people. The kind words and encouragement I have received along the way have been so instrumental in moving and pushing me to complete this series. Hearing the words *When's the next book coming out* or *Hurry the hell up, dammit* is always music to my ears. Words cannot express the appreciation I have for each of you. Thanks to you all!

Special thanks go out to my editor, Jan Lee. She has been invaluable, not to mention incredibly patient, in helping me construct these books. She has helped me stay on the straight and narrow, and, more importantly, she has been a significant influence in helping me find my voice. Thank you, Jan.

To Joy Jockell, my bride, partner, and first reader, I couldn't have done any of this without you. Your markups of all my shitty first drafts are always humbling and a pleasure. Your love and encouragement has been nothing short of amazing. I can't thank you enough. Love you, forever and a day.

KIRK S. JOCKELL

PROLOGUE

It was an early Monday, and still dark outside when he came into the office. The detective bullpen was for the most part empty, just a few folks scattered here and there and the smell of fresh coffee. Most folks wouldn't start rolling in until sometime after the donuts arrived. He liked the quiet and wanted to take advantage of it before the room got too loud. It was set to be a big day. One that's been a long time coming and Detective Larry Anderson wanted to go over everything one last time. Not that he needed to. He's been through it a million times.

He poured a cup of black coffee and took it to his desk. He took a seat and leaned back in his chair. He put his feet up, crossing his ankles like he always does. He pressed his thumbs and fingertips together and rested his chin on his index fingers to think.

He thought about it a lot. He couldn't help himself. It was by design. Reminders were kept all around his cubical. A copy of the file was always close at hand, either somewhere on his desk or in a drawer, usually right up front so he couldn't miss it. The biggest reminder, though, was the large white case board that stood in front of the windows just a few feet away from his desk.

In the bureau, resources are tight. There are multiple, ongoing investigations at any one time, some more significant than others. Some warranted the use of a case board, others didn't. Anderson's case was old and on life support. After some time, his boss ordered him to pull the plug and clear the board. Anderson protested and lost. He took a picture of the board with his phone and placed everything in a box. Before noon of that day, the board was already being used for an auto theft investigation. Anderson left that day in a huff. The next morning Anderson was recreating his case board when his lieutenant showed up to work. "Anderson! Goddammit ... What did I tell you about that board?"

"My board, Lieutenant. Bought it myself. The other ones are over there," Anderson said pointing to the three well-used case boards on the other side of the room. "I'll keep this one over here, out of everyone's way." That was over two years ago.

His board displayed the relevant key points of the case file, but in a format easier to understand. Reader's Digest versions of all the notes were written within little black boxes scattered about the board. Depending on their relevance and importance, some boxes were connected by colored lines. Green lines meant a direct, indisputable connection. Red lines meant a highly-suspected connection. Blue and yellow lines indicated stages of the investigation still being developed: yellow for plausible theories, blue for hunches. But it was the green lines that had his attention.

He reached over and grabbed his coffee and took a sip. Then he slung his feet off the desk and got out of the chair. He stood there drinking more coffee before walking over to the board. Among all the boxes and connective lines were four photos arranged in the shape of a diamond. These four pictures served as the board's center-piece. He let his eyes follow the pictures and the lines that connected them.

At the bottom of the diamond was a picture of collected evidence, a Beretta 92 FS, a 9mm semi-automatic pistol. Up and to the right was a picture of Terrance "T-Daddy" Lundsford. Ballistics proved the connection between the gun and Lundsford. It was the weapon used to take his life. A green line connected the two.

Across the board and to the left of Lundsford was the third picture. It was of a beautiful young lady, a high school portrait. The girl was Grace Matthews. A green line connected Ms. Matthews and Lundsford. He was to stand trial for her beating and rape, but it never came about. The mishandling of cornerstone DNA evidence, along with other circumstances, gave the Virginia Beach District Attorney cause to drop the charges. Lundsford walked.

The father of Ms. Matthews is a Navy Captain. At the time of the beating and rape and the later murder of Lundsford, he served as the commanding officer and close friend of the man at the top of the board. Another green line connected Ms. Matthews to the last picture at the top of the diamond, Nigel Logan.

Anderson stared at Logan's picture and sipped his coffee. He actually liked the photo. It was an official navy portrait. He was in uniform, no smile, no frown, all business. His head was framed by the stars and stripes of the American flag. It was a very patriotic image.

A red line connected the images of Logan and Lundsford, and a vertical green line connected Logan with the pistol. The Beretta was registered to Logan. It was his weapon. The same weapon Logan had reported stolen only two weeks before Lundsford's untimely death. As Anderson looked at the gun, a familiar thought raced through his mind: *Stolen ... how convenient*.

He looked at the picture of Logan and said, "It's a different game now, Logan. A different game. We have a whole new set of players."

It was true, new players had come onto the field. One in particular, Virginia Beach District Attorney, Patrick James. With a stellar record as a prosecutor, he had served under his predecessor, Blair Westhoven. Upon learning of his advanced prostate cancer, Westhoven decided enough was enough. It was a diagnosis fit for retirement. After filling the seat for over thirteen years, he wanted to spend more time with family and fight the disease in private, outside the public eye. Who could blame him? A special election was held and James won in a landslide.

He never spoke of it publicly, but, as Westhoven surrendered his office, he had but one professional regret. The botched rape and battery case against Terrance Lundsford. It was the only real scar on his record. His team had screwed up. The victim, Grace Matthews, never saw the system deliver the justice she was due. Instead, she watched the system crumble and fail her. To Westhoven, that was unacceptable. He had lost other cases, but those were fought and argued in the courtroom. It's different when you know a son of a bitch is guilty and he gets primetime news coverage as he walks free. Yeah, if he could have a mulligan, that would be the one. Instead, Grace Matthews got her justice at the hands of a vigilante.

The vigilante, Nigel Logan; he thought about that failure from time to time, but to a much lesser degree. It had bothered him a great deal at first. The idea that the Grand Jury wouldn't hand down an indictment still boggled his mind. He had gotten indictments on less. In all his years of practicing law, he'd never seen a Grand Jury so willing to look the other way. While he didn't like their decision, he knew it had nothing to do with him or the members of his team. His team did good work. They did their job.

It took a while, but he came to terms with it. If the Grand Jury could look the other way, so could he. He was able to reconcile the matter in his mind, because he knew Lundsford raped and beat that poor girl. He had seen the DNA results, and the evidence was ironclad. Lundsford had to be punished.

With every fiber of his being, Westhoven also knew Logan killed Lundsford. He was sure of it and confident he could have proven his case. He would have gotten his guilty verdict, no doubt. But that didn't happen. Logan walked.

In a way, Westhoven felt he was done a favor. As wrong and unlawful as it was, Logan dished out a punishment to Lundsford that he couldn't deliver himself. Not that Lundsford's crimes would have warranted a death sentence … but … *It is what it is.* Like so many other people, Westhoven wasn't losing any sleep because Lundsford had departed the land of the living.

There was something else Westhoven felt comfortable with. Logan may be capable of violence, but he wasn't a threat to peaceful society. He had studied Logan's naval record. He interviewed many of his peers and the officers that he served under. In the end, he determined Nigel Logan to be, at the center of his being, a good man.

Had he been given the opportunity to try Logan, he wouldn't have passed it up. He would have been trying the crime, not the man. Had he been awarded a guilty verdict, he would have taken it, but Logan's sentence wouldn't have made the world any safer. If anything, perhaps a tad more dangerous. Westhoven's pragmatism told him *Like it or not, it was guys like Logan that helped keep the world in check.* He would never admit it, but, with Lundsford dead, he was able to sleep at night. Justice had been delivered and served for Grace Matthews. And for that reason, he was able to let it go.

For Detective Larry Anderson, there was no letting go. Which is why he maintained his own personal case board in the bureau and worked the case in his spare time. He was determined, and, with Westhoven out of the picture and Patrick James sitting as the new DA, he felt good about his chances to get another shot at Logan. He would soon find out. He and his lieutenant had a meeting scheduled for later that morning. It was time to discuss knocking some dust off that old file.

Nine hundred miles away, Red and Nigel were sitting on the tailgate of Nigel's truck. It was going to be a perfect morning. The sun was creeping toward the horizon, ready to start another gorgeous day. The colors of dawn cast an orange glow about the beach and water. Slight wave action brought an occasional rogue breaker crashing down on the sand. They sat in silence while watching for mullet out on the horn of Cape San Blas, their cast nets at the ready in the bed of the truck.

Red broke the quiet and got Nigel's attention, "I want to ask you something."

They looked at each other and Red said, "You know … I don't mean to pry, but…"

"But … you're going to anyway?"

"Yes ... how long's it been since you last spoke to Candice?"

Nigel looked back toward the water and spoke to the surf. "Three weeks."

"That's quite a long time."

Nigel looked at his friend and said, "A fucking eternity."

"Why don't you call her? She may be scared."

"I want to. I'm giving her time and space. She knows where to find me. And besides, she has no reason to be scared of me. She knows that."

"But what if she is? You know, scared. Maybe not of you, but of the whole situation."

Nigel said nothing.

"What if you are both scared to call the other and never do? Think about that for a minute."

"Listen. That's how we left things, okay? If she was still interested, she could call me. If she didn't, I would understand."

Red said, "You mean … that's how *you* left things."

Nigel said nothing and Red changed the subject.

"It's almost time," said Red. He dug into the cooler and dug out a couple of bottles of Coors Light. He handed one to Nigel and used the other to point to the horizon. "Wait now."

It seemed to boil at that spot where the water meets the sky. It grew more and more intense. As the top edge of the sun broke the plane of the horizon, Red and Nigel twisted the tops off their beers. They tossed the caps into the bed of the truck and clanked the bottles together. Together they said, "To a new day!" They drank deep and long until the cold and the carbonation forced them to come up for air. "Ahhhh! That was good," said Nigel.

Red nodded his head in agreement and pointed his bottle toward the water. He was catching his breath when he said, "Swirls. There!" They both watched, and sure enough, there was activity just about fifteen or twenty feet beyond the gentle breakers. Then a lazy mullet broke the surface and flopped on its side. "Mullet! Let's go!"

They both jumped off the tailgate and started gathering up their nets.

Nigel said, "You want to make a little wager?"

"Like what?"

"Let's say that whoever catches the most gets out of cleaning?"

"Sounds like a fool's bet. You better get your knife ready."

Under his breath, Nigel mumbled, "Yeah, right."

Red was about to head out toward the water when he stopped and said, "Hey, Nigel. Listen. What I was talking about earlier. I just want to say…"

Nigel interrupted, "Don't worry about it, Red. You don't have to apologize. Everything will work out."

"Oh," Red said, "I wasn't going to apologize. I was just going to say, 'Don't be a stupid asshole,' that's all." And he tore off toward the water. "Come on!"

Instead of staying seated behind his desk when Detective Larry Anderson and his lieutenant entered his office, Patrick James got out of his chair, walked around to the front of his desk, and stood. After handshakes and good mornings, DA James opened his palms and directed the two detectives to the chairs in front of his desk. "Please … please, take a seat."

They did, and the DA leaned back on the front of his desk crossing his ankles and his arms across his chest. "So," he started, "give me the pleasure of one guess to figure out what this is all about."

Detective Anderson looked at his boss and asked, "Did you tell him?"

"Nope," his boss said with a half-grin. "This is all on you, Detective Anderson."

"Detective, excuse my flippant comments. I know you want to discuss something serious; otherwise you wouldn't be here. It is the Terrance Lundsford case, correct?"

Anderson looked again at his boss who shrugged his shoulders at the detective's stare. *I don't know. Don't look at me.*

"Listen, Detective Anderson. It is no secret that you have taken this case personally. It is important to you. You feel all your good work has had no closure. That it all slipped away without being taken seriously."

The DA paused, held his gaze on the detective and continued, "Wouldn't you say that is a fair assessment?"

"I just want justice to be served," said Detective Anderson.

"Justice for who?"

Detective Anderson started to say something but paused. He wasn't expecting that question to be coming from the mouth of the DA

The detective was about to answer, but the DA interjected, "Because, you see ... I get the sneaky suspicion that you have possibly transferred the injustice from Lundsford to yourself. That, in the back of your mind, it is you that has suffered a great injustice and not necessarily Lundsford."

His boss grabbed his arm when Anderson stood, but he jerked away. The DA never flinched and stood his ground. "Listen," Anderson started, "I worked hard, damn hard on that case. And yes, I'm man enough to admit, I took the fact that the case went nowhere as a huge and personal *Fuck You*. But you need to be clear on one fact."

The DA said nothing. He was listening; giving the detective the floor.

"I didn't work hard on that case because *I* wanted a conviction. *I* worked hard because a man had been killed, murdered. And despite however unsavory Terrance 'T-Daddy' Lundsford was to the community, his murder needed solving."

When Anderson stopped talking, he was mad and out of breath. Anderson maintained his own stare at the district attorney. There was awkward silence in the room. After a few seconds, the lieutenant stood and said, "Perhaps we should go, sir. Sorry to disturb and waste your time." He looked at Anderson and said, "Let's go detective."

"No. Not at all," the DA replied. "Please ... take your seats again."

The DA got to his feet and walked around the desk to his chair. He was about to take his own seat when he noticed the two were still standing. He smiled and said, "Please. I mean it. Sit."

Everyone did.

The DA shuffled through a few folders and stopped on the one with a picture of Nigel Logan paper-clipped to the outside. He looked at the picture for a second or two then opened the folder and asked, "So ... where are we?"

Anderson went to great length to tell the DA everything he knew about the case and why they should proceed in obtaining another Grand Jury decision.

Attorney General James listened, and when Anderson was done, said, "So, in the years you have been keeping the burners warm on this case, you really don't have anything new? Is that what you are telling me?"

The detective looked over at his lieutenant in search of a good answer. He didn't find one. All he got was a raised eyebrow. He turned back to the DA. "That is correct, sir. My workload. I have had other cases, and to be honest, I didn't want to waste department dollars and time on something that might not go anywhere."

The DA looked at Anderson and nodded his head. With a half-grin, he looked at the detective's boss and said, "And he's thrifty, too."

Anderson's boss said nothing.

Anderson leaned forward and asked, "So, what can we do? You agreed to see us, so you have to have some interest in the case."

The DA took a pencil from a coffee cup that was loaded with pens and pencils. He held it tight and upright between his fingers. He brought the eraser down and tapped it on his desk calendar three or four time until his forefinger and thumb reached the desk. Then he flipped the pencil over and did it again, this time tapping the point of the lead. He did this several times as he thought.

Without saying a word to each other, both detectives observed the condition of his desk calendar and determined this behavior to be an old habit. They also noticed that the DA only tapped the pencil within the square that indicated that day of the week. The future days on the calendar were clean while most past days were littered with dots of lead and small pieces of eraser.

The DA jabbed the pencil back into his cup and said, "Yes, I do have interest, but not without something new to bring to the table."

"But sir," interjected Anderson, "we've gotten indictments on less."

"True. But I don't want this office to be embarrassed again, detective."

Anderson found himself speechless. He took the comment as a personal stab, as if it were his shoddy work that brought disgrace to the office. It wasn't meant that way.

The DA leaned over his desk and said, "Turn up the heat, detective. Find something. Bring me something new."

The DA turned to his boss and said, "Turn him loose. Give him the time and resources to work this case."

"Yes, sir."

The detective sat up a bit straighter in his chair. Then he and his boss stood. The detective extended his hand and the DA took it. They shook and Anderson said, "Thank you, sir."

As they were walking to the door, the DA had some parting advice. "And I would try to keep the investigation close to the chest. Try not to garner too much attention. It seems Logan's popularity and Lundsford's lack thereof may have caused the media to favor Logan. I'm sure that played to his advantage."

The two nodded, then slipped out the door.

CALL ME LAMAR

Nigel doesn't believe in traditional luck, not in most cases. He is amazed, though, to see so many people, especially those that can least afford it, place so much faith in the idea that Lady Luck is just one paycheck away. For the ignorant, the idea that one can obtain gross amounts of wealth by scratching a ticket or by playing a few numbers is a dream come true: one dollar at a time. The state lotteries are magical at marketing to the simple-minded.

Nigel is a *make your own luck* kind of guy, and you can't make your luck from a roll of tickets or playing the nightly drawings. There is no strategy when it comes to winning the lotto, even though there are some who would like you to think otherwise. There are little booklets for sale revealing the hottest numbers, the ones that come up most. They are utter nonsense at a price and printed for suckers that don't understand the math and statistics behind a game of lotto. *Bless their hearts*.

The only actual strategy to increase one's chances of winning is to buy multiple tickets for each drawing. But this is a fool's tactic. Buyers find some psychological comfort in buying $20.00 or more at a time (some buy much more), over just a single $1.00 ticket. Like it places them in a better position to reap the benefits of a multimillion-dollar windfall. It really doesn't, not in a practical sense anyway.

If you take into consideration the overwhelming odds against each ticket, each additional ticket purchased doesn't do much of anything to increase your actual chances of winning it big. Take the simple Florida Lotto game for example. A player selects six numbers between one and fifty-three. All you have to do is match all six numbers in the random drawing to take home the millions. The problem is the odds of winning: 1 in 22,957,480. And those odds are great if you stack them up against the odds of the Powerball game: 1 in 258,890,850. So, buying extra tickets doesn't help much, but it does, without fail, guarantee that you'll piss away a bunch of money. Week after week after week.

Playing and winning at Texas Hold 'em is another pure luck game, where Nigel is concerned. He isn't a student of the game like everyone else around the table. He hasn't read all the books or watched all the videos. He hasn't taken the time to learn how to *make his luck*. Hell, Nigel knows for a fact that Joe Crow has at least ten books and an entire DVD collection covering the subject. These guys are serious about their poker. Nigel, not so much. He shows up for the food, the friends, and the camaraderie. He doesn't mind and fully expects he'll be leaving some money on the table. He doesn't give a shit, and the other guys love him for it.

Tonight's game was different for some reason. He could do no wrong. He was winning everything without even trying. Lady Luck was showing him some serious love and dealing some red-hot cards. It was pure poker porn.

During one game the pot had grown into a hell of a pile. Most everyone looked quite confident about their hands as they stayed in and placed their bets. Nigel's hand was only decent, but had potential. He stayed in anyway. With all the bets in, Joe placed the last card up on the table. Nigel's two pair turned into a full house. The room erupted into sighs as Nigel smiled, racked his winnings, and started piling up chips.

Red, Nigel's partner in mischief and shenanigans, was at the table. He said, "Son of a bitch, Nigel. With how you're playing, you could win without looking at your cards."

"Ha!" Nigel said with much excitement. "This winning stuff feels pretty good. I can see why you guys get so excited."

"You should try it," said the guy next to Nigel.

It was Sheriff Mark Watts. He often drops in, usually just to eat and watch, but sometimes he can't resist temptation and will grab a seat at the table. And he never plays in uniform; that wouldn't look good.

In general, a gambling house in Florida is illegal. However, there is reasonable flexibility built into the statutes to allow for friendly, penny-ante games. So, while sitting at the table may be legal, Sheriff Watts would never bring discredit to his position by playing in uniform. Nigel respected him for that.

Legal or not, poker is a cardinal sin in the minds of many. If the ladies at church ever caught word of Sheriff Watts playing poker, he could kiss the next election goodbye. Some things cannot be tolerated, even though they would always welcome him to play a card or two of Bingo on Tuesday nights.

At the table, he felt safe. He knew everyone pretty well, and he trusted nobody would ever say anything, especially Pastor Eddie who sat next to Red.

"Try what?" asked Nigel.

"Play a hand without looking at your cards," said Sheriff Watts. "Let's see just how lucky you are."

"Sure," said Nigel. "What the hell?" Nigel looked up and saw Pastor Eddie giving him the eye. "Sorry, 'bout that, Padre."

"It is quite all right, son," he said with a thin, straight smile as he shuffled the cards. It was his turn to deal. "We all have our weaknesses and misgivings."

"Really? What are yours?"

"Well ... there are many. I'm a sinner, just like everyone else at the table..."

Pouring from his handle of Jim Beam, Red piped up and said, "Hey, now! Come on, Eddie. Easy, boy. Don't toss me in your basket of spiritual transgressors."

"I'm sorry, Red," said Pastor Eddie in his calm Sunday morning tone. "Even someone as angelic as you isn't pure in thought and action."

Red said nothing but lifted the bottle of bourbon to offer the pastor a drink.

"Just a bit, please. Thank you. As I was saying, Nigel, every man has his weaknesses. I, for one...," He paused to think for a moment before looking Nigel in the eye to say, "Tonight, when I get home, I will ask for forgiveness because I'm praying like hell you will lose this next hand."

"Deal 'em, padre."

Pastor Eddie looked at Nigel. He licked his thumb and went back to shuffling. There were five at the table: Pastor Eddie, Joe Crow, Nigel, Sheriff Watts, and Red. The small and big blind bets went to Joe and Nigel. With the bets on the table, Nigel said, "Let's do this."

The pastor dealt the hole cards and everyone took a glance at their cards. Nigel didn't, but he slid them off the table and held them face down in the palm of his hand. He kept his eye closed as he suspended the two cards in the air.

Joe looked over at Nigel and asked, "What the hell are you doing?"

Nigel relied, "Shhh. Give me a sec."

Red said, "Oh shit, boys. We may be in trouble."

"What makes you say that, Red?" asked Sheriff Watts.

"He's weighing the cards in his hand," said Red.

Nigel said, "Shush!"

"Don't shush me … he knows the amount of ink and the density of the colors needed to make each card. They vary. A king weighs more than an ace, and so on. He's figuring out which combination of cards he might have in the hole."

"That's bullshit," said the sheriff. "Nigel, quit the crap and let's get going."

Nigel gave the sheriff a slight grin and placed the cards down on the table and said, "Start your betting."

The bets were called all around the table until Joe Crow decided to raise the stakes by doubling the high-blind bet. Everyone else took another look at their cards, a natural thing to do when someone raises. Nigel put his palm on top of his cards covering them. The betting continued and everyone called.

Pastor Eddie didn't hesitate and dealt the Flop, three cards up: an ace of diamonds, a seven of clubs, and a five of diamonds. Red put on a pair of sunglasses and went stone-faced. Everyone except Nigel looked at their cards. Joe Crow started the betting by doubling the high-blind bet again. Everyone paid up to see another card and Pastor Eddie mumbled some scripture as he dealt the Turn, a seven of hearts. The betting started again and Joe didn't hesitate, doubling up on the high-blind bet again. Nigel cut him a look and called his bet. Sheriff Watts called and Red took his time to think and look at his cards. He was acting all Vegas-like, cool as a cucumber. Nigel chuckled under his breath and started to hum the tune from Jeopardy. Red said, "I'll see your bet Joe," as he tossed his chips in the pot. Then he grabbed another set of chips, "…and raise you another."

Joe said, "You're bluffing, Red."

The betting continued around the table and everyone called until it came around to Sheriff Watts. He looked at his cards and he looked at the top of Nigel's cards. He took another quick peek at his own then pushed his cards forward and said, "I'm not going there. I'm out."

Pastor Eddie said, "Is everybody ready?"

Nigel said, "Cry me a river, Padre."

The last card was placed on the table and eyebrows of both curiosity and disappointment were raised, but it was difficult to distinguish between the two. It was a three of diamonds. Joe stayed in, but checked his bet. Nigel looked over at him and said, "Where's all that earlier enthusiasm, Joe?"

Joe returned a thin smile and shrugged his shoulders.

Nigel said, "Okay. I'll start things off. He tossed in the high-blind bet. Red called. Pastor Eddie called. Joe called and raised another double-blind. Nigel looked at the top of his cards. *What's under there?* Then he looked at his stack of chips. He was having a great night. It was so great, in fact, that this hand didn't matter. He was having a blast. He said, "I'll see your raise and double that."

With Sheriff Watts out of the game, Red had a decision to make. He studied his hole cards then the cards face up and staring him in the face. He looked over at Nigel and found him weighing his cards again, eyes closed, head tilted back, a sheepish, but confident smile on his face. Red studied his buddy a moment or two more and said, "Ah, hell no!" He pushed his hole cards away. "No way. I'm out. I know that look."

Pastor Eddie looked at Nigel and said, "I guess I'm gonna have to pay to see those cards, huh?"

Nigel said nothing. He was still feeling his cards in the palm of his hands.

"I'll take that as a yes. I'm in. Call."

Joe called Nigel's raise and said, "Okay, let's see 'em."

Nigel said, "Show me yours and I'll show you mine."

Pastor Eddie flipped his hole cards and said, "Three Aces."

Joe gave a smile, then he turned his cards over: a four of hearts and a six of spades. "It's a straight, boys."

Sheriff Watts said, "Nice."

Then everyone looked at Nigel. Pastor Eddie said, "Well … whatcha got?"

Nigel flipped over the first card, a ten of diamonds.

Red said, "Uh, Oh!"

Nigel flipped his other card and Red sang out, "Spaghettios!"

It was the King of Diamonds, a neat little flush. Everyone laughed out loud as Joe Crow's heart sank.

As the group continued to laugh and chortle in disbelief, the cell phone of Sheriff Watts vibrated in his pocket. He answered it at the table and nobody paid any attention to the one-sided conversation. "Hey, Lamar." It was Franklin County Sheriff Lamar Williamson. "That's okay. It's probably a good thing. I'm losing my ass. How is the wife?" ... "Good, good. So, what can I do you for?" ... "Uh huh, I remember." ... "Really?" As Sheriff Watts held the phone to his ear, his deportment shifted. He went from poker player to an officer of the law. He listened with a calm intensity. Then he turned his head and eyes toward Nigel who was still laughing and stacking his chips. "As a matter of fact, I do. I'm quite familiar. Hold on a sec."

Sheriff Watts put his hand over the receiver and pushed back from the table. "Guys, I need to take this outside. I've had enough for one night, fellas. It's been fun." He held up the phone and said, "Department business."

"I'm not far behind you," said Joe Crow. "I can't stand the idea of taking another beating."

Red threw a hand in the air and waved without looking.

Pastor Eddie said, "See you Sunday morning, Mark. Don't be late."

Right before he got to the door Nigel said, "Come on, Sheriff. Don't go. I'm on a roll. My luckiest night ever."

The sheriff looked at Nigel and thought *It looks like your luck is about to run out.* Then he stepped out into the dark.

Nigel was driving home from the game. It was late, and he was happy. Every now and then, he would pat his left breast pocket. It contained his winnings for the night, a nice, double-folded stack of cash. He hadn't even counted it yet and probably wouldn't. He laughed at himself, because he knew it was pure luck. There was no way in hell he would ever repeat a night like that. Without question, the money he won would find its way back into the pockets of future players. Losing at poker was what he did best, and he didn't care.

As he turned onto his street, his headlights lit up a vehicle parked in his yard. Nigel slowed to inspect. It was an unmarked squad car. Nigel crept closer. He could see the bar of blue lights hidden behind the rear window and the collection of special purpose antennas and cameras not found on production cars.

When he pulled into his drive, the driver's door of the squad car opened. It was Sheriff Watts. He got out and leaned up against the front fender of his car.

Nigel stopped and put the truck in park. He sat still there for a few beats and watched the sheriff through his rearview mirror. He was standing there, waiting next to his vehicle. Nigel could tell by his posture and the hour of the visit, this wasn't a social call. Nigel swallowed and got out of the truck.

Neither one of them said a word as Nigel leaned up against the fender to join the sheriff. They both stared ahead with their arms crossed. After a few moments, Sheriff Watts asked, "So, is there anything you need to tell me, Nigel?"

Nigel said nothing.

Sheriff Watts continued, "I got a call tonight. The one I took at the table. It was from my good friend Lamar Williamson. He's the sheriff of Franklin County..." Sheriff Watts paused to see if Nigel would volunteer anything.

Nigel stood quiet.

"Sheriff Williamson is investigating a rather bizarre situation that occurred in Tate's Hell. An abandoned vehicle was found and a search of the area discovered a handgun and some other disturbing things."

Sheriff Watts didn't want to say too much, so he didn't mention the various body parts that had been found scattered about the surrounding woods. They both stood there in the dark: quiet and thinking. The sheriff's brain raced in one direction, while Nigel's flew in another.

"It seems Lamar is having a hard time pulling all the pieces together. He's kind of stumped and feels like you might be able to help fill in some of the blanks." He let that cook in Nigel's mind before saying, "Nigel, I like you. You seem like a stand-up kind of guy. So ... I'll ask you again. Is there anything you need to tell me?"

Nigel stood up, faced the sheriff and asked, "Do I need a lawyer?"

Sheriff Watts thought about it a bit and said, "I guess that all depends. You probably will when you speak with Sheriff Williamson, but not tonight. It's late and I just want to chat about it."

Nigel said, "Come inside. I need a drink."

Nigel held up the bottle of Four Roses Single Barrel and said, "Sheriff?"

Sitting on the couch, he threw up a hand and said, "No thanks. I can't."

Nigel said, "Bullshit. I hate to drink alone and a little snort isn't going to kill you. And besides, we're just chatting, right? It's not like this is an official visit."

"Okay. Just a little."

Nigel pulled down a jigger and two old-fashioned glasses from the cupboard. He poured a full shot glass and a splash for the sheriff and a four-finger long pour for himself.

Nigel handed him his whiskey and took a seat, saying, "So ... I guess it's safe to assume that, if they had enough, there would already be a warrant for my arrest?"

"Right now, they just want to talk to you. You are currently just a person of interest."

Nigel took a deep sip and said, "Yeah, I already know how that feels."

The sheriff picked up his own shot glass and before taking a small sip said, "Uh huh. I was shocked to learn that myself. I wouldn't have suspected."

Nigel wasn't sure how much the sheriff knew, but it was obvious. He knew enough about Virginia and Nigel's difficulties with the Terrance Lundsford murder. If he didn't know everything, it wouldn't be long before did.

Sheriff Watts pulled a folded picture out of his shirt pocket and spread it out on the coffee table. The picture showed an old, purple Buick 225. The driver's side door was open, as was the trunk. "The vehicle is registered to a James V. Waters. Does that name mean anything to you?"

Nigel was shaking his head no as he studied the picture. He concentrated mostly on the big trunk where he had been stowed for the ride. Till now, he had no idea what kind of car had taken him to Tate's Hell. It had been so dark, and it could have been any trunk of any big vehicle as far as Nigel knew. But as he stared at the picture, his brow began to furrow. "Wait a minute," said Nigel. "I remember seeing that car. It was behind me in traffic. It must have been following me that day." He looked up and continued, "...to the marina."

"So, you admit to being there?"

"Yeah. But it wasn't by my choice. They took me out there in the fucking trunk."

Sheriff Watts threw back the rest of his bourbon. He set the glass down and said, "Damn, you got good whiskey."

Nigel said nothing.

The sheriff stood and said, "That's enough for now. It's late. I'll let Lamar know that you'll speak with him about this tomorrow. Does that sound alright?"

Nigel nodded his head.

"Meet us at the county building. Let's say, around eleven. We can grab an empty room at the clerk's office. Sound okay?"

Again, Nigel nodded his head and took another drink.

As Sheriff Watts started to leave, he said, "Keep your seat. I can show myself out. Thanks for the drink, and you may want to go ahead and line up an attorney."

"Thanks, but I won't need one."

Sheriff Watts stopped and turned around. "And why is that?"

"Because, I didn't do anything wrong."

The sheriff headed for the door and said, "I hope not. I like you a lot, Nigel Logan."

A few minutes later he heard the swing and slam of the pet door. He looked up to find Tom, his cat, sitting and staring at him. "Don't look at me like that, dammit." Tom ran and jumped into his lap.

Nigel arrived fifteen minutes early and waited in his truck. It was quiet in the cab. It was a good thinking-quiet. He had done a lot of that since waking from his three-and-a-half-hour sleep.

The events of that day in Tate's Hell ran through his mind. He had to sort through what he should disclose and the details he should exclude. He decided to go through the events one last time. He closed his eyes and thought. First the ambush, then the sight of Tom unconscious with blood oozing from his nose and ears. Then everything went black and he woke up in the trunk of a car, bound by duct tape. He remembered the pain from the beating he took, how his head throbbed with every heartbeat.

Nigel thought about the several stops, the ones he can remember anyway. Many of the details were still so fuzzy. He had taken quite the beating. Then the quiet and his train of thought came to an abrupt end. His thoughts and memory were replaced by the signature guitar riffs of Deep Purple's *Smoke on the Water*. He opened his eyes and turned his head toward the music. It was Red, his Ford Exploder pulled alongside. Red sat in the car and let the song finish. Before Red shut down the SUV, Nigel heard the voice of Oyster Radio's Michael Allen say, "Now, let's take a look at your weather." Red joined Nigel in his truck.

Red slammed the truck door and said, "Morning, buddy."

"Just *Morning*, not even a *Good Morning*, Red?"

"Well," Red said, "given the circumstances, I figured I'd let you fill in the blank there."

"Thanks! It certainly is morning. You got that part right."

"Are you ready?"

Nigel gave the question brief consideration and said, "Yeah. Come on. Let's get this over with."

They approached the security checkpoint. Sheriff Watts was waiting for them on the other side. They emptied their pockets to go through the metal detector. Nigel walked straight through and got the green light. Red was still taking off his belt.

Sheriff Watts stepped up and shook his hand. "Good morning, Nigel."

"Good morning, Sheriff."

Then the sheriff said, nodding toward Red, "I thought I said it would be a good idea to bring a lawyer? Why's he here?"

"And I told you I didn't need one. It was Red that drove out to Tate's Hell and picked me up. I figured Sheriff Williamson might..."

Sheriff Watts and Nigel were interrupted as Red walked through the gate and was greeted by red lights and alarms. A young deputy taking his duties very seriously, especially with his boss looking on, stepped forward and asked, "Is everything out of your pockets?"

Red did a quick pat down and said, "Yeah. It seems so."

The deputy took out his metal detecting wand and said, "Spread your arms and legs out."

Red did as he was told and the deputy started at the legs and moved the wand around. Nothing there. Then he started at his wrists and checked his arms. As the deputy checked his chest, the wand

25

screeched a warning. The deputy was able to isolate an area around Red's left breast pocket moving the wand back and forth. The deputy stepped back and said, "What do we have here?"

"An old battle injury," said Red. "A bullet lodged next to my heart, too risky to operate. Got it during the Korean War."

Nigel said, "Red, you would have been what? Like nine or ten during the Korean War."

Red looked at the deputy and said, "Okay, maybe it was Vietnam."

"Red! Would you please quit screwing around?" Nigel looked at Sheriff Watts and said, "Maybe bringing him wasn't such a good idea."

The sheriff answered with a grin and raised eyebrows.

Once Red removed the quarter from his pocket, they were able to proceed.

Sheriff Watts led them into a conference room with a large table. A man in uniform stood and Nigel went directly to him with an outstretch hand, "Sheriff Williamson, I presume?"

The sheriff reached out and nodded as they shook hands. "And I assume you are Mr. Logan?"

"That would be correct. Please, call me Nigel."

Nigel and Sheriff Williamson were the only ones in need of introductions. Since Red runs a D.U.I. school in Port St. Joe, he already knew all the other players in the room.

Williamson looked at Red and acknowledged him saying, "I wasn't expecting to see you here this morning."

Watts injected, "According to Nigel, it seems Red is mildly involved."

"Involved," Nigel said, "is too strong a word. Red isn't involved at all. I called him first chance I got. He merely came and picked me up off the side of the road."

Sheriff Williamson said, "Well, let's not get ahead of ourselves. Nigel, what do you say we both grab a chair and talk." Nigel took a seat directly across from him. Williamson looked at Watts and said, "Sheriff, would you take Red in another room and gather his statement?"

Red and Sheriff Watts left and shut the door.

In the beginning, there was some awkward silence, then Sheriff Williamson started things by saying, "Well ... thank you for agreeing to meet with me today. This entire investigation has been quite disturbing. I'm hoping you can fill in some of the gaps."

"I'm curious. How did you find me?"

Sheriff Williamson thought about it for a few seconds and said, "DNA. We found your DNA in the vehicle. Ran it through the database and found a match."

"I'm still curious. DNA from what?"

The sheriff didn't say anything.

"Come on," Nigel insisted with a slight sound of aggravation in his voice. "I'm here, ain't I? You want me to fill in a few holes? Fill in a few of mine."

"Hairs," the sheriff said. "Hairs in the trunk. We found loose samples scattered about plus matching samples attached to a few wads of duct tape."

"So, you figured someone was in the trunk, right?"

"It seemed a logical assumption."

"Well," Nigel said, sarcasm pouring from his lips. "You can drop the assumption. It was me."

"Tell me about it."

"In a minute. One more thing first." Nigel saw some impatience seep through the sheriff's expressions, so he backpedaled a little. "I'm sorry, Sheriff. You're just trying to do your job. I just want to know how you knew I was in Port St. Joe. But you don't have to answer that. We both know how you found me."

"Nigel, I can't help you if you don't help me. I need to know what happened and it seems you are the only one that has any answers."

"Sheriff Williamson ... don't take this the wrong way, but I don't need your help."

They stared across the table at each other in silence. It was a moment of understanding and appreciation for each other, both sides only wanting the truth. After a few moments, Sheriff Williamson put his pen down and said, "Fair enough. No offense taken. Just do me a favor and help me."

It was small, but a thin smile stretched across Nigel's face for the first time, and he said, "I'll try, but much of it is still pretty foggy."

The sheriff said nothing.

"It was early evening. I arrived home after sailing. That's when this big guy ambushed me. I never had a chance."

"What day was this?"

Nigel thought for a few moments, shaking his head. Then a light came on. He reached for his wallet and opened it. He shuffled through several receipts until he found the one was looking for. He studied it and slapped it on the table and said, "It was the seventh. The seventh of August. I had lunch with a friend. This is the receipt where I bought barbecue."

Sheriff Williamson read the receipt and took notes. He looked at Nigel and said, "Paul Gant. That's damn good barbecue."

They both nodded in agreement.

"So, do you know who ambushed you?"

"I don't know. Never seen them before. He hit me so hard the first time that I could never recover to defend myself. He just kept coming after me. He pounded my head into the floor until I was out. I thought I was dead for sure."

The memory of that moment brought back the clear image of his cat motionless on the floor. He lowered his eyes to look at the table. His hatred for those two returned, and he was doing his best to contain his anger. But it wasn't enough.

"I see it upsets you to think about," said the sheriff.

Nigel looked up and glared into the sheriff's eyes and replied, "The sons of bitches tried to kill me. I think I have the right to be upset."

The sheriff nodded and waited with patience, giving Nigel time to collect himself. After a while, he coaxed. "What do you remember next?"

"Waking up in the trunk of a car, hot, sweating, and bouncing down the road. They had bound my wrists behind my back and bound my ankles. They used duct tape. My head ached so bad, it hurt to think." He stopped to collect more thoughts and continued genuinely, "There isn't much I remember about the ride. I was concentrating on getting out."

"Do you remember any stops?"

"I remember one." His eyes opened wider and he said, "No ... it was two. Two stops along the way."

"I should have asked this earlier, but do you remember how many were in the car?"

"There were only two that I saw once I got free." Then he paused for a minute and said, "But ... I half expected three."

"Why three?" asked the sheriff.

"Because on one of those stops I remember hearing a lot of discussion outside the car. I tried to listen, but couldn't make out much. Then, when they got back in the car, I heard and felt three doors slam."

Williamson finished up some notes and said, "Let's take a break. Can I get you anything? Coffee? Water?"

"Coffee sounds good."

Sheriff Watts was talking to Red in the hall when they noticed Williamson come out of the room. Watts excused himself to join him. When he walked up, Williamson was already on the phone with someone.

"Yes ... that's what I said. Every piece of surveillance video available. Maybe we'll get lucky."

"How's it going in there, Lamar?" asked Watts.

"I don't know, Mark. I just ordered my guys to collect any and all security video along Highway 98 from local businesses. That might tell us something." Pointing down the hall with his head, he said, "How's it going with Red?"

"Ah, nothing much there. He's telling it pretty straight. Say's Nigel called him up in the middle of the night and needed a ride. Red found him walking on the side of the road. Says Nigel was a mess, looked like hell. He just got in the car and didn't say anything the whole way home."

"Do you believe him?" asked Williamson."

"I don't have any reason not to."

"Well ... we should look at his phone records, just to be sure."

Sheriff Watts pulled out his note pad and said, "Red showed me his phone and the incoming call. But the thing is, it didn't come from Nigel's phone." He tore out the page where he wrote down the number and handed it to Sheriff Williamson. They looked at each other. "It's a Virginia area code. I already checked."

"What about afterwards? In the days following, has Logan said anything?"

Sheriff Watts smiled and said, "Probably. But it's hard to say. Those two are thick as thieves ... in a good way I might add. So, there is a chance that Red isn't being fully upfront. But, he says Logan doesn't like to talk about what happened that night."

Sheriff Williamson said, "Thanks, Mark."

Nigel was up stretching his legs when the door opened and the sheriff returned. They took their seats and Nigel began the next round of questioning. "So, do you have an idea who was involved? Who did this to me?"

The sheriff thought about it for a few seconds, then opened a briefcase and produced two pictures. They were mug shots. He put them on the table and slid them toward Nigel so he could see them. "Do either of these men look familiar?"

Nigel didn't hesitate. "That's them. Sure as shit." He continued to stare at the pictures, then asked, "Who are they?"

Pointing to one of the pics the sheriff said, "This one is James Victor Waters. It was his car we found."

Nigel studied the shot. It showed a large bald head, eyes full of anger and contempt. A vein bulged across his forehead and the muscles in his neck were tight.

Sheriff Williamson added, "He has quite a rap sheet. He's spent a lot of time inside and is known to be violent. He's one bad mother."

Nigel tapped the picture hard with his finger. "I can confirm that. He's the one that jumped me at the house and pounded my head."

The sheriff moved his finger to an image of a much smaller individual. He had cornrow braids, and a smart-ass look that showed through his tilted head, half smile, and gold teeth. "This is Willie B. Anderson. He's no stranger to trouble either. Mostly petty stuff though. His prints were all over a handgun we found."

Nigel nodded his head as he looked at the picture. He almost smiled when he thought of the rattlesnake that bit him and the big gator that took him as a prize. He shifted his eyes to the big guy. There was nothing to smile about in that picture, and he felt himself getting angry again.

Nigel slid the pictures back across the table and said, "Bastards. The both of them."

"And you don't know them? Never seen them before?"

Nigel was a little annoyed that he was having to repeat himself and it came through when he replied, "That's what I said. I've never laid eyes on them, ever."

"Why do you think they were here? Why would they want to come all the way down here from Virginia to do this to you?"

The sheriff and Nigel looked at each other. Nothing was said at first. Then Nigel said, "I think you already know the answer."

"Well, I have my ideas. I just want to get your take on it."

"Let's not play games, sheriff. I hate games. I really do. If you have a specific question you want to ask me, then clear the air and ask it."

"Okay ... I'm sorry." The sheriff pulled out a piece of paper, looked at it and put it back in his pocket. "Terrance 'T-Daddy' Lundsford. Is this about him?"

"It's the only thing that fits. I have no enemies except for maybe the vermin closest to that worthless piece of shit."

"But what were they after?"

"Hell, sheriff. I don't know. Goddamn revenge, I guess."

"Revenge on an innocent man?"

Nigel got quiet. He was controlling his anger. He stared across the table and, in a softer tone that shifted the direction of the conversation, said, "Sheriff, I'm not revisiting Virginia. Period. I left all that behind, or at least I tried, when I set out on my boat."

"But, if the two are connected..."

"There is no if. They are connected. There's no other explanation. So what? It doesn't change anything. Please. Don't let the history of my past fog your perception of the current reality. I'm not one to take on the role of a victim. I can take care of myself, but it was me that was attacked. I was beaten and thrown in the trunk of a car. I was taken to Tate's Hell to die, but didn't."

The sheriff said nothing.

After a few moments of silence, Nigel said, "Listen. I'm sorry all this happened. Trust me. I didn't ask for this and neither did you. So, let's get back to why I am here, to help you fill in some gaps."

Now it was Sheriff Williamson's turn to stare at Nigel. They were both leaning in across the table, quiet in their examination of the other. Williamson studied Nigel with over thirty-five years of law enforcement experience. Even in a rural, small-town environment, the one thing Sheriff Lamar Williamson prided himself on was the ability to read people. To him, it's one of the most important parts of the job. To serve only by the strict letter of the laws means to give away part of your practical application of common sense. Justice isn't always black and white. After all, the laws we live under were written by men as flawed as the men that break them. Nobody's perfect and everybody's guilty of something.

Then he thought about his retirement, only a few months away. He thought *How do I want to spend my final days?* Preparing for a life of leisure, or wasting my time chasing after some case with a probable pointless outcome. Justice may have already been served.

The sheriff relaxed and smiled. Then he sat back and said, "May I call you Nigel?"

Nigel sat back himself. He even went so far as to rock back on the rear two legs of his chair. "May I call you Lamar?"

"No," said Sheriff Williamson with a grin.

"Good then!" Nigel said with his own smile. "I'll call you Sheriff. And you can call me Chief."

"Fair enough."

Nigel didn't say anything.

"So, Chief. Earlier you said, 'I was the one taken to Tate's Hell to die, but lived.' Tell me about that last part, about how you lived."

And he did, at least for the most part.

Nigel started, "It was strange. Everything happened so fast and so slow at the same time."

He described the lengths he went through to escape from the duct tape that bound his wrists and legs. He relived for the sheriff, the best he could, how he surprised them with the tire iron when they opened the trunk. He shuddered a bit at the memory of the handgun going off as he knocked it away. He shook his head to help remove the memory of being so close to being shot, then said, "After knocking the big guy unconscious, I was able to bust the other one's ribs and escape the trunk."

"So," the sheriff said, "there was a tire iron? What happened to it? We never found it at the scene?"

"You should have," Nigel said. "I dropped it on the ground." This was truthful, but not the full truth. He wasn't about to go there.

Nigel went on to explain how dark it was and how he hid in the grass as the one named Willie searched the area for the gun. He half-smiled as he described the rattlesnake bites and how the skinny one discharged all his rounds in a fruitless attempt to kill it.

"Hmmm ... that makes sense then. We found the bullets grouped together tight in the ground."

Nigel said nothing.

"What happened next?"

"That's when I stood up with the tire iron."

"Did you kill him?"

Nigel looked away toward the wall and said nothing.

"Well?"

Talking to the wall Nigel said, "No. No I didn't." Then he turned back toward the sheriff and continued, "But I was going to. No doubt."

"What then?"

"He tried to run. His only escape path was the water. That's when the gator took him. It had to be the biggest gator I've ever seen. I've never seen such a splash. Just like that he was gone."

"What about the other one?"

"I really have no idea." Which was a lie. He had his ideas, but he wasn't going down that road. He continued, "Hell, the guy could still be alive for all I know."

"He's not."

And as the sheriff began to pull some more photos out of his briefcase, Nigel said, "Excellent."

The sheriff slid the pictures across for Nigel to see. As Nigel studied the shots, the sheriff said, "That's how we found him. Scattered about the woods. He'd been ripped apart."

The sheriff said nothing and watched Nigel's face as he went through all the photos. Nigel never displayed any sign of shock or surprise. He had that look one has when forced to look at somebody else's wedding pictures. Stoic and uninterested. When he finished, the photos were stacked up and slid back across the table. "Good riddance, motherfucker."

The sheriff put the pictures back into the brief case and asked, "How could this have happened? For him to have been torn apart like that?"

"I don't know. At some point the big guy regained consciousness. He snuck up and grabbed me in the dark. He was squeezing the life out me. He cut off my air supply and I couldn't breathe. I passed out."

The sheriff said nothing.

"Believe me when I tell you, I was shocked when I woke up on the ground. No one was around, so I searched the car, grabbed my stuff and a cell phone I found, and got out of there."

"Is that the phone you used to call Red?"

"Yeah."

"Do you still have it?"

"No," Nigel lied. "I ditched it in the trash."

There was silence between them. They were both thinking. Then Sheriff Williamson said, "Let's back up a bit. You said that there might have been three of them."

"I only saw two."

"Yeah, but you said that you half-expected three."

Nigel thought about it. The memory of the one unexplained gunshot flashed across his mind. He couldn't be sure of anything, so he said, "I guess I was wrong."

More silence followed before the sheriff said, "I'm not sure how else you can help. This is all you remember?"

Nigel didn't get a chance to answer before the sheriff asked, "You don't remember seeing or hearing anything strange or out of the ordinary?"

Nigel was quiet before answering, "No. But everything was out of the ordinary that night."

The sheriff was quiet and studied Nigel's eyes. Then he opened the briefcase again. He pulled out two more pictures and asked, "Are you sure? Think hard. This is important."

Nigel didn't take two seconds to look at the pictures before handing them back. "Nothing."

The sheriff looked at the two pictures then pulled an old snapshot from his breast pocket and handed it to Nigel. "I took this one myself. About ten years ago. Pretty amazing, wouldn't you say?"

Nigel handed back the photo and said nothing.

The sheriff put the crime scene photos back in the briefcase and closed it. And with great care he put the other photo back in his shirt pocket, patting it flat to create a mental note that it was there.

"Nigel..." The sheriff chuckled and said, "I'm sorry. Chief. Chief ... I've lived in Franklin County my entire life. I have seen a lot, just about everything. I've fished every stream, hunted every acre, and driven every mile of road. There hasn't been much get by me." He patted his breast pocket again and said, "I was in a deer stand when I took this one. You are one of the very few I have shared it with; not even my wife has seen it."

Nigel said, "To preserve the good impressions others have about us, some things are better left unmentioned, even if it's caught on film from a deer stand, or witnessed while standing in the middle of Tate's Hell. Some things need to remain a mystery."

The sheriff was nodding his head in agreement. Then he said, "So I guess we've both seen a lot in our times."

"Yes, sir. That seems to be the case."

"Oh, shit. Just call me Lamar."

THE STORM

The late afternoon light gave way to dusk sooner than normal. Ominous, heavy cloud coverage crept eastward, saturating the western sky with moisture and activity. Rumbles of thunder could be heard in the distance. Storms were coming.

Nigel took refuge in an Adirondack on the front porch of his little cottage. He was substituting his normal evening beer for club soda and lime. He had already consumed more than his recommended daily allowance of Coors Light and needed a change. It had been a long day at the beach fishing with Red. Not rod and reel fishing, but cast net fishing for mullet.

As he relaxed, clean from a fresh shower and wearing nothing more than a pair of well-loved khaki shorts, he felt the air move across his skin. He could differentiate between the artificial wind created by the ceiling fan and the outside breeze that was building and coming through the screen.

It had been a long, but satisfying day. He loves to eat mullet, and he's addicted to tossing the net. And since the only way to catch mullet is with a net, the combination of the two make for the perfect pastime. Sitting there under the fan gave him pause to think about the day he learned to throw.

There's a long-standing joke. If Nigel were a castaway, alone on some deserted island with all the world's finest fishing gear and an unending supply of bait, he would starve to death in a week. He can't catch a fish to save his life. He's a hopeless case, even the fish in a stocked pond are safe. Everyone has something, a skill or talent that escapes them. For Nigel, it's fishing ... but not completely.

Throwing a cast net is an altogether different matter. It was a couple months before the incident in Tate's Hell that Red gave Nigel his first and only cast net lesson. Red spread the net out making a big circle on the beach and said, "When you throw it, that's what you want, to open the net up out over the water." He showed Nigel the series of lead weights along the circumference of the net and explained the importance of not getting them tangled. Then he gave Nigel the hand line and attached it to his right wrist. He had Nigel coil the line and portion of the net in one hand. Then he had him gather up about half of the remaining net and place it with the coil. With the net all made up in one hand, Red showed him where to grab one of the weights with his free left hand. Red looked Nigel over and said, "That's it. You're ready to throw. Just make sure that weight in your left hand is the last thing to leave your body. Let the rest of the net clear before you let go."

Nigel said, "Show me the motion of throwing."

Red pretended to throw the net twice and said, "Let her fly."

Nigel gave it a whirl out over the sand. As it launched, it opened up in mid-air and landed as a perfect pancake on the beach. They both looked at it for a long while. Then they both looked at each other. Nigel asked, "That's good, right?"

Red said, "Do it again!"

And he did, and not just once. Each throw resulted in the lead-line expanding to full capacity, the weights thumped in unison as they landed on the beach. Red made him throw it over and over again, until he was sure it wasn't just beginner's luck. It wasn't. Nigel was a natural. Red shook his head and said, "Give me that damn thing."

Red made up the net and threw a banana. "Dammit," he said. He pulled the net off the sand and reached out to Nigel. "Here, throw it again."

He did, and it was perfect. Red said, "What the hell. You've been holding out on me."

"I've been trying to get you to show me."

"Nigel ... I think this is the beginning of a beautiful relationship."

They wasted no time after that first lesson and jumped into Nigel's truck to roll down the beach. They were headed toward the horn of the cape, keeping a close eye out for the lazy, less-than-acrobatic, flopping jumps of mullet. "There!" Nigel said pointing. Two mullet had taken to the air at the same time. Red looked and found a third.

They got out of the truck and Nigel made his way out into the water with the net. As he stood in the surf, Red stood in the back of the truck looking for activity in the water. He called out a command to Nigel. "To your right," hollered Red. "School at two o'clock!"

Nigel let the net fly. It spread out like a dancing girl's dress as she spun. It landed wide across the water's surface. As Nigel took in the line, he felt the pull of the catch. It was strong, more powerful than he would have expected. He looked back at Red. They were both smiling. Red said, "Drag it on out here. Let's see what we got."

The catch flipped and flopped around on the sand. Red started to throw them in a five-gallon bucket. There were nine mullet and a couple pin fish that got tossed back into the surf. Red was staring into the bucket overcome with happiness. You could almost see tears puddle in his eyelids. "Dinner!" he said. Then he looked up at Nigel and said, "Get my filet knife. It's in my other bucket."

Nigel did and Red went to cleaning the mullet, being careful to extract the gizzard. Mullet are vegetarians, which is the reason they must be caught with a net and the reason they have a gizzard. Red extracted the first little jewel and held it up to the light. "Yummy." And threw it in with the beer and ice.

"Seriously," said Nigel. "I can't believe you like that shit."

Red ignored the comment, and said, "What the hell are you doing just standing there? Grab that net and get your ass back in the water."

He did, and in less than one hour, he netted more fish than he had ever caught in his entire life. Three shy of the limit. For fifteen more minutes, he continued to throw looking for those last remaining fish. No dice. The mullet had moved on. So, on his first outing with the net, Nigel dragged a total of 47 mullet to the beach.

Working the net today was quite different than that first day. Today was more about stamina and persistence ... and nourishment (beer). The schools were small, as were the catches. But they both stayed after it, each throwing, each taking turns to clean. Red had the biggest single catch between the two of them: three. Most other catches, when there was something in the net, were brought in one at a time. Most of their throws came up empty except for the pin fish, sting rays, and an occasional whiting.

Throwing a cast net for any extended period of time can be exhausting. After a while the lead weights that make up the skirt of the net start to get a little heavy, but Nigel has the shoulders and arms needed for such punishing activity. Over the course of the day, he must have thrown over 200 times, but there were plenty of beer breaks in between.

Regardless, it doesn't matter how big and strong you are, anyone that throws a net like that will pay the price of soreness in the morning. Nigel knew what to expect, so he washed down four Advil PM with his club soda. Eight hundred milligrams of Ibuprofen for the pain and 100 milligrams of Diphenhydramine for a good night's rest. It was just what the doctor ordered.

He sat back and listened to the wind and the gentle thumping of the ceiling fan as it chopped at the air. The quiet led him to think too much. His thoughts turned to Tate's Hell and other recent troubles. He tried to ignore the bad memories, replacing them with happier thoughts, but it was no good. Every bad memory flooded his mind. He needed a distraction, so he got up for some more club soda and tuned in Oyster Radio.

As he was pouring, another reminder of the night in Tate's Hell came into the kitchen. It was Nigel's feral cat, Tom. He decided being inside was far smarter than facing the elements of the approaching storms.

It wasn't long after that dreadful night that Nigel installed the small pet door, so Tom could come and go as he pleased. It took a while for him to get used to it, but the cat's a pro now. Putting in the door was the least Nigel could do, especially after Tom almost surrendered his own life protecting him and the cottage.

The memory of that day remains fresh in his mind. Nigel relives parts of it every time he sees the cat. He guessed the cat's memory is pretty good too. The way Nigel sees it, they are in this to the end and are bound by ties thicker than the blood, sweat, and tears that were shed that day.

"Hey, buddy. Whatcha been up to?"

Tom jumped up on the counter and Nigel went to grab the cat's entire head with his hand. The cat met him halfway and pressed back as Nigel rubbed his face, neck, and ears. "Well, it's good to see you too." Nigel moved his hand to scratch the cat's back and he approved, arching high and pointing his tail toward the ceiling.

Nigel headed back to the porch, and Tom made chase. He settled back in his chair, and waited on the weather and sleep to come. Tom jumped up on the porch swing, walked around in three tight circles, scratched a bit at the cushion and flopped down. Shaking his head Nigel asked, "You comfy over there?" He slouched down in his chair and slid a pillow behind his neck and head thinking *Crazy damn cat.* Billy Joel's *Piano Man* was playing on the radio and he could hear the weather off in the distance. He closed his eyes.

The air was saturated with humidity. When the rains arrived, they did so as a suspended mist, struggling to reach the ground. Then the first successful sprinkles started to land, clearing the way for others. The pace of the light rain increased. The wind briefly stopped blowing and the bottom fell out of the clouds. The rain came as an all-out downpour. The drops of rain were replaced with a solid column of water dropping from the sky. The sound of the rain was loud but relaxing, and the heavier storms were still out of town. The edge of the storm brought cloud-to-ground lightning off in the distance. Its thunder caused Nigel to open his eyes and look around. The cat hadn't moved. The thought of heading to bed crossed his mind, but he was comfortable enough, so the idea was dismissed. He laced his fingers in his lap, leaned his head back on the pillow, closed his eyes and found sleep again.

It was around midnight when the slow-moving storm got on top of them. The wind had returned and the lightning was heavy and active, strikes all around. The trees and palms danced in protest as the wind pushed their tops around at will and in every direction. Somewhere on a nearby block a transformer blew. The background music of Oyster Radio went quiet and everything else dark.

The Advil PM was doing its job. Nigel slept through just about everything, only cracking an eye every now and then at the close lightning strikes. It wasn't until the cat began hissing and howling that Nigel opened his eyes wide and became alert.

He sat up straighter, rubbed his eyes, and looked around. He couldn't see anything. It was pitch black. He might as well have had his eyes closed. There was no difference. He couldn't see Tom, but he could tell he was off the swing. He was in front of Nigel, somewhere between him and the screen door uttering a long, skin-crawling yowl.

"What is it?" Nigel whispered. Then he stood up to look out toward the front yard. He could hear the heavy rain splashing in the small pond that always collects in his yard, but he saw nothing.

A flash of lightning provided a brief moment of illumination. Then it went pitch black again, but something caught his eye. Nigel said nothing and kept his eyes trained on the area where he thought he saw something. Then some cloud-to-cloud lightning bounced around and cast a glow about the yard. There, standing in the middle of the grass, was a single figure watching the house. It was Candice.

Without lightning, nothing was visible. When the next round of flashes came, she was still there, but he could tell she had backed up several steps. He opened the door and stepped out into the rain. He called out, "Candice!" He walked toward her. He still couldn't see her, but as he moved closer he began to hear her gasping for air. She was crying. A crack of lightning confirmed she hadn't moved. When he reached her, she was barely visible in the darkness.

He reached out to touch her face and she let him, tilting her head into his palm. He ran his fingers across her cheeks and his thumb underneath an eye. He could feel her viscous tears, even through all the rain. He withdrew his hand letting his fingertips caress her chin.

"Candice. How long have you been out here?"

She didn't answer, and he didn't see her shoulders shrug. *I don't know*.

"Please," he said. "Come inside. Let's get you out of the weather."

Again, she said nothing, and he couldn't make out the fact that she was shaking her head.

Nigel reached out for her hand, but, the second he touched her arm, she pulled away. Then she spoke. Her words were barely audible over the rain and wind, but Nigel heard every word.

In the darkness she asked, "Is all this true?"

Several thick bolts of lightning stretched across the clouds in several directions, looking for a place to land. They lit up the sky like an early morning sunrise. Candice held something soggy and wilted in her hand. Nigel recognized it immediately. It was the newspaper article he had left with her the last time they were together. That was over a month ago.

The article was written by Sherry Stone, a reporter from Tidewater Virginia. In it, she provides surprising, if not shocking, details about Nigel's past. A period and history that no one else on The Forgotten Coast, except Red, knows about. In particular, the shroud of suspicion regarding Nigel's involvement in the murder of one Terrance "T-Daddy" Lundsford.

There was silence between them. Nigel could barely see movement, but she was shaking the article in the air. "Come on, dammit. Tell me!"

He answered her, but a crack of lightning drowned out his answer. But in the flash of light she could read his lips. She looked to the sky and began to cry even harder, even though she was empty of tears. Nigel stepped in closer and took her in his arms and pulled her close. She hesitated, but gave in as they held each other tight in the rain. His lips found her neck and he kissed her over and over again until he reached her waiting mouth. As they kissed, her mouth became more welcoming and they became consumed with one another.

As they kissed in the yard, the rain began to let up. The lightning became less frequent, the thunder more distant. They came up for air and looked at each other in the dark. Their breathing was as heavy as the wind. Nigel whispered, "I do love you." Candice didn't hear him, nor could she see to read his lips, but she didn't have to. Nigel reached down, picked her up, and carried her back to the cottage. The storm was over ... for now.

BOWERY STATION

It must be a combination of sun, sand, and alcohol, or perhaps there is something in the water, but, whatever the cause, Florida shenanigans are the best. It was a Saturday afternoon and Nigel was on his way out to St. George Island. He was headed to Paddles, a seaside watering hole to attend an album release party for his good friend Brian Bowen. Brian was promoting his newest release, *10 Mile Smile*, a collection of six coastal tunes that celebrate the area and people of the Forgotten Coast. A few of the songs were already getting quite a bit of air time on Oyster Radio and becoming popular with the locals and many tourists. Nigel didn't have a copy yet, so he figured attending to support his buddy was the proper thing to do. Plus, on more than one occasion, Brian had mentioned the bikini eye-candy was worth the trip. Not that Nigel was in the market, but it never hurts to look.

Having never been to St. George, Nigel wasn't exactly sure where he was going. As a navigator by trade, he was confident he could figure it out. It's just an island after all. It's a busy island, though, as Nigel came to find out, especially on Saturdays. He should have taken that into consideration. It was turn-around day. The mass of tourists ending their vacation and trying to leave the island collide with their replacements that are eager to get on and get started. It makes for quite the cluster.

It didn't take long for Nigel to realize that he missed his turn. He turned down a little side street so he could turn around. He was about to borrow a driveway when he noticed some commotion at the end of the street. Two Franklin County Sheriff squad cars had their blue lights flashing and a collection of onlookers had taken to the street and gathered around. Curiosity got the best of Nigel so he eased on for a better look himself.

As he got closer, it was obvious things couldn't be too serious. Folks in the crowd were smiling and laughing. Nigel still couldn't see. The squad cars were blocking his view, but he could see the erratic movements of the two deputies on the other side of the cars. Nigel got out to join the others. As he walked up, he asked anyone that would listen, "What's going on?"

A guy turned and said with a grin, "Crazy shit, man. This guy has flipped his lid."

As Nigel stepped around the cars, he took in the scene. The two deputies were dancing around trying to corral another fella into the squad car. "What the hell?" said Nigel.

"Told you, dude," the guy said. "This fella is bat-shit crazy."

The guy the deputies were trying to apprehend was buck naked. Well almost, he had inserted his pecker into the sleeve of an extra-large curling iron cover and was holding it tight underneath his little pot belly. When anyone tried to approach him, he would bark a maniacal laugh and rush toward them wagging it back and forth and up and down. The deputies had on rubber gloves, but would sidestep and dodge like bull fighters anytime he got too close.

Nigel asked the other guy, "Who is he?"

"Don't know," the guy said. Best I can tell, his name is Frank. That's what the deputies and that woman on the porch keep calling him."

Sure enough, there was a woman standing on a porch screaming, "Frank! Frank! Get your ass back in the house. You are embarrassing me! Now, Frank ... get in here."

All the while one of the deputies was trying to coax him, "Come on, Frank. Either get in the car, or go back in the house, so we can talk about this. We don't want to hurt you, now. But we've had just about enough of this nonsense."

This went on for another couple of minutes and Nigel found himself getting bored with it all. He was walking back to his truck when he heard one deputy say to the other, "Shoot him, Jimmy." That was enough to rekindle Nigel's attention.

"Hell no," deputy Jimmy said. "You shoot him. I don't want to have to deal with the paperwork."

The woman on the porch was screaming, "Did you hear that, Frank? Did ya? They's about to shoot your ass. You better get in here."

But Frank wasn't going to have anything to do with it. In a defiant last stand, he bowed his back, pointed the curling iron sleeve up in the air, and wiggled it back and forth while he barked like a dog. The deputy not named Jimmy said, "Oh, hell. Enough of this."

The barking and the wiggling ended and was replaced with a girlish scream the second the two, small, dart-like electrodes penetrated his belly. Neuromuscular incapacitation took over and his entire body wiggled and jerked around in the street. He looked like a freshly caught fish that had been dropped in a boat. As the curling iron sleeve was let go and all his glory was made available for view, none of the women looking on were too impressed. Nigel heard voices from across the street. *That's it? That's all you got?* The crowd dispersed to mind their own business. The excitement was over.

As the deputies were getting the situation under control, the woman on the porch ran inside the house. Moments later she reemerged with a dirty pair of blue jeans and an old stained tank-top. She ran out to the curb and threw the clothes out on the street and said, "Here! He's your problem now. And don't bring him back until he can bring two handles of vodka and enough weed to replace what he smoked."

The two deputies looked at her as Nigel walked back to the car. He was thinking *She probably shouldn't have said all that.*

When Nigel parked his car at Paddles, he still had the image of a naked Frank dancing around with the curling iron sleeve containing his little junk. As he got out of his truck, he could hear Brian just starting a song off his new album, *Beach People Problems*. Nigel laughed as he thought *Well, that seems appropriate* .

Nigel entered the deck and walked up to where Brian was playing. He threw a ten-spot in the tip jar and Brian ad-libbed a "thanks, stranger" into his lyrics. Nigel settled himself at a back table and listened. Brian was having a good afternoon. The tip jar was filling and the CDs in the box were being replaced with cash.

When he closed out his last set, he opened a fresh Miller Lite and entered into casual chit-chat with patrons as he made his way over to Nigel's table. He took a seat. It was a hot afternoon and sweat oozed out his pores. "You should hydrate better," Nigel said.

"I am," said Brian, "there's water in beer."

"I guess there is. Are you done for the day?"

"Nope. I'm playing at B.S. from six till whenever."

B.S. is an acronym affectionately used for obvious purposes. But it's also the short name for the Bowery Station, where there is plenty of good-time B.S. to go around. It's back on the mainland in Apalachicola. When it emerged on the scene a couple years ago, it wasted no time becoming the hottest spot in town, creating a sense of community that welcomed everybody across all walks of life. There is no shortage of characters to make the party.

B.S. is a small, cozy venue like no other. Finding a seat can be a chore, but that is no problem. There is plenty of space on the sidewalk benches and picnic tables where the B.S. often overflows.

The operation is pretty simple: cold beer, wine, roasted peanuts in the shell, and great music. That is a combination that is hard to beat, especially when it is run by good, honest, hardworking folks that have as much fun as the patrons.

Nigel looked at his watch, "Well, it's after five; you better get your ass in gear and tear down. Can I help?"

"No, brother. I have a routine."

After settling his tab, Nigel was headed to his truck. He was following as Brian was hauling a speaker back to his vehicle. Nigel called after him, "Oh, shit. I almost forgot. I need a CD."

Nigel was reaching into his pocket when Brian put the speaker down and tossed one to him. Nigel tried to give him money, but Brian held up his hand. "Your money isn't any good here. Happy Birthday."

"My birthday was back in February."

"Well, damn then. I guess I'm a few months late."

Nigel smiled and didn't argue. "Thanks, dude."

Driving across the bridge, Nigel reached over and picked up the CD that was sitting on the console. He ripped the plastic cover off with his teeth and popped the disk into his stereo. With the windows rolled down, he had to turn the volume up, but he would have cranked it up regardless.

As he sat at the light waiting to turn left onto Highway 98, back toward Apalach and Port St. Joe, something caught his eye. Hell, it would have caught anybody's eye. A scraggly-looking guy sporting knotty dreadlocks and a scarlet macaw parrot on his shoulder was across the street with some obvious tourists. Most locals don't dress to the pastel, preppy standards of IZOD and Vineyard Vines. *Thank God!*

TALES FROM STOOL 17 – DARK DAYS OF JUDGMENT

When Nigel saw the exchange of money and merchandise, he snickered and laughed. As he pulled through the intersection he thought *Somebody's getting high on the beach tonight.* Perhaps an altered state of mind will help them realize just how silly they look in baby blue on yellow and pink on chartreuse. *Hey Biff and Babs, it is not 1985 and you're not on Martha's Vineyard anymore.*

Logan doesn't smoke pot. He hasn't smoked any since before he shipped out to boot camp. Two months prior to his departure date his friends threw one hell of a farewell party. It had only three ingredients: Beer, Weed, and Pizza. He got more fucked up than the Cheshire Cat and spent most of the evening in a big La-Z-Boy recliner. The next morning, he was still in the chair; his head still a little foggy with a slight pounding. One of his buddies was on the couch. He was rolling a new one. He fired it up and brought it to Nigel. Logan waved it off. "No thanks. I had enough last night. I'm done. No more." He hasn't smoked since, and that morning was a new beginning to a most disciplined Navy career.

Having the party two months prior was important. His recruiter told him, if he was going to partake in any recreationals, he didn't want to know about it, and, more importantly, there should be none taken 60 days prior to shipping out. "You want to show up with a clean system," his recruiter said. "You will piss in a bottle when you get there, and you don't want them throwing your ass back on the bus to send you home."

Logan's recruiter didn't lie. The day after arriving at the Recruit Training Command in Great Lakes, IL, the Navy's newest boot camp company was lined up for their first of many tests. The little piss cups were handed out.

In the days after they surrendered their samples, it was during a Smoke and Coke break that one of Logan's shipmates began to brag about how he was able to pull the wool over the Navy's eyes. His name was Patterson, and he was good at talking a big game. He was from New York, the Bronx, and spoke in terms of absolutes and matters of fact. His farewell party, he claimed, was the night before he got on the bus. He boasted about getting all messed up the night before he left for the Navy. The difference, however, was that he drank two quart bottles of white vinegar the morning after. In his thick, over-confident accent he swore, "Makes you piss pure spring water."

Most of Logan's first shipmates were fresh out of high school. Three of them were only seventeen years old. Their parents had to sign a waiver for them to join. Essentially, they gave up their parental custody and the Navy became their new mommy. Those that were listening to Patterson were awestruck and gullible. They were eating it up. Logan was a little older than most. He was only a few weeks from tuning twenty-one, so he wasn't buying. He didn't say anything, but thought ... *Patterson, you're an idiot*.

It was about a week and a half later. Most had already forgotten about their little piss test, those that didn't have anything to worry about anyway. It was morning. Everyone was standing at attention at the foot of their rack, ready for inspection and breakfast. Their chief, the company commander, came out of his office. He walked up and down the floor with a piece of paper in his hand. He was squinting and his bottom lip was puffed and curled out, his signature look of discontent.

After three or four passes, he stopped at the head of the room and with heightened rage started reading names. "I need the following three pieces of shit to take two steps forward. Wilson," he paused for dramatic effect. There were two Wilsons in the company. The sphincter of Tim Wilson loosened up when the chief finally said, "Wilson! Allen Wilson."

The next name caught Logan a little by surprise. When the chief called out, "Martin," Logan flinched a bit. Martin's name was the last in the group that he would have suspected to be connected with any sort of trouble. Eddie Martin was kind and calm and spiritual. He had started a Bible reading group with a few of the others. He had a religious soul about him, but he wasn't overbearing or pushy with that crazy, glazed-over look. You couldn't help but like the guy. He was the guy that, if things went to shit, you'd want in your corner.

Logan was beginning to wonder what this was all about. Hell, if a guy like Martin was involved, any of their names might be next. Logan began to riffle through his memory of the past several days. Had there been something he screwed up on? Did he miss something? Then he heard his chief call out the last name on the list, "Patterson!" Nigel snickered and thought *Vinegar. White Vinegar and Spring Water*.

48

The chief announced, "Everybody take a look. These are your company dopers!"

The chief went on to bark and lecture on the need for trust, responsibility, accountability, loyalty, and dependability, but all Logan could think about was Martin. *Damn.* And, of course, that he was getting hungry.

The three were escorted away by the Gestapo, two muscular first class petty officers from the Master at Arms shack. Many were certain that they would be marched to some stone wall to be readied and blindfold for a firing squad. As they walked by, the faces of Wilson and Patterson were drooped and defeated. Martin held his head up and maintained an *I got Jesus glow* about him. That made Logan smile.

Well, it turns out "the sending your ass back home" comment made by Logan's recruiter was a bit of a stretch, at least for back then. When the company got back to the barracks from their evening meal, there the three sat polishing their shoes at the foot of their rack. Turns out the Navy doesn't send you home, but they sure as hell strip away everything else. All the professional schools and training and advancements that had been part of their contracts, *poof,* they were gone, only to be replaced by a guaranteed gig of chipping paint off some old tin can. The Navy needs those guys too.

Nigel took his time heading home. With music blaring and his left arm draped out the driver's side window, he took in the sights of the Apalachicola Bay. As he crossed the bridge, he counted three shrimp boats steaming home in front of a sun that was dropping fast before a western sky. He brought a knuckle to the brim of his visor and rendered a salute to their job he so appreciated. Tough work.

As he came off the bridge and into Apalach, he rolled to a stop at the flashing light. He had a decision to make: Hang a left and stay on Highway 98 toward home, or cruise straight through and find a cold beer. He chose the latter.

Nigel parked in front of Bowery Station but remained in the truck so he could finish listening to Brian's song, *Ode to Port St. Joe.* He drummed on the steering wheel with his fingers as he sang along. *St. Joe Beach, Cape San Blas, Money Bayou, and Indian Pass ... Ain't life great, on Highway 98, and 30A too. Oh, Port St. Joe, Florida, USA ... Y'all come back soon*.

49

It was still a bit early and the bar traffic was a little light as Nigel entered the Bowery. Lisa was serving up beers and conversation to the handful of patrons milling about. Matt sat at the bar, studying some paperwork with a concerned look and furrowed brow. Nigel took stool 17 opposite him and Matt looked up and offered a smile. "Howdy, Nigel."

"That's more like it," said Nigel. "What's with the troubled look?"

Lisa slid a pint draft of Oyster City Blonde Ale in front of Nigel, to which he tugged at the bill of his visor and said, "Thanks, doll."

"Shrinkage," Matt replied.

"Oh, Hell," Nigel said. "That can't make Lisa very happy either."

"You guessed right there. She's more upset about it than I am."

Nigel knew what he was referring to, but couldn't pass up the opportunity to lighten the mood some. "Well ... I don't know if you have seen it advertised or not. There's a great TV infomercial about this little pill. It's supposed to help a guy and his equipment perk up and bring overwhelming satisfaction to the opposite sex. They're like steroids for your pecker."

The joke wasn't received well as Matt said, "My inventory, Nigel. I'm talking about my inventory."

Lisa stuck her head into the conversation and said, "I saw the infomercial last week. I already ordered him a 30-day supply."

Nigel and Lisa both busted out laughing.

Matt said, "Dammit, you two. This is serious."

That made the two of them laugh even more.

Behind a thin, straight-lined smile, Matt did his best to maintain a controlled look of seriousness, but said nothing.

"Hey Matt, if they don't work out for you, can I give them a try?"

Referring to a recent silly stunt where Red and Nigel streaked past hundreds of music lovers outside the Forgotten Coast Shrimp and Raw Bar, Lisa said, "Word travels fast in these parts. I hear you don't need no pills, Nigel."

"Trust me," Nigel said through his laughter. "That was nothing more than an optical illusion. The sun was casting just the right amount of shadow."

Now all three of them started to laugh, but Matt maintained some level of seriousness. Through his own chuckles, he said, "Shit, guys. Give it a break, will ya? I'm trying to work here."

"Okay ... okay, Mr. Businessman. Go about your number crunching."

Matt went back to studying the numbers and rubbing his head. Nigel was about to take a sip from his beer but stopped at the last second and asked, "Hey, Lisa ... that's all you ordered, really, a 30-day supply?"

"Goddammit, Nigel. Knock it off!"

"Alright ... alright." And Nigel pulled an imaginary zipper across his lips to signify he was done.

The two of them sat in quiet for a while. Nigel sipped his beer while he watched Matt rub a shiny spot on his temple.

"Okay," Nigel said. "I'm no money man, but what has you so perfluncted?"

Matt looked up, "Per what?"

"Perfluncted. It's a word. I just made it up. It means ..." Nigel thought for a second and said, "Ah shit. I'll give it a definition later. What's wrong, my friend? Talk to me."

"Something isn't right. My numbers are way off."

"Like how?"

"Like ... according to my sales data, I should have more beer in my inventory than I currently have."

"How bad is it?"

"From what I'm looking at, about fifteen cases of beer." Matt went back to rubbing his head. "I run a tight ship, Nigel. I do have some built-in expectations for some losses. You know, as a regular part of running the shop. Taking that into consideration, my numbers are always spot-on every month. But, for the last month or so, shit just don't add up."

"What about the draft beer station? I would think it might be tough controlling that?"

"Nope," Matt said, "Everything on that front looks to be in line. No, I think it is in the bottles."

"Do you think someone is stealing straight from the cooler?" Nigel asked.

"Naw. Hell, I'd notice something like that if it were happening. I'm usually the only one that goes back there. This is something else."

Nigel got up and patted him on the shoulder and said, "You'll figure it out. It's probably nothing but stupid math."

Nigel moved to the other end of the bar to give Matt some space. Lisa recharged his Oyster City draft while he went to the barrel of peanuts to grab a double fistful to crack and eat. By the time Brian showed up and started hauling in his gear, Nigel was on his third draft and had created quite an impressive pile of shells on the floor. Nigel was leaned up against the bar talking with a couple of the local fishing guides when he heard Lisa say, "Sorry guys. Happy hour is Monday through Friday, five to seven."

Nigel looked back over his left shoulder. A guy wearing a pair of Ray-Ban Wayfarer sunglasses, a chartreuse button-down, and a smartass smile, asked, "Is that am or pm?"

Lisa ignored the idiotic question and moved on. She was way too busy. The place was starting to get crowded; even Matt had put his troubles away and started to work the bar.

Nigel turned the rest of the way around and looked at the guy. It was one of the preps he saw earlier on the corner of Highway 98 and the bridge road to St. George Island. The GQ dudes dealing with the parrot boy. Nigel looked around the room and found the others. They weren't hard to spot. Three attractive gals accompanied them in like attire. Their hair was done just so, and great thought went into their outfits, all the way down to the huge bug-eyed sunglasses and floppy hats. They could have been models for some New England fashion magazine. The gals improved the guys' appearances, but it didn't make them look any less stupid.

Charles, one of the fishing guides, saw the guys too and said, "Hey, fella. That's a great color you're wearing there."

The preppy guy at the bar said, "Excuse me?"

"Your shirt. That color is great ... on the tail of a pearl-white Gulp bait. Otherwise ..." And he started to laugh.

The GQ boy had no idea what Charles was talking about. He kind of chuckled to himself behind a sheepish smile as he grabbed his happy hour token off the bar and rejoined his crowd.

At Bowery Station, people don't have to look at their watches to know if happy hour is on or not. Matt has a yellow ball cap attached to a halyard that runs to a block in the middle of the ceiling. At the commencement of happy-hour the cap is raised with great celebration, bell ringing, and cheers from the crowd. The BOGO party is on.

The Bowery Station happy hour token is used to keep up with the freebies. They're wooden nickels with the B.S. logo stamped in the middle and Bowery Station, Apalachicola, Fl. spelled out around the edge. During happy hour, patrons get one with each beer or wine purchase. As long as the hat is flying, the tokens can be used in exchange for a refill. And if you forget to use a token one day, you can use it some other time. A pretty smart gimmick that everyone enjoys, just listen for the bell and watch for the cap.

Brian was playing to an enthusiastic crowd behind the two tip jars provided by Matt and Lisa. Each jar has a handwritten sign hanging out front. One says *Keep Playing*; the other says *Stop Playing*. Most of the tourists don't pay much attention to the signs. If somebody drops a tip into the Stop Playing bucket, the locals will start a jolly ruckus and give them a good-natured ration of shit.

That's what happened when one of the New England beauties dropped a ten-dollar bill in the wrong bucket. *Boooo! Boooo! B.S., B.S., Bullshit, Move it, Move it over!*

It didn't take long for her to realize almost everybody in the joint was yelling at her. But once she did, she couldn't understand why. She caught more hell than most, especially from the guys, probably because she was so damn pretty.

It got so rowdy it interrupted one of Brian's new songs, *April, May, June*. He stopped playing. She stood there with her hand over her mouth, embarrassed. Playing along Brian said, "Sweetheart, if you go ahead and fill that jug up, I'll be happy to pack up all my shit and be home by six."

She looked at Brian but remained clueless. Nigel walked up to her. She was pouting and pulling on her bottom lip. She looked like she was about to cry. Nigel smiled and winked and pointed to the sign. She read it. Then Nigel pointed to the other sign on the other bucket. She read it. Then a light came on and she rushed to move her tip from one bucket to the other. The place went crazy with cheers and whistles, while Matt banged on the ship's bell. Now everyone was laughing and she started crying tears of happiness.

She turned and hugged Nigel. Then she gave him a big kiss on the cheek, then on the lips. At first, he just stood there. Then he played along and kissed her back, but, at the same time, was thinking of how he was going to explain this to his girlfriend Candice. And he would have to, no doubt. Shit ... chances are she would know about it before he even got home.

The kiss lasted a bit longer than either Nigel or her boyfriend expected. After about five seconds the boyfriend came off his stool yelling, "Hey, you son of a bitch. Take your hands off her." One of his other buddies followed along as back-up. The guy in chartreuse stayed behind.

After about four steps in, a huge fella reached out and placed a wide palm on the chest of the boyfriend stopping him, "Whoa. Whoa, pretty boy. You don't even want to think about it."

The boyfriend looked past the big guy. His girlfriend and Nigel were still kissing. He said, "Screw you," and tried to push past, but the massive fingers never budged.

"She's a little drunk. Everybody is having a good time and everything is going to be all right. Now go back to your seats."

From the stage, Brian was patient but said into the mic, "Get a room. I'm trying to do a show here."

The boyfriend's buddy said, "Yeah, Chip. Come on. Give it a rest."

The big guy chuckled. "Chip? ... really? You've got to be kidding me."

That's when the girlfriend ceased her lip lock on Nigel. The crowd erupted into cheers again. She looked up at him with glazed-over eyes and said, "Damn. Thank you."

"You're welcome."

She tried to kiss him again, but he smiled as he held her off at arm's length, "Okay, darling. I think that's enough; your 60 seconds of fame are over. Let's get you back with your group." Nigel looked over his shoulder at Brian and said, "From the top, brother."

Nigel put his arm around her waist and escorted her back. That's when Nigel saw the massive body of Luther Collins standing in the crowd. Otherwise known as Little Bit, Luther is a shrimper from Port St. Joe. He's also the guy that protected Chip from a possible beating of his life.

As they walked by, Nigel stopped and said, "Hey, Little Bit. Whatcha doing in Apalach?"

"Just working. Ned Carlson needed someone on *Miss Molly*."

"Good to see ya."

Nigel and the girlfriend made it back to her group. The boyfriend was still mad. "Hey, guys. I think she is one of yours."

The girlfriend did the right thing and walked up to the boyfriend and kissed him. He lightened up a bit after that.

Over the music, they made their introductions. Nigel looked over at the boyfriend and said, "Sorry 'bout that kiss. I guess she got a little carried away."

The group was not from New England, but Charleston, South Carolina. All six of them had recently graduated from the College of Charleston and decided on a road trip. While talking with Zane, the guy in a powder blue polo and pastel yellow shorts, Nigel learned they had just gotten into town that morning and they had never been to the area before.

Nigel looked at Duke, the guy in chartreuse, and thought of the B.S. token. *If you've never been here before, where did you get the token?* Then he remembered the corner transaction and the parrot boy.

Nigel reached into his own pocket and found a token of his own. He brought it out and asked Duke, "Hey, did I see you drop this earlier?"

Duke said, "I don't think so and produced a handful of tokens from his own pocket. He held them out for Nigel to see and said, "I think I'm set. Must be somebody else's."

Nigel looked at the pile of tokens and said, "Yeah. I see that."

Nigel bid them a farewell and headed back to his stool which was now occupied by someone else. Move your feet, loose your seat. There was, however, a fresh draft waiting on him. Lisa slid it to him and said, "Here. You're going to need this."

"Thanks, Lisa."

Nigel took a sip of the beer and turned around to listen to the music. As Brian was finishing up a John Prine song, Nigel heard his phone bong. It was a text from Candace. He opened it up and read the short six-word message in all caps: I HOPE IT WAS WORTH IT!

Nigel spoke to his phone, "What?" Then his phone bonged again. Another text, this time an image. It was of him and the girl kissing. *Oh Shit.* Nigel looked at the picture again and took a sip of beer. His head snapped around remembering what Lisa said when she slid him the beer. *You're going to need this.*

He looked toward the bar to find Lisa grinning and laughing. She said something to him, but he had to read her lips: *You are in big trouble.* Then she gave him a wink.

Lisa had taken the picture and sent it to Candice. Unbeknownst to Nigel, she also called Candice and explained everything. He would have a lot of explaining to do, and Candice was going to love every minute of it. She planned to work it for all it was worth.

Nigel reached into his pocket and found a twenty-dollar bill and a couple of tens. He flipped thirty bucks on the bar and dropped the other ten in Brian's tip bucket. Brian gave nod of thanks while he strummed his guitar and played the harmonica. Nigel showed him the picture as he played. Brian's eyes got wide and he stopped his mouth harp just long enough to announce, "Trouble in paradise, folks. Give my love to the missus, brother." He went back to playing as Nigel headed to the door, dialing his phone.

The next morning Nigel was quiet in his bed. A diagonal path of light stretched across the bed as the early morning sun found its way in through a gap in the curtains. He had been awake for hours and had already been up once to have a pot of coffee. But, he had decided to be lazy and slip back into bed. With his fingers laced behind his head, he starred at the ceiling.

A little later he felt movement. He turned his head to find Candice studying him. She slid a hand across the mattress and up across his chest. She moved closer and slung her right knee over his legs. She continued to scoot in until she rolled on top of him. She kissed him on the neck and sat up so she was on her knees, straddling his hips.

She was gorgeous and perfect in her nakedness, even first thing in the morning. He reached up and touched the side of her face and slid his hand down her neck and across her beasts.

Candice bowed and stretched her back and as she rubbed the sleep from her eyes said, "Whatcha think'n 'bout? Your new girlfriend?"

Nigel smiled and said, "No. Not exactly."

Candice squeezed her thighs on Nigel's hips and said, "Well, let's see if I can't get your mind off whatever troubles you." She reached down and grabbed the back of his legs and began a slow grind and wiggle. It didn't take long for Nigel's body to react. Candice made a slight adjustment or two. She took him with her hand and raised her hips. She gasped as she settled back down. As she caught her breath, she said, "Well, there you are. Good morning to you too."

Candice worked her magic and Nigel was happy to put off his thoughts of the Bowery Station tokens, the gang from Charleston, and the parrot boy. With a ten-mile smile, Nigel reached back and grabbed the curtains and slung them together closing the gap.

Later, Nigel slipped out from under the covers and left Candice to her dreams and pillow hugging. He took a quick shower and donned a fresh uniform: shorts, Columbia fishing shirt, flip-flops, visor, and Calcutta sunglasses. Minutes later he was having more coffee with Brian in his apartment. Nigel could squeeze in one more cup. It was 0945 and he has a personal moratorium on coffee after 1000.

They made small talk about the day before, and Nigel congratulated him on two successful shows. "Right on, brother! Right on! It was a good day all around," Brian commented.

They both laughed like hell as Nigel described the little, naked, potbellied guy running around the street chasing people with his curling iron sleeve over his pecker. And Nigel rolled his eyes when Brian brought up the gal from Charleston and the tip-bucket kiss. It did, however, serve as a reminder for his visit.

"So, Brian, do you know anything about an unsavory-looking cat with a parrot that runs around the Apalach and St. George Island area?"

Brian's face went sour. "Scrawny looking little shit with dreadlocks?"

"That sounds like the guy," said Nigel. "Has one of them Doctor Doolittle parrots, except it's red."

"I don't know much, but I know enough. His name is Jessie or Jess, at least that's what folks tell me. More importantly, he's a pain in my ass. I don't like him."

"Really?"

"The son of a bitch is a bum. He shows up with that damn parrot and disrupts my show. He asks for money or beer from the tourists in exchange for having a picture taken with that nasty bird. The tourists love it, naturally, until he starts asking for money. Matt and Lisa had to tell the fucker to stay away. Folks were complaining."

"Really?" Nigel said again. "How long ago was that?"

"I don't know. Maybe three or four months ago."

Nigel didn't say anything.

"But that's not the big thing. I could give a rat's ass if the guy gets a free beer from time to time. It's that fucking bird. It's loud as shit and won't shut up while I play."

"Maybe it wants to hear more Buffett covers."

Taking slight offense to the Buffett comment, Brian said, "Screw you, Nigel!"

Nigel laughed and said, "Easy, brother. Just poking at you."

"I'm sorry. I just don't like that guy or his damn bird. And to make matters worse. I can probably expect to see the bastard later today."

"Why's that?"

"Because I'm back on the island this afternoon, playing at Parrothead's and the owner likes it when he shows up."

"Forget about him. Sorry I brought him up."

"Why did you bring him up?" asked Brian.

"Ah nothing." Nigel changed the subject, "So ... what time do you start playing?"

Oyster Radio was playing on the radio as Nigel's truck headed back toward St. George Island. *Lost in Florida*, a Tom T. Hall song finished up right before the local news. He glanced at the stereo and smiled as Michael Allen reported.

"A Georgia man, identified as Frank Little of Darien, GA, was arrested on St. George Island yesterday after the Franklin County Sheriff's Office responded to calls of a naked man chasing a woman around a house on Baker Avenue. When deputies arrived, the man was in the middle of the street wearing nothing. Little did show some discretion by containing his penis in a large black tube. The deputies described the incident as bizarre with one deputy stating, 'he was running around performing lewd and obscene gestures with the tube, laughing like a hyena the entire time.'

"After refusing several requests to surrender quietly, Little was brought down with a Taser, taken into custody, and charged with public intoxication, indecent exposure, and false advertising. The black tube was later identified as a curling iron sleeve belonging to his girlfriend. The girlfriend refused to press assault charges, but became angry with the deputies when she learned the black sleeve wouldn't be returned immediately. Little was later released on a twenty-five-hundred-dollar bond."

As Nigel stepped on the back deck of Parrothead's, Brian was well into his first set. Nigel took a corner table way in the back to listen and observe. The place was packed with tourists and from the looks of the tip jar, Brian was having another good afternoon. Brian didn't even notice Nigel was there, but with all the bikinis and tanned skin running around, Nigel would have been disappointed in him if he had.

It wasn't until he was about to start his second set that Nigel piped up and yelled, "Play that Colorado song."

Brian found Nigel in the back and said, "Right on! You got it, stranger."

Colorado is more than an original Brian Bowen song; for Nigel, it carries a special significance. As Brian was introducing the song and providing insight to its inspiration, Nigel strolled to the front, made a contribution to the tip jar and moved to an empty bar stool so he could hear better.

It was through this song that Nigel first met Brian, not face-to-face, but by radio-to-ear. Nigel was poring over nautical charts while at the CPO Club on Key West Air Station. He was just passing through, sailing his boat and putting distance between himself and a murder for which he remained a suspect. The barkeep was streaming Oyster Radio over the Internet and, for some reason, when Nigel heard the song, *Colorado*, it stuck.

The next morning Nigel and his boat, *MisChief*, got underway, heading 270 true. The only destination was the western horizon in front of them. He had no idea where he wanted to go. He didn't know. The only thing he knew were a few catchy lyrics from a song he heard from a Forgotten Coast radio station out of Apalachicola. That was enough, and he changed course for Port St. Joe.

In many ways, it was Brian and Oyster Radio that were responsible for Nigel stopping and dropping a hook in St. Joe Bay.

Had he not changed course, had he continued heading west, he would have never met Candice, or Red, or Trixie, or any of the other characters, including Brian, that were now such an important part of his life. It was by way of *Colorado* that Nigel found this sleepy part of the Florida panhandle. It was *Colorado* that brought Nigel home.

Nigel was kicked back, sipping his beer, and enjoying the song when he noticed Brian get distracted. He didn't sing the upcoming chorus. He continued to play behind scrunched eyebrows and gritted teeth. Then everybody on the deck became startled. A screaming squawk filled the air, followed by immediate whistling and laughter. Nigel turned his head and there he was, the guy believed to be named Jessie and his scarlet macaw.

Brian was right. Their presence was a complete distraction. Had it not been for the bird's incessant chatter, it might have been okay. After all, the bird was beautiful and the guy seemed to have a modern-day pirate charm about him. It all fit the mood and environment of Parrothead's. The problem, though, was it wasn't okay. The guy was a pirate, and, to make matters worse, he and his parrot were fucking up Nigel's favorite song.

When Nigel came off the bar stool, Brian smiled and started to sing, picking up where he left off.

By the time Nigel got to the parrot boy, the bird was already sitting on a lady's shoulder and laughing in her ear as she posed for a selfie with her phone. Others were around awaiting their chance to play with the bird, even though the parrot boy reeked from the freshness of last Thursday's bath.

Nigel ignored her and spoke to the parrot boy, "Your name is Jessie, right?"

"Yeah. Who wants to know?"

"The guy who can no longer hear the song he requested because your bird won't shut up."

The parrot boy said nothing and shrugged his shoulders.

"Both your nasty asses, you and the bird, need to leave now."

The lady finished her selfie with the parrot and brought the bird back, slipping the guy a five-dollar bill.

Above the bird's whistling and laughter, again Nigel said, "Leave. Now ... before I lose my patience. Get out of here."

In her *I'm-not-from-around-here* accent the lady looked at Nigel and said, "Maybe you need to leave. This bird is sweet and gorgeous."

"Lady," Nigel said. "To start with, I'm not talking to you. And no, *they* are not sweet. He hasn't showered in days, and, if you had been paying any attention at all, you would have noticed that sweet and gorgeous bird shit all down the back of your blouse."

Her tone seemed to change when another woman confirmed the fecal splattering with a thin-lipped smile and a nod of the head.

The lady took off, yelling, "Harold! Oh my God! Harold! Back to the house."

Nigel turned his attention back to the parrot boy. "I'm not going to say it again. Leave!"

"No."

Nigel said, "Wrong answer." He grabbed a handful of dirty dreadlocks, clenched down tight, gave them a half-twist and headed for the deck steps.

The parrot hung on but was flapping its wings and screaming in protest. The parrot boy was screaming and yelling as loud as the bird. They were almost to the steps when this fella intervened, "Whoa! Whoa! Whoa! Knock it off before I call the sheriff."

Nigel slung the parrot boy around and released him.

The fella said, "I'm the manager here, pal." Looking at the parrot boy, he asked "Now what's going on, Jess?"

The parrot boy shrugged his shoulders, so Nigel explained, "I tipped your guitar player and requested a song. I was listening to it just fine until shithead here and his bird showed up."

Parrot Boy started to smile big when the manager said, "Listen, pal. You're going to have to leave. The customers love Jess and the bird. They get to stay. I can't have any trouble here, so, unless you want me to call the sheriff, you got to leave."

Nigel looked at the manager, then to the parrot boy who was now wearing a smartass grin. He looked back at the manager who said, "Now. You have to leave, now."

The parrot boy said, "Listen, fella. I'm sorry about your song." He reached into his pocket and continued, "Here. No hard feelings. Go to Bowery Station. These are worth a few free beers at the bar."

The parrot boy held out and opened his hand. It was full of B.S. tokens. Nigel studied them, said nothing, and turned to walk away. A handful of folks applauded as he walked down the steps. The manager followed him and stopped at the edge of the parking lot.

From the microphone, Nigel heard Brian say, "Nice try, fella. See ya another time."

Nigel didn't leave.

When he got to his truck, he never looked back but figured the manager was watching. He jumped in, started it up, and pulled out of the parking lot nice and slow, no sign of anger or emotion.

Before pulling back into the parking lot, he made an easy-going drive around the block, stopping at a convenience store to pick up a six pack of beer, a bag of ice, and a can of Copenhagen pouches. He found a great place to park in the shadows that provided a good view of the parking lot and bar.

The old Ford F-150 isn't as comfortable as it used to be, but Nigel didn't mind. A new truck payment is far more painful, and he has sat and waited in far less comfortable conditions. It was hot and muggy, but he had beer, a little dip, and the radio. He settled in for the wait.

After about an hour and a few beers, Nigel observed several folks come and go from the bar, but no sign of Parrot Boy. The one thing he could see was the need to empty his bladder, so he got out and stepped around the back of the truck. He was finishing his business when he saw the red parrot bouncing along between cars. Nigel ducked down to watch as he zipped up his pants. When he was sure he hadn't been seen, he crouched down and began to follow, keeping a couple rows of cars between.

The bird stopped moving next to an old Ford Taurus station wagon. Nigel crept closer and watched as Parrot Boy put the bird into a cage in the back seat. Nigel was only a row and a few cars away. When Nigel saw his target open the door and jump behind the wheel, he took off in a sprint. He gave a quick glance around to see if anyone could see him. There were a few people in the lot, but he was confident he wasn't drawing their attention.

As he got closer, he could hear the engine begin to turn over. As the tired engine fired off, Nigel opened the passenger side door and jumped in, knocking a collection of empty fast food bags and a box into the floorboard. Parrot Boy jumped back startled, saying, "What the..." Nigel reached for the ignition, took the keys, and said, "Shut up and don't move. We're going to have a little talk."

Nigel hoped he could do this without drawing much attention, but the parrot was excited by the commotion and began squawking and flapping its wings. Parrot Boy made a quick move for the door handle, but Nigel grabbed his wrist, twisted it back on itself and said, "Not so fast, Jess."

Jessie shifted in his seat. He was much smaller than the six foot three inch, 230 pound Logan. He contorted his body as Nigel twisted. "Okay! Okay! Dammit ... just let go."

Nigel did.

Jessie shook his wrist in the air and with fear in his voice said, "What do you want?"

"Tell the bird to shut the fuck up."

He did, but it didn't.

Nigel took the keys and started the car. As he did, he noticed the contents of the box that were now scattered about the car. He reached down and picked one of them up.

Jessie said, "What's going on? What do you want with me?"

"Buckle up. You're driving. Let's go."

"Where to?"

Nigel held up the bootleg B.S. token and said, "Bowery Station, bitch. You have some explaining to do."

Parrot Boy hesitated. Nigel reached for his cell phone and said, "Or ... I can call the Franklin County Sheriff."

He put the car in drive and made for the street. Above the chatter of the bird, Nigel said, "You're doing good. Keep it nice and easy, no funny business."

They were halfway across the St. George Bridge when Nigel asked, "How many more boxes of these fake tokens do you have?"

The parrot boy said nothing.

Logan looked around at the surrounding traffic. There weren't any cars around, so Nigel reached over and grabbed his driver by the throat and clenched his fingers and thumb around his windpipe. "Jessie. I asked you a question, goddammit."

Parrot Boy let go of the wheel and tried to pull Logan's hand away but couldn't. The car started to roam over into oncoming traffic, so he let go of Logan's hand and swerved back into his own lane. Logan released him and said, "Don't piss me off. Keeping me happy is in your best interest."

With one free hand, Parrot Boy rubbed his throat and, with a strained voice box, coughed the words, "You're crazy."

"No," Logan said, "I'm just crazy enough. Now answer the question."

The answer didn't come quick enough, so Logan began to reach for his throat again.

"Two!" he screamed. "There are two more full boxes in the back."

"Are there more anywhere else?"

"No. That's all I have left."

"Good."

They were quiet, but it was awkward. Nigel's quiet was cool, calm, and collected, offering an occasional smile to his driver. Parrot Boy's quiet smelled of nerves and fear. He wasn't smiling.

They were now crossing the bay bridge toward Apalach. Nigel broke the silence, "So how much were you selling them for?"

Jessie said, "Does it matter?"

"Guess not."

As they were closing in on town, Nigel said, "Okay. This is how this is going to work. You are going to find a parking space outside Bowery Station and we are going to serve you up a heaping helping of humble pie."

"How do you mean?"

"You are going to tell Matt everything. Confess and apologize."

"But what if he wants to call the cops and have me arrested?"

"He probably will, but that won't happen. I am going to advise against it."

The parrot boy looked at Logan with jittery eyes and asked, "Why would you do that?"

"For two reasons. First, you are not worth the county tax dollars it would take to prosecute your worthless ass."

Parrot Boy tried to park across the street, but Nigel saw an open spot in front of the bar. "No. No. No, asshole. Park over there, in front."

He did. After he put the wagon into park, Parrot Boy asked, "What's the other reason?"

Logan looked at him with cold eyes and said, "Because, if Matt and Lisa ever even suspect you're up to your old tricks, I promise, I will find you. And when I'm done, you will have wished you were locked up in jail, safe in the loving arms of some fat, burly inmate. Are we clear on that point, Wilma?"

Parrot Boy said nothing, but he offered a nod.

"Now pick up all those tokens and put them back in the box."

He did as he was told and Nigel looked around. It was already shaping up to be a busy afternoon at the Bowery and the music hadn't even started. A lot of folks were socializing outside on the bench and picnic table, which meant the seating was limited inside. The parrot mumbled and chattered to itself. Nigel turned toward the cage and said, "Shut up back there. I need to make a call." Nigel pulled out his cell phone and dialed Matt's number. Just before it went to voicemail, he answered.

"I'm a little busy, Nigel. What's up?"

"I see that. Good crowd. Things look like they're hopping."

"You're here?"

"Yep."

"Then why the hell are you calling me on the phone?"

"I need for you to come out front. It's important."

Nigel hung up, reached across, took the keys out of the ignition, and grabbed the box of tokens. As he was getting out of the wagon he looked at Parrot Boy and said, "Don't go anywhere, Wilma."

Matt walked out drying his hands with a bar towel, then slung it over his shoulder. He found Nigel leaning against the fenders. As he approached, he leaned his head over to the side to look through the windshield. When he recognized who was behind the wheel, he pointed his finger and said, "What the hell is he doing here?"

Nigel raised a hand and said, "It's okay. I brought him." Then he paused a beat and said, "Well, it's actually not okay, but I'll get to that in a minute." Nigel turned and looked at Parrot Boy to deliver a silent message. *Don't even think about it.* They moved to the hood of the wagon and Nigel placed the box on the hood.

The parrot boy sat behind the wheel and watched and listened best he could. He saw Nigel open the box to let Matt reach in for a sample. All the while Nigel was explaining everything he knew. Parrot Boy sat up straighter and pressed his back against the seat to add distance when Matt looked at him with a furious gaze. Matt was pacing now, back and forth in front of the wagon, talking with his hands, but he wasn't loud. Parrot Boy could hear bits and pieces, but he didn't have to hear anything. Actions speak louder than words.

When Jessie saw Matt grab his cell phone, he got nervous. He turned his head and started to eye the door handle. He contemplated his chances. *If I'm quick about it...* Then he almost pissed his pants when he was startled by a slap on the hood. He looked up to find Logan staring at him, shaking his head, and wagging a finger. "Don't even think about it, Jessie."

Nigel talked Matt into putting the cell phone away. They talked a bit more, then they walked around the back of the wagon and confiscated the other two boxes out of the back. When the back was open, Matt spoke to the back of Parrot Boy's head, "Jessie ... you're a slimier bastard than I imagined."

The slimy bastard said nothing.

As Matt carried the two boxes back into the bar, Nigel walked along the driver's side of the wagon and opened the door. In a calm voice said, "Get out, Jess. Get the parrot and come with me."

Parrot Boy hesitated so Logan reached in and grabbed a handful of dreadlocks and started to pull. "I said, 'Get out,' dammit."

Parrot Boy began to yell, "Okay! Okay, goddammit. Let go!"

All the hollering upset the parrot. It was back to its hell-raising mode, but calmed down some after Jessie got it out of its cage. And while those that were outside already had a casual interest in what was going on, now their full attention was squarely on the wagon and the commotion. They stopped their drinking and conversations as Logan dragged Parrot Boy out of the vehicle.

When he was out of the wagon, Logan let go of his hair. He grabbed the back of his shirt. "Get moving, Jessie," Logan demanded. "Inside."

As they passed the hood of the wagon, Nigel reached over and grabbed the open box and carried inside. Everyone that was outside now fell in line to follow them in. Nigel marched Parrot Boy straight to the stage where the microphone stand stood hot, always at the ready for some impromptu open mic performance.

Matt went back behind the bar with Lisa. She asked, "What's going on?"

Matt put his finger to his lips and said, "Just listen."

Nigel tapped on the mic a few times with his finger and made a crisp popping noise through PA speakers. People winced. He leaned over and said, "Is this thing on?"

Everybody in the room said in unison, "YES!"

"Oh, good," Nigel paused for a beat then continued. "Well, it is Sunday after all. And if any of you are like me, you probably missed your church service this morning. So, I was thinking we could have ourselves a little service this afternoon."

Moans and groans and lack of interest filled the room. Nigel said, "Now don't be so down on me. We are going to have communion too. So, grab a fresh beer and some peanuts." That brought a little life back into the group.

"Now, I'm not a very religious man, so humor me a bit here. Are there any good Catholics in the room?"

Several hands went up.

"Good. You guys will have to forgive me now, because I'm sure to go off script."

Nigel reached over and put his hand on the parrot boy's shoulder and said, "How many of you know Wilma here?"

Parrot Boy gave a frustrating look to Nigel and said, "Jessie, dammit. My name is Jessie."

Several hands went up.

Nigel looked at Parrot Boy and said, "Sorry about that. So, tell me, do you see any familiar faces out there, Jess?"

Parrot Boy slowly nodded.

"Good," Nigel said. "That means this will be all the more meaningful for some, because we are going to start this little service off with a real confessional."

The parrot boy looked at Nigel and with a surprised crack in this voice asked, "What?"

Nigel ignored him. "That's right folks. Master Jessie here is going to share his deepest secrets, transgressions, and sins, many of which are crimes against society."

The room began to play along. Gasping sounds, as well as ooohs and ahhhhs filled the room. One guy in the back hollered, "Say it isn't so."

"Yes, I know. It is shocking," said Nigel. "So ... how many of you in the house want to hear a confessional?"

The room cheered with excitement.

"All right then. Let's get to it."

For Nigel, the fun and games were over. The fun-loving, gregarious attitude was over. In a stern, more serious, business-like tone, Nigel looked at Parrot Boy and said, "Jessie, the floor is yours."

As Nigel stepped away and offered up the mic, Parrot Boy could see the seriousness in Nigel's eyes. He made his way to the microphone and looked out at the crowd. They were smiling, anticipating whatever came next. He looked behind the bar. The look on the faces of Matt and Lisa were of anger and frustration. He looked at Nigel who offered one word, "Now!"

He stepped closer to the mic and said, "Ahhh. Hey y'all. I'm not sure where to start..."

He got quiet, thinking of what to say next and a woman from the bar yelled, "Just tell it, young man. The truth will set you free."

That was followed by a few Hallelujahs and an amen or two. He was about to say something when somebody with a rough voice said, "Hey! Look, Bubba. It's the bird guy."

Everyone turned around to look. A group of bikers, not of the Huffy or Schwinn variety, had entered the bar. Parrot Boy looked at Nigel and said, "Oh shit."

"Friends of yours?" asked Nigel. "I don't care. Stop stalling. Get on with it."

Parrot Boy replied with a slow shake of his head.

Nigel pushed him out of the way and took the microphone. "Okay folks, enough with the kidding around." Pointing toward Parrot Boy, he said, "Jessie, standing here, is a shithead."

Nigel told the crowd what Jessie had done. How he'd counterfeited the Bowery Station happy hour tokens and sold them as bootleg copies to tourists, essentially indirectly stealing from the B.S. coffers.

A few in the crowd took a sneak peek at the tokens they had in their pockets. Most slipped them back into their pockets and said nothing. Regardless of the circumstances, they didn't want it known that they had been active participants in the conspiracy.

That was how most reacted. The biker gang, on the other hand, wasn't worried with what others might think or say. Guilt by association didn't weigh heavy on their minds. The biker called Bubba said, "So ... what you are saying is," and he held up three quart-freezer bags of tokens, "these are worthless?"

"Did you buy them from little Rasta boy here?" asked Nigel.

"Yeah. Exactly."

"Well," Nigel said, "I'm sure they will make great poker chips, but that's about it. They won't get you beers around here."

The bikers started to grumble. Their anger grew and they started to ease their way through the crowd and toward the stage. Nigel watched the advance and spoke to Parrot Boy, "Jess, if you were ever thinking of running, you're behind by about five seconds. Just remember what I said in the car, I meant every word."

"Got it ... here ... hold Ruby for me." He put the parrot on Nigel's shoulder and dashed off the stage and exited out through the beer garden, a courtyard which empties out on a side street. It was his only option as an escape route. The biker gang was in full pursuit. Nigel stopped the one called Bubba and said, "Do me a favor. Hand over the bags. They're no good here."

Bubba was reluctant, but surrendered the tokens anyway saying, "The little bastard." Then he took off to join the chase.

Once the parrot boy and the bikers left the building, it only took about ten seconds for the place to return to normal. Matt turned the music back up and people went back to their beer drinking and peanut eating.

Nigel put the parrot on the tip jar that said *Stop Playing* and walked over to the bar and dropped the bags of bootleg tokens on the bar. Lisa said, "I wonder how many more are out there?"

Matt joined them and Nigel said, it doesn't really matter. You'll both just need to be careful for a while when folks turn them in. He opened one of the bags and dumped the tokens out on the bar. He picked one up and said, "They look pretty damn good, huh? But lookie here, he spelt Bowery wrong. The 'e' is missing."

Matt reached over into the box that supposedly contained the authentic tokens. The third one he looked at was a forgery. "I guess we'll have to go through and check all of these."

They all said nothing for a bit, then Nigel said, "Where's the entertainment? They should be here by now, shouldn't they?"

Lisa said, "They can't make it. Their van broke down in Sopchoppy."

"Well, that sucks."

"Not so bad actually. Matt got in touch with Brian. He should be here any minute. He is heading straight over from Parrothead's."

"Parrothead's ... shit! That reminds me. I need a ride. I left my truck over there."

Matt said, "Let me get my keys. It's the least I can do."

"Thanks," said Nigel. "While you do that, I need to put Jessie's car keys back in the wagon. I'm guessing he will be coming ..."

Then somebody at the door yelled, "What the hell is this, some kind of sick joke?"

It was Brian Bowen, looking flabbergasted.

Matt said, "What is it, buddy?"

Brian pointed, and through gritted teeth said, "What is that fucking parrot doing on my stage?"

Nigel mumbled, "Uh Oh. Not good."

And, as soon as the parrot saw Brian, it walked around the lip of the tip jar, weaving its head back and forth screaming, "Stop Playing! Stop Playing!"

Nigel, Matt, and Lisa busted out in laughter. Brian not so much.

EL DIABLO ROJO

The melodic high-pitch shrill of the boatswain's whistle moved up and down the notes and filled the entire room. After a few cycles, it quit altogether. Within a few seconds, it was back. He did his best to ignore it, but he couldn't. That was the whole idea. It was a command, a call to action, an audible specifically designed to get your attention. It worked every time, whether you wanted it to or not.

Nigel raised his head and looked at the clock on the nightstand. He shook his head and thought *Son of a bitch. You have to be shitting me.* In that moment, Nigel realized that downloading a boatswain's whistle call as a ringtone was one stupid idea. As much as he loved naval nostalgia, the idea of it being forced down his throat at 0115 wasn't something he had thought about.

He reached for the phone, squinted to read the caller ID and found the button to answer. "Damn," he grumbled. Then he sandwiched the phone between his pillow and ear. He answered with a clearing of his throat, but said nothing.

The voice on the other end of the line asked, "Nigel. Are you there?"

Nigel said nothing. As a matter of fact, he never even heard the voice on the other end of the line. He was back to sleep. The caller recognized the subtle snore and breathing pattern.

"Nigel. Wake up, dammit. This is important."

Moments later, after never getting a response, the call was ended. The phone went dead and all was quiet again. Until ... the caller dialed Nigel's number again.

Now, with the phone right next to his ear, the boatswain's whistle pierced right through one side of the brain and exited out the other. Startled was an understatement. The adrenaline rush caused his heart to stop, then race and sent his body into convulsions as he attempted to lift himself off the pillow. His eyes were wide open, but they had not adjusted to the darkness. He couldn't see anything. When the phone cycled through another whistle, he swatted the phone off the pillow and against the wall. He half-hoped the phone was broken, but no luck. The Otter Box case did its job and protected it from certain destruction. The phone, now on the floor with the screen up, continued to whistle.

Nigel swung his feet out of bed and onto the floor. He was panting, breathing hard from the sudden excitement. He looked down at the phone and the Caller ID. He reached down and picked up the phone to answer it. He rubbed his head with his free hand and cleared his throat before growling a single question, "Have you been drinking?"

That was a dumb question. He realized it the second it came out of his mouth, but he wasn't thinking clearly. It was either too early, or too late ... however one-fifteen in the morning should be described, so he followed up with a more logical question, "What is it, Red?"

"I need your help. Trouble's brewing."

"Trouble is something I'm trying to stay away from. You should know that better than anybody."

"Yeah, but that still doesn't take away from the fact that I need your help."

Red was being serious. Nigel could hear it in his voice. He wasn't being his usual casual and carefree self. Nigel could also hear wind noise and Black Sabbath playing in the background, an Oyster Radio classic, especially after dark.

"Where are you?" asked Nigel.

"About a mile from your house. Get dressed. I'll be there in one hundred and eleven seconds."

Red ended the call.

Nigel remained on the side of the bed. He was bent over holding his head shaking it in disbelief. Then he reached down and grabbed a pair of drab olive cargo shorts off the floor and slipped into them. He stood, stretched and headed to the coffee maker.

After dumping out the old grounds from the filter, he poured the old coffee out of the pot and started to rinse it out. That's when he noticed the headlights of Red's Explorer turn into the drive. Nigel turned on the machine and was pouring fresh water into his Mr. Coffee when Red walked in the back door to the kitchen.

"What are you doing?" asked Red.

Nigel turned his head as he continued to pour, and with cutting sarcasm said, "What the hell does it look like I'm doing?"

"But we don't have time for that."

"You must have a rat in your pocket, because I'm not sure which 'we' you are referring to. But there's one thing for sure, I'm not doing shit until I get some coffee and you tell me what this is all about."

"Can you make it a cup to go? We may already be too late."

With slight aggravation, Nigel said, "No. I can't. Now what's this all about?"

Red said one word that got Nigel's immediate attention, "Poachers."

In the time it took for the coffee maker to gurgle, spit, and drip a fresh pot, Red explained enough to satisfy Nigel's needs. Red was still providing details when Nigel interrupted, "So why did you wait until one o'clock in the morning to call?"

"I hadn't planned to call at all, but I was up late watching old reruns on the television. That's when I saw some activity down by the beach."

Red and Trixie's place is on Cape San Blas. It's beach front on the Gulf of Mexico side, a beautiful location with a great view of the beach and surf.

"Red," Nigel said. "It's tourist season. People are on the beach at all hours."

"I know, but..."

Nigel saw the concern and worry in Red's eyes. He is a true lover of nature, but he isn't a tree-hugging wacko by any stretch of the imagination. For example, Red often wears a t-shirt that says, *I Love PETA* on the front, but the back says *People Eating Tasty Animals*. For Red, it's all about balance.

Aside from all of Red's crazy and silly antics, Nigel has come to understand him as one of the wisest and most rational men he has ever known. Red understands man's position as Earth's dominate species, and for man to survive, it will come at the expense of others. But he also believes there are times when man has an incredible responsibility to preserve its resources from abuse, so his interests in protecting what should be left alone runs deep. Nigel could see this was one of those times, so, if Red was concerned, so was he.

As the coffee was finishing up, Nigel said, "To your right, first door under the counter. Get my Thermos and fill it. I'll go throw on a shirt and grab a few things. You can tell me the rest in the car."

When Nigel got back to the kitchen, he was dressed. He had slipped into a black t-shirt and was carrying a large, heavy-duty canvas bag. Red had a cup of coffee waiting for him on the counter. Nigel grabbed the cup and took a quick sip and looked at Red and said, "Thanks, man." That's when he saw Red standing at the door. In one hand, he held Nigel's Thermos bottle, in the other his handle of seven-year-old Jim Beam. Nigel's eyes shifted several times back and forth between the bottle and Red's face. Then he said, "Really?"

"What? It could come in handy."

Nigel brushed by his partner shaking his head and said, "Come on, dammit. Let's go."

In the vehicle, Red explained everything. The day before, he attended a meeting with the Port St. Joe Sea Turtle Patrol. The group is made up of passionate volunteers that help in the protection, recovery, and preservation of the ocean's endangered and threatened species. Red isn't a volunteer, but he provides financial support, appreciation and respect for their work. He has a financial and emotional interest in their efforts, so he often shows up at meetings to check on their current activities and progress. His attendance and input is always welcomed.

"Nigel, someone has been raiding nests. Poachers have been preying on fresh lays after the females crawl ashore."

"That sucks," replied Nigel.

"Yeah. It sucks and it's also illegal as hell. Twice this week, as volunteers were making their morning turtle-walk rounds, fresh nests were discovered to have been disturbed, the eggs snatched away and removed."

"And you think they are out there now?"

Red shrugged his shoulders and said, "I don't know. I got a bad feeling."

Nigel thought *A bad feeling, huh?* But didn't say anything. He could see this wasn't one of Red's crazy shenanigans, so Nigel was all in. He poured more coffee from his Thermos.

The entire Forgotten Coast of Florida is an active sea turtle nesting region. Unfortunately, states that are lucky enough to share in the wonder of sea turtle reproduction do not have the resources to monitor and protect their activity. This is why the work of the turtle patrol is so important. If not for the volunteers, the nests would go undocumented and more importantly unprotected.

Each morning, during the laying and hatching season, volunteers patrol the several miles that makeup the shoreline, from Indian Pass to the tip of Cape San Blas. In the early weeks of the season, they look for the distinctive tracks made by females that have returned to the beach from which they themselves had once hatched. If this is a female's first visit to lay eggs, it may have been twenty to thirty years since she last made the crawl to the ocean as a hatchling. If she is successful, she will make her way into the dunes to lay her eggs, which could be in excess of one hundred. During a female's laying season, which occurs every two to four years, every few weeks she will return to dig another nest and lay more eggs. She may do this six or seven times before she is done.

There are several things that could impair a female from a successful lay. All of which are avoidable as they are created by man. One is unnatural lighting on shore. The other is shit left on the beach by tourists.

The unnatural lighting confuses the turtles, both nesting females and hatchlings. Light pollution around nesting beaches make it difficult for females to find and select the dark and quiet spots necessary to lay her eggs. After emerging from their nests, the same unnatural lighting will cause the internal navigation system of hatchings to become confused and draw them away from the water's edge and toward certain death.

Items left on the beach serve as obstacles the turtles can't easily navigate. The path to their nesting site is driven by instinct, not by individual choice. They make their landfall in the dark of night, so they are not prepared to deal with obstructions in their path. More times than not these result in false crawls. The turtles are simply unable to reach their nesting destination, so they give up and head back to sea, in hopes of being able to try again later.

This tourist effect hasn't always been a problem, but in recent years it has increasingly grown. A trip to the beach used to mean a few chairs, maybe an umbrella, and a cooler. Now, with the development of the popup tent, a family's footprint on the beach has grown to a full-scale campsite. If several families vacation together, it is less of a campsite and more like a hideous beachfront monstrosity.

They become so massive that it is impractical to set up and teardown each day. It's ridiculous.

During the height of the summer tourist season, the beaches can be littered with these large obstacles decreasing a female's chances of success when she finally comes ashore. This is an obvious, great concern to the turtle patrol, plus … it makes the beaches look like ass.

For this reason, the county has enacted a "Leave No Trace" ordinance, which has become popular with other beach communities that have developed concerns with tourist clutter. Basically, if you bring it on the beach, you take it back with you each night. Doing so keeps the beaches clean, plus it opens a clear path for the turtles.

It is bad enough that a female has to deal with shore lighting and a cluttered beach, it is another when scumbags are raiding nests and poaching eggs. That raises the level of human intervention from inept and ignorance to harmful and malicious. A complete game changer.

Red was turning his Explorer onto Cape Road when Nigel asked, "So, where are they finding the raided nests?"

"Between the gate and the horn of the cape."

"Ah … makes sense."

A large section of Cape San Blas, from the Gulf of Mexico across to St. Joe Bay is owned by the Air Force. It is part of Eglin, AFB. There are no planes or runways, but the property is active with just about every type of satellite dish and antenna of varying frequency. It's a top-notch communication center.

There is no development on this section of the base and access to it after dark is limited to foot traffic. At dusk, the gate is locked to prevent vehicles from driving on that section of the beach. All this means, no unnatural shore lighting and no tourist compounds are left on the beach. It provides the best of all worlds for any female drawn back to this spot to lay her eggs. It also creates a secluded, well-hidden playing field for some bastard looking to stock up on eggs.

Red eased into Salinas Park. The park has an access for permitted vehicles to drive on the beach, plus it was the most practical spot to enter the beach given where they were going. They weaved their way through the property, and as soon as they reached the beach access Red shut off his headlamps and left his parking lights on.

The sky was blanketed by heavy overcast. There would be no stars or moonlight to drive by, so visibility was going to be a huge problem. Nigel reached into the backseat and grabbed his bag. He pulled it up front in his lap and said, "Turn off all the lights."

"Then I damn well won't be able to see. It was going to be bad enough driving by parking lights."

Nigel opened his bag and grabbed a pair of spooky looking goggles. He placed them on his head and flipped a switch on the side. He moved his head, looking around the vehicle. He took them off his head and handed them to Red, "Here put these on."

Red took the goggles, "What the hell?"

"N.V.G., Night vision, you'll be able to see just fine."

Red slipped them over his head and adjusted them for fit. "Son of a bitch. These are awesome. Where in hell did you get these?"

"Doesn't matter. They come in handy when sailing at night. As do these..." Nigel reached back into his bag and produced a pair of bulky looking binoculars, also of the night vision variety. He wrapped the strap around his neck and turned them on and used them to look around. As he gazed around, he added, "And they eat the shit out of the batteries." He rested the unit against his chest and turned toward Red, who looked utterly ridiculous and out of place wearing the military grade night vision goggles.

Red was looking around at all the various shades of green stopping to focus on Nigel's face and huge smile. Red said, "What the hell is so funny?"

"Nothing, Red. Nothing at all. Let's get moving."

Red pulled out on the beach and took a right toward the horn of the cape and the gate that marks the beginning of the Air Force beach. Before long they were riding past Red and Trixie's and moving quicker than normal, much faster than they normally would have during the day.

"Can you see okay?" asked Nigel.

"Sure, but if I didn't have these on I would be running over all kinds of shit."

"Just keep an eye out for holes."

"Yep," Red replied.

Large holes dug in the sand are another significant danger to the female turtles. Holes left overnight are found by the turtles during their historic crawl. Once they fall in and get stuck, the game is over.

Not to mention, a significant hole will cause huge problems for some Jeep or pickup truck out for an evening ride. That is why beach holes were included in the Leave No Trace ordinance. It isn't brain surgery. *You dig it. You fill it.* Leave each night as if you were never there.

Running down the beach was like an obstacle course. Tents, piles of beach chairs, holes dug by children, and the occasional kayak littered the beach. While Red navigated the clutter, Nigel scanned ahead with the binoculars. Something got his attention.

"Whoa!" Nigel said.

"What is it?"

"I don't know yet. Just slow down and keep driving."

Red was inspired by whatever Nigel may have seen and was influenced to press the Explorer a bit harder down the beach. This made for a bumpier ride and made looking through binoculars more difficult.

"Whoa, brother. Slow it down some. Slow it way down."

Nigel kept the glasses to his eyes and said, "Up there. That next beach camp. Stop the truck there."

"Oh, shit!" said Red. "I see it now." And even though they were almost there, Red pressed hard on the accelerator before standing on the brakes and sliding to a stop. They both jumped out of the vehicle and ran down to the crawl tracks and followed them into the middle of a canopy tent.

The beach camp was a monstrosity. It must have accommodated five or six different families. Three canopy tents were strung together like a triplex apartment building. Each tent contained more shit than anyone should have at the beach. The only thing missing was the color television that they apparently took back with them, because they found a remote control resting on a cooler. *If you need this much shit at the beach, why bother.*

"Come on," Red said as he panted with excitement. "She's still in here."

Red didn't hesitate. He started grabbing beach chairs and whatever else he could snatch and slung them out of the way. He looked up at Nigel and yelled, "Help me, dammit."

When enough gear had been cleared away, they found her underneath a table and wedged between two large coolers. She was confused and frantic to find her way. The table was slung to the side by Red as Nigel pulled the coolers out of her way. Once she was free, she stopped her struggling to rest. There was more stuff piled up between the female and the dunes, so Nigel made short work of clearing a path.

Nigel was panting himself. "What now?" he asked.

"We wait," said Red.

As they waited, they gathered the stuff they slung around and piled it all up in one of the other canopy tents. That's when they found the television remote control, and of all things a marine porta-potty. As they were dragging the last cooler under the tent, in a deflated tone, Red said, "Damn! Stupid motherfuckers."

From the other side of the tent, Nigel asked, "What is it?"

"The anxiety was too much. She's headed back to sea."

Nigel found Red's silhouette. They walked over to where the turtle was marching back toward the surf, getting close enough that Nigel could now make her out in the darkness. He asked, "Will she try again?"

She moved under the effects of exhaustion, but as the surf began to slide up wet beneath her fins and shell, she picked up her pace. As the first wave crashed upon her head, Red said, "We can only hope." And he turned and walked back to the vehicle with Nigel in tow. They settled back in the seats and Red said, "Hand me that bottle of Beam."

Nigel reached behind the driver's seat and produced the handle of whiskey. Before giving it to Red, he unscrewed the cap and took a deep swig of his own. Red took a sip and said, "She looked young."

Nigel listened.

"This may have been her first visit since she herself hatched somewhere along this stretch of dunes," Red paused then continued, "decades ago. All to be screwed up by a bunch of humans." Red took another healthy sip and said, "Stupid bastards."

Nigel said, "Stupid? Probably not. Ignorant, maybe. They aren't being malicious, just..."

Red said, "Stupid," finishing Nigel's sentence. "You saw all that shit they drug out on the beach. For crying out loud, the place is looking more like a goddamn, cheap-ass trailer park every year. It's just stupid."

"I hear ya, brother. You've made your point, Red," Nigel conceded.

They passed the bottle back and forth a couple times. They sat in silence for a few minutes. Nigel's neck was resting on the head rest and his eyes were closed. He was on the edge of sleep when Red said, "Well, I guess it's a good thing we came out here, huh?"

Nigel's eyes popped open. He was about to say something smart, but he saw something down the beach. Small lights danced on the edge of the dunes. He blinked a few times to help focus then he grabbed the binoculars. The magnification and night vision brought the green and black action much closer.

Red noticed Nigel's interest and gazed down the beach. "Hey, what do you see?"

"Can't be sure," said Nigel. "But there is one thing I can be sure of..." Nigel stopped to look at his watch. "At fifteen after three, I'm willing to bet it isn't good."

The action was down where they expected to find it, on the Air Force beach. They were maybe a couple hundred yards away and Nigel didn't want to spook them by driving closer. The access gate would be locked anyway, so they wouldn't be able to get there by vehicle.

Nigel handed the binoculars to Red and said, "Let's trade. I want to get closer."

Red handed over the night vision googles and Nigel adjusted them for his head. After snugging the fit, he said, "Use the binoculars to get closer. Don't let them see you. I'll catch up to you later."

Nigel opened the door and slipped away. Red half-yelled, half-whispered, "What are you planning to do?" But it was too late. Nigel had already disappeared into the dunes. "Dammit, Nigel."

Nigel dashed about thirty yards or so into the dunes before turning toward the target. The rolling hills of sand are not huge, but, coupled with the healthy stands of sea oats, they created good cover. He kept a low profile as he darted between and around the dunes. After a while, to get his bearings, he crawled atop a dune to gage his progress. They were still there and he had made up more than half the distance. He eased backwards off the dune and set off again.

He ran faster. Head down, bag in hand. When he had a pretty good idea he was getting close, he slowed, to a stalking speed. He stopped and listened. He could now hear voices. He crept closer and closer. The voices were travelling over the dunes much clearer now. They were Latino. Not a word of English was being spoken.

Logan looked around and found the highest dune between himself and the voices. Head down, he dashed to its base and sniper crawled to the top for a better view. There they were. Three of them. Four of them if you counted the female loggerhead that was depositing eggs right into the hands of the poachers. They were transferring the eggs into a medium sized cooler, plenty big enough to handle the hundred or more eggs that were to be expected.

Logan was patient and vigilant as he watched. To get more comfortable, he twisted and dug his elbows and body down into the soft sand. He snapped a twig or something doing so, and it caught the attention of one of the poachers. He looked up saying, "Alto! Alto!"

He pointed his flashlight toward the noise. Logan remained perfectly still. He didn't even breathe.

Perhaps it was by design to prevent drawing too much attention to themselves, but all three of the poacher's flashlights were weak and dim. The light pointed at Logan wasn't powerful enough to illuminate the dune, but bright enough to cause a blinding effect through Logan's NVGs. All Logan could do was squint and watch for movement.

The poachers whispered back and forth. A conversation Logan couldn't hear or understand. Finally, the light moved off him and they went back to the task at hand, transferring eggs into the cooler.

Logan remained still and quiet in the sand contemplating his options. It was three on one. He liked the odds. He had a huge advantage: sight. He could see them, but they couldn't see him. The thought of weapons crossed his mind, but he was betting they weren't armed. He asked himself in thought *What to do?* And the answer came. He told himself *Be patient. See what happens. You can always attack later.*

Logan began to wonder about Red. *Where was he?* That was something else he had to consider. If Red charged the nest in anger, then it would be a game changer. He turned his head and body to look back down the beach. It took a while but he finally caught movement. Red was creeping up the dune line.

As Logan turned back toward the nest, one of the poachers had stood. After brushing sand off his knees and legs, he started to make his way inland through the dunes. Nigel smiled. Now the match-up was two on one, or one on one. It was his pick. He went with the conventional predator playbook, prey on the one who has strayed from the herd.

Logan watched the lone poacher stroll away at an easy pace. He was in no hurry and neither was Logan. He waited and allowed some distance to build before backing off the dune. He opened his bag and pulled out a pair of closed finger sailing gloves and slipped them on. He got to his feet and crouched as he walked away. The further away he got from the nest, the faster his pace. The pursuit was on.

Like before, he stayed low as he dashed around the dunes, but as he traveled inland, there was less coverage from the dunes. Long before either one of them reached the stand of pines that stood between the dunes and the Cape Road, the coverage would be all but gone. Logan still had darkness on his side.

He decided not to follow the poacher, but to run around and ahead. He wanted to enter the woods first adding the cover of trees to his advantage. Logan began to pick up his pace, standing straighter as he picked up speed and making more noise in the process. He went wide to create some distance and as Logan was passing some forty to fifty yards or so to the right, the poacher had stopped. Logan slowed to a walking pace and then stopped to watch his target. The darkness was still overwhelming. Logan watched the poacher's light dance around, and point in the wrong direction. Logan smiled and dashed to the tree line and took cover behind a big pine. He peeked around to check on the poacher. He had resumed his slow and casual pace. Then Logan pushed off the tree with his hand and disappeared further into the woods.

The poacher had been sent back to the van for cigarettes. He didn't smoke, but the leader of the group did. He drew the short straw which was part of the reason for his lackadaisical stride. Once in the woods, he heard more movement and picked up his pace. He knew of the feral hogs that roamed at night. He was aware of their temperament, but it wasn't a wild hog he had to be concerned with.

The weak light did little to pave his way forward, but it was enough to move him quickly through the makeshift trail they had forged over the past few nights. In short order, he found the dirt road, and where they had parked the van. The poacher reached the driver's side door and grabbed the door handle. He became startled by the sound of a stick or twig snapping somewhere behind him which caused him to stop and turn around. He peered into the darkness, his heart rate increased, his breathing already labored.

Logan was watching from Earth's shadow, almost complete darkness. He was standing still in the open, only twenty or twenty-five feet away, but invisible to the poacher. Logan sized up the target through the night vision googles. No big deal. The green image showed a guy of average height and on the thinner side of a medium build. It would be easy to take him.

The poacher called out in Spanish, but Nigel could only understand the names, "Carlos? Miguel? Is that you?"

There was no answer. Only silence. He remained still and cautious for several moments before returning to the van. He opened the door and the interior light came on. Logan moved close and crouched behind the van. He reached up, turned off his NVGs, eased them from his head, and placed them on top of his bag. The sudden light was blinding to the poacher, but he found the cigarettes on the seat. He squinted as he grabbed the pack and put them into his pocket. Then he opened the console and found a switchblade. He popped it open in the cab and rushed to back out of the van. He turned around toward the pines and pointed the knife at the darkness, moving it from side to side.

With the van door still open, the poacher stood in a small, glowing, basket of light. The very instant the poacher glanced off in the wrong direction, Nigel engaged. By the time the poacher saw the movement and his attacker to his left, it was too late. He brought the blade around and actually penetrated Logan's midsection, but the stab wound remained shallow. The blade exited Nigel's body as the clenched fist of his left hand delivered a powerful blow to the poacher's face. He was propelled backwards, and when the poacher bounced off the open van door, Logan connected with an even more destructive, debilitating right. The poacher collapsed in a heap on the dirt. Lights out.

Logan stood in the glow of the van's interior light and pulled up his shirt to inspect his injury. It was minimal, maybe an inch deep. The bleeding was light. Logan realized it could have been a lot worse and looked down at the target. "Dammit," he said and delivered a swift kick to the poacher's midsection. "You little fucker. You ruined my shirt."

Logan moved to the back of the van and opened the rear door. "Oh, shit," he said to himself. The back of the van contained several small Styrofoam coolers, some empty, some closed tight with duct tape. To make matters worse, two turtle shells cleaned of their meat hung from racks on the side of the van. He took a knife from his bag and opened one of the coolers. They were full of eggs, iced down for travel. He opened another and it contained eggs and meat packaged in gallon sized freezer bags. Another cooler contained nothing but fins. Not only had they been stealing eggs, but they also had an evisceration operation as well. "You slaughtering bastards," Logan mumbled.

Logan's thoughts turned to three things: The other two poachers on the beach, Red, and the time. He looked at his watch. It was 0345. There was still time, but soon the sun will begin to paint the edges of the horizon with color. He needed to work fast.

Logan pulled the unconscious poacher by the collar to the back of the van. There was plenty of rolls of duct tape, so he used it to tie up his target. As he secured the poachers wrists behind his back, it brought back a recent memory of when he himself had been bound by duct tape and thrown in the trunk of a car. In his mind, he relived the steps he took to escape. As Logan applied wrap after wrap around the ankles, he looked up at the lifeless form and said, "You won't be that lucky, bitch."

Logan left the poacher leaned up against the back, left wheel well. He was closing the back of the van when someone shouted out in more Spanish. "Jorge. Where are you? Come help."

Logan grabbed his NVGs and bag and dashed toward the pines. He looked back at the van and the interior light was still on. He had left the driver's side door open. *Shit!*

He donned the pair of NVGs and looked toward the dunes. He could see the two other poachers, moving slow through the pines. They were carrying the cooler. Logan moved from tree to tree to get closer.

One of them yelled something, "Jorge. Bring me my goddamn cigarettes and run to the beach. Get the shovels and other gear. We are done here."

Jorge was taking a nap.

"Jorge! Goddammit, answer me!"

No answer. There was only silence. Then as the poachers came out of the woods and onto the dirt road, they saw the van. They saw the door open and Jorge leaned up against the van. The two looked at each there and lowered the cooler to the ground. They took off running toward the van. They were also running toward Logan who was watching from behind a tree. The one bringing up the rear would be Logan's next target.

The poacher in front zipped by first. Then, right before the next poacher reached Logan's position, he stepped out and with his right arm extended and loaded with power. The poacher ran full speed into a clothes-line that took him off his feet and landed him on his back, head first. Had the road been asphalt the poacher would have been out, but the softer sand only stunned him. He tried to get back up, but Logan was ready and met him with a full right hook to his temple. The poacher went to the ground and Logan followed. He grabbed the poacher by the collar and was about to deliver another damaging blow when the third poacher jumped on Logan's back and grabbed him tight around the neck. Logan collapsed on top of the other poacher and his night vision goggles came off his head.

At six foot three, Logan was much bigger than any of the three and that gave him an advantage, especially if he could keep them isolated. The poacher held on tight and squeezed as hard as he could. Logan pushed off the ground one hand at a time and got back up to being on all fours. The poacher around his neck, squeezed and squeezed and twisted back and forth with violent action. He thought he was chocking Logan, but he wasn't.

Moving one leg at a time Logan began to stand. When he got to his feet, the poacher was like a determined bull rider. He still had his hold and was dangling off Logan's back waiting for an eight second buzzer. He got his full ride when Logan ran backwards and drove the poacher into a big pine and bounced his head off the bark.

The poacher slid down to the ground. Logan leaned down and grabbed the front of his shirt, raised him off the ground several inches and delivered another blow to the head. Then another. The next thing Nigel heard was the unmistakable sound of a hammer being cocked followed by the pressure of a barrel being pressed into the back of his head.

Logan dropped the other poacher with a thud and raised his hands high. "Okay! Okay! Easy now. Don't do anything stupid."

The poacher yelled in Spanish, but Logan couldn't understand a word. Logan tried to straighten up and he quickly learned that understanding Spanish wasn't necessary. The increased pressure of the muzzle against the back of his head told him everything he needed to know. *Get down. Down on the ground!* Logan winced as he hit his knees.

Logan could just make out the shadows of his target moving around him, and the poacher never stopped talking. Logan could tell by the way the poacher was repeating his words, getting angrier and angrier each time that he must be asking a question.

Logan yelled, "I don't understand Spanish, asshole."

Then a voice from the darkness said, "I do, bitch."

The poacher turned to look and was met on the side of his head with the flat end of a shovel. The poacher dropped the gun and fell to the ground.

Logan remained on his knees as more Spanish was being spoken, but it didn't take long for him to pick up on the Gulf County accent. As he scrambled to his feet he said, "Red! Dammit. Is that you?"

"Just call me, El Diablo."

"Son of a bitch, Red. You speak Spanish?"

"Yeah. It's a little something I picked it up while doing some time in a Tijuana prison. It was the summer of '76. Jimmy Carter was running for president against Ford. Some friends and I crossed the border..."

Whether it be fact or fiction, Nigel could tell that his buddy was about to spin one hell of a yarn. A yarn neither one of them had time for, so he interrupted. "Red! We don't have time for this. We have work to do."

"But it was a trumped-up charge. We were in this bar..."

"Later, Red. Later." Nigel found his pair of NVGs and continued. "Help me drag these guys over to the van. And don't touch anything."

Red chuckled.

When they got to the van, they dropped the poachers in the road. Nigel said, "There is plenty of duct tape in the back of the van. We're going to bind these two just like the other one."

Nigel was setting the poachers up against the van when he looked up to see Red standing behind the van. He was still, staring, his vision fixed through the back window. Nigel walked up to Red and peered into the back of the van too. Nigel put his hand on Red's shoulder and said, "I'm sorry. I didn't mean for you to see that. Honest."

Red gazed at the hanging shells and shook his head. He mumbled under his breath, "The bastards."

"Come on Red. We got to focus."

Red helped as Nigel bound the other two with duct tape. Not only would they never escape, it was going to take forever for someone else to cut them free. Nigel searched the inside of the cab and found a cell phone. The screen was locked, but he put it in his pocket anyway. He ran around to his bag and pulled out a portable GPS and powered it up. Once the unit had a fine lock on their position, he created a way-mark to record the van's coordinates.

Nigel found Red scribbling something on the side of the van with a sharpie pen. "Red, what are you doing? We don't have time for this. We got to go."

"We can't go yet."

"What do you mean, we can't go?"

"The eggs, Nigel. We can't just leave them."

"Red, the eggs in the van are iced down. There is nothing we can do for them."

"Not those eggs." And Red pointed down the road. "I think there is still time. We can get those in the ground where they belong."

Nigel wasn't crazy about prolonging their stay in the area and said, "Red. Brother. We got to go."

But Red wouldn't leave. He walked past Nigel and picked up the shovel and said, "You go. I understand. I can take care of this by myself."

Nigel watched Red hurry to the cooler, grab one end, and start dragging it back through the woods. Nigel looked around the van one last time, surveying the scene. The interior light was still on casting a glow about the area. He found the switchblade on the ground which reminded him of the stabbing. He quickly covered the wound with his hand. Then pulled his shirt up to check the bleeding. It was still at a minimum, but it made him think: *DNA*. He wasn't going to make that mistake again, so he picked up the knife and stuck it in his pocket. He gathered his bag and other items and donned his night vision googles. He turned and looked toward the woods. Red was still making his way.

Red was more than half way through the woods when he felt the other end of the cooler lift off the ground. Red turned around and Nigel said, "I can't leave my wingman."

Red said nothing.

"This really means that much to you?"

Red answered with a single word, "Everything."

Nigel said, "Then it means everything to me. Let me go first. I can see."

They were quiet on their jog back to Red's car. The car doors slammed and Red fired up the engine. It was still dark, but visibility had improved. The eastern sky was beginning to cast a familiar glow at the horizon's edge, but the sunrise was still some time away.

Nigel said, "Do you think they'll make it. The turtle eggs, I mean."

"There's no doubt in my mind. They'll be fine."

But there was doubt, how the eggs had been affected by the ordeal was uncertain. All they could do is hope and convince themselves that everything was going to be alright.

Nigel pulled out the poacher's cell phone and called 911. Even a locked phone can be bypassed to dial 911. A young-sounding female dispatcher answered the call. "Gulf County 911. Who am I speaking with? What is your emergency and location?"

Nigel refused to identify himself, but told the dispatcher about the poachers. He told her what they would find once they got there. He told her where they were and read off the GPS coordinates. He made her repeat them back to him twice. When he was satisfied that she was taking him seriously, he said, "And you will want to hurry and send an ambulance. One or all three may require medical attention."

The dispatcher made one last plea, "Who is this...?" But Nigel ended the call.

A few minutes later they were rolling down County Road 30A toward Port St. Joe. They rode in silence. Red's thoughts were glued to the slaughtered turtles and scores of eggs that would never hatch. He thought of the eggs that he and Nigel placed back into the warm sand. That made him smile. He looked over at Nigel, his head was leaned back and his eyes were closed. Red said, "Thanks for everything."

Nigel kept his eyes closed but offered a smile. He raised his head and opened his eyes when Red said, "Here they come."

At the far end of the long straight road, flashing blue lights were approaching. The squad cars were moving at a high rate of speed. They zipped by, one right after another. There were three of them and they had to be going at least ninety miles an hour. Red watched them disappear in the rearview and Nigel checked them out in the side mirror. When they were gone, they looked at each other and Nigel asked, "Where's that bottle of Jim Beam?"

Red smiled and said, "I thought you'd never ask."

By the time the sun was up and off the horizon, the scene at the van was crawling with county deputies, members of the base security team, and FWC investigators. Two of the poachers were sitting in the back of squad cars, while the third, *shovel head*, was being transported to the emergency room. He was conscious, but bleeding out of his left ear. One of the county crime scene photographers stopped to capture an image of the words written on the van. He was checking out the image on his LCD screen when an FWC officer of Latino decent approached. The photographer asked, "What does it say?"

The FWC officer replied, "El Diablo Rojo estaba aqui. *The red devil was here.*"

LEAVE NO TRACE

In big cities, such as Chicago, New York, or even Atlanta, from a daily news perspective, there is no shortage of murders, rapes, gang activity, or multi-million dollar political scandals to fill up the news feed. If anything, it is often difficult to select which murder, robbery, or scandal will be most newsworthy. After all, it's all about what sells, not what's most important.

Small towns that run weekly newspapers don't generally have this problem. *Thank God.* The news cycle of Port St. Joe is no different. *Thank God, again.* The big cities can keep their sewer news. Neither the local paper, *The Star*, nor its citizens want or need big city drama in their backyards. *The Star* hits the pavements every Thursday morning, and if the readers had their choice, they would pick happy and boring over tragic and exciting any day.

However, even from the news desk of a sleepy town, a savvy editor would like to have, on occasion, something juicy and substantive to report on. There is only so much mileage a paper can get out of a first-ever release of a coveted and secret muscadine preserves recipe, or the occasional complaint of discolored water coming from the new, fancy schmancy, high-dollar water treatment plant, or even the repeated reports of black bears dumpster diving out on The Cape and Indian Pass. And, as entertaining and content rich as it can be, people get bored with the repeated name calling, childish shenanigans, and antics coming out of the Gulf County Board of Commissioners.

One of the fun things about having a weekly paper is how the local rumor mill will take a story and twist it around before the facts can be published on Thursday. If something really newsworthy happens over the weekend, the locals have several days to play with, spin, and distort the facts and details. This was one of those weeks.

"Son of a bitch!" Nigel lamented.

He lost the coin toss, again. When he and Red are at the Forgotten Coast Raw Bar, they will often flip to see who has to pull the first round of beers from the draft station. Red normally does the ceremonious flip. Being a creature of habit, Nigel found himself at a great disadvantage. Over a year earlier, Red picked up on how Nigel always chose tails for the coin toss. This sent Red searching online. He found a coin dealer and paid way too much for a double-headed quarter. The motivations were simple: to drive Nigel nuts and, of course, to always make Nigel pull the first round of beers.

Nigel jumped off stool 17 and marched away bitching. Red chuckled to himself, feeling not the first inkling of guilt. Then he slapped the bar to get the attention of Bucky, one of their favorite shuckers. "Let me taste one, Buck."

Bucky shucked an oyster and slid it down the bar. Red took it and slurped it from its shell. He looked at Bucky with a hint of disapproval and asked, "Texas?"

"Louisiana," replied Bucky.

"Nothing from Apalach?"

Bucky shook his head, went back to shucking and said, "We haven't been able to get anything out of Apalach in weeks."

The estuarial waters of Apalachicola bay produce the World's finest, most coveted oysters. The largest natural oyster fishery in the nation. The fresh water from the Apalachicola River coupled with the rich, salty waters from the Gulf of Mexico that are held hostage by the bay's barrier islands, creates the ideal balance of salinity for oysters to thrive. The oyster industry in Apalach is so prolific, it supplies ten percent of the nation's entire oyster harvest. Or at least, it used to.

Many factors have changed the face of the industry over the past several years. Lack of fresh water coming in due to extended drought and over-usage upstream raises salinity levels allowing natural predators easy access to the beds. The opposite extreme with excessive flooding lowers salinity and drowns the beds. Then, of course, there was the tragedy with the Deep Horizon oil spill of 2010.

The ambiguities of how the oil would affect the fragile waters of the bay caused the Florida Wildlife Commission to relax the harvest restrictions. The oystermen were told to harvest what they could; the oil was coming. They did, and the oil never came. The beds were decimated and the bay's recovery has been slow and painful ever since.

Red leaned over and stuffed a five-dollar bill in the tip jar, "It is what it is, Bucky. Two dozen raw, please."

A few stools down, Red recognized one of the turtle patrol volunteers. She was having a bit of lunch with a friend after a busy morning of marking and documenting new nests. Red didn't know her name, but had seen her around the volunteer network.

Nigel was sitting back down with the beers when one of the gals said, "The FWC told Jennifer that the van was loaded." Jennifer was a name Red did know. Jennifer Hilton works closely with the conservancy and heads up the turtle patrol effort. Nigel and Red sipped their beer and listened. "They counted almost five hundred eggs and they had slaughtered several turtles and put their meat on ice."

Bucky interrupted the gals and said, "Oh. You talking about the poachers they caught? That's just crazy."

The volunteer put both her hands on the bar leaned forward and said, "Yes. They say it was the weirdest thing. Just bizarre."

Bucky slid the tray of oysters in front of Red and Nigel and said, "I heard they found them naked."

That was Red's cue. "Nakedness! I love me some nakedness. What are you talking about, Buck?"

The volunteer beat Bucky to the punch, "Oh, you haven't heard? They caught three poachers morning before last. They had been raiding fresh turtle nests. Very sad."

"Really?"

"Yes. It is all so mysterious. They have no idea what actually happened, but it appears somebody caught them in the act and called 911."

Bucky was chomping at the bit to jump in and said, "But, Red, the crazy thing is what the cops found when they got there. The poachers were naked and duct-taped around pine trees."

The volunteer gals said, "Oh, my. I heard they found them tied up, but not naked."

Red was drinking his beer with a smile as he listened to Bucky, "Yup. Somebody caught them, beat the shit out of them, stripped them down, and taped them up. One of them had been busted up so bad, they had to call an ambulance. I think he died later at the hospital. The other two are sitting in the pokey."

Sounding shocked and concerned, the volunteer gave out a slight gasp and said, "Died? Oh, dear." Then she reminded herself of what the poachers had done. She straightened up on her bar stool and exclaimed, "I guess the bastards got what they deserved."

Nigel said, "Naked and dead, huh? Where'd you hear all this Buck?"

Bucky said, "Sammy."

Sammy is one of Bucky's best friends from high school. Bucky and Sammy are just two points of a harmless trouble-making triangle. The third is Blair. The three of them are thick as thieves and run together almost all the time. Their ambitions don't stretch too far beyond their high school graduation and beer drinking on the beach. Youth, beer, and idle time often breed trouble as they scheme to find ways to entertain themselves. Boys will be boys.

"Sammy, huh?"

"Uh huh. His mom's sister has a friend whose daughter works in the cafeteria at the jail. She says one of the inmates told her all about it."

Red said, "Well, I guess you'd be hard pressed to find a more reliable source."

Not catching Red's sarcasm, Bucky said, "Exactly."

Nigel ignored Bucky and looked down at the two women and asked, "Do they have any idea who did all this?"

"My friend Jennifer said they're clueless. And who really cares, right? Whoever caught these guys did us all a huge favor. They were heaven sent."

Red was drinking his beer and thinking hard. In an *aha!* moment, he slammed his cup down and announced, "The Teenage Mutant Ninja Turtles. That's who did it."

Everybody had a good laugh. Red got up, recharged the beers, and sat back down. He extended his hand toward the two gals, "My name's Red. And this ugly mug behind me is Nigel."

Nigel offered an awkward smile and a little finger wiggling as a friendly wave.

The turtle girl took Red's hand and said, "I've seen you around some of our meetings. My name is Sally. This is my friend Tina. She's from the mountains of North Carolina. This is her first time visiting."

Red looked past Sally and spoke to Tina. "You thought you were going to come down here and relax, didn't you? I'll bet the turtle Nazi has been working you to death."

Both ladies laughed and Tina said, "It's been great. This morning I got to watch as one female was depositing her eggs. It was magical. We don't have this sort of thing in Asheville, where I'm from."

He already knew the answer, but Red asked Sally anyway, "Any improvement from the tourists? Are you seeing any impact from the "Leave No Trace" ordinance?"

"Not really," said Sally. "Many just aren't aware of the new law, others just don't care. We had two false crawls this morning due to stuff left on the beach. It's sad. I mean, it's great they passed the ordinance, but what good is it, if it isn't enforced."

Red wanted to say something about the false crawl he and Nigel encountered while on their little operation, but didn't want to put them in the vicinity of the scene. Instead he said, "Somebody just needs to drive through each night and collect all the shit. They'll learn fast that way."

Bucky stopped shucking to listen.

Sally asked, "Wouldn't that be like stealing?"

Nigel chimed in, "I don't see how it could be. By leaving the stuff out there each night, they're in violation of the law, right? Essentially, the stuff is being abandoned, so it's available for picking and profitable repurposing."

"You know what they say," interjected Red. "Possession is ninety-nine percent of the law."

Red looked up and saw Bucky staring off into the distance and said, "Damn, Buck! Stop your daydreaming, boy. You have orders to fill!"

Startled, Buck said, "Yeah ... Thanks, Red." And went back to shucking.

Nigel's phone vibrated and buzzed across the bar followed by a, *Bong!* It was a text message.

As Red continued his conversation with the ladies about the early failures of the "Leave No Trace" ordinance, Nigel looked at his phone. The message was from Candice. *I am home for lunch...*

Nigel was typing her a message to explain that he was at the raw bar with Red when ... *Bong!* ... a second text came through. *And I'm horny* .

Before he got through reading the second message ... *Bong!* ... he got a third. *It would be a terrible thing to waste. YOU NEED TO HURRY!*

It was a comical combination of excitement and hyperventilation. Nigel worked the back-button fast to deleted the message he had already started. As his thumb worked the keyboard, he said, "Red! I got to go!"

"What! I thought we were going to throw the nets?"

Nigel always feels a little foolish when he does this, but he replaced all the worthless words with a single emoji, the big smiling face showing all the teeth. He hit send and said, "Nice meeting you ladies. Sorry, brother. I got to run."

Red said, "Where's the fire, dammit?"

Nigel winked and said, "Now you're getting personal."

Red took a sip of his beer and mumbled, "Oh, shit. I can't compete with that."

Nigel got up and flipped a ten-spot on the bar and said, "Adios, Buck."

As Nigel headed toward the door, Red yelled, "In the morning. First light, dammit. Pick me up. We got mullet to slay."

"First light. Got it." And Nigel Logan was out the door.

She stood at the window and watched for his truck. All the lamps were off. The only light filtered in through the blinds that were left half open. She watched the old Ford F-150 turn on to her street, and, when it pulled into the drive, she walked over to the stereo and started a song she had already selected. The she stood in the middle of the room and faced the door.

Moments later Nigel's signature three knocks played on the old wooden door. Two quick knuckles ... followed by a pause ... then the harder third. He opened the door and stepped inside. They weren't alone. Singer-songwriter Jessica Rand was singing her new country hit, *The Whiskey on your Breath*, as Candace stood waiting. He eased the door closed behind him.

They stood facing each other and Nigel gazed up and down her gorgeous body. She wasn't naked, but getting that way would only

95

take slipping the unbuttoned, long-sleeve oxford off the back of her shoulders. She was having fun with her hair this week. Now a blond with streaks of blue highlights here and there. She wore it well, and it matched her smile that was full of naughty mischief.

Her long, tanned legs walked toward him in time with the music. Nigel swallowed hard as she moved in close and took his hands. She moved closer and reached behind her, placing his wide palms on the cheeks of her tight ass. She helped him pull her in tighter. Then she pinned him against the door and kissed him. She let him come up for air, and they both stared at each other. Their minds and lungs raced with serious anticipation.

Nigel asked, "What's for lunch?"

She tilted her head and formed a small smile accentuated with a little pout. She moved closer and whispered into his ear, "You." Then she took a gentle bite of his earlobe.

Candice backed away a bit and let her blouse fall to the floor. She closed in tight and took her knee and ran it up and down Nigel's leg as she sang the last few lines of the song. "Love me, baby ... Love me to death ... Take me baby, with fresh whiskey on your breath."

Nigel smiled and said, "Thank you, sweet Jesus. I love country music."

She kissed him again. He slid his hand down the back of her thigh and grabbed behind the knee of her lifted leg. He pulled her in tight, pivoted around, and pinned her to the door.

The rising sun was just beginning to paint the morning horizon when Nigel parked outside the house. He looked up toward the windows. Everything was dark and quiet looking. He smiled. It wouldn't be for long.

Nigel cracked the front door open. He stuck his head in, shook it a couple of times and said to himself, "Figures as much." He put the key back under the old, weathered ceramic pelican and went inside, being careful that the screen door didn't slam shut.

Now that he was inside, he started moving around like it was in the middle of the day, no longer trying to be quiet. He found the light switches and lit up the kitchen. He went to making a pot of coffee. He turned the water on in the sink and rinsed out the pot and filled it with water. He emptied the filter basket banging it extra hard against the inside wall of the trashcan.

Red never uses paper coffee filters; the metal screen that came with the coffee maker works fine for him. To Red's credit, paper filters are an unnecessary form of the pollution that fills our landfills. He'd say, "It doesn't sound like much, but if everybody did their part..."

Nigel opened the cupboard and found the whole bean coffee. He filled the grinder up with beans. He was about to make it sing when a grin flashed across his face. He stopped and unplugged the grinder.

He moved with great stealth. He eased into the hallway and found an electrical plug right outside Red and Trixie's bedroom door. He moved the grinder as close as he could to the door. With a half-smile and teeth clenched, he let it rip.

The screeching, high-pitched sound of the motor coupled with the racket of the beans being reduced to powder is loud enough in the kitchen. But in the close confines of a hallway, the racket is amplified as the noise bounces off and around the walls. Now laughing internally, Nigel stood there and shook the grinder as it did its work. He could hear nothing but the grinder. Once the grounds were made, he stopped and listened.

As soon as the blades stopped turning he heard Trixie completing a thought. "...ucker. Son of a bitch!"

Through the door, Nigel could hear the commotion of a moving mattress, bed sheets being flung around, and feet moving across the floor. He reached down and unplugged the coffee grinder anticipating the need to run. Seconds later the door flung open and revealed a bright and early, naked version of Red. He stood, not saying anything.

Nigel winced at the sight and moved his head around Red to look into the room. Trixie was on her back, still under the covers but with a pillow pressed tight to her ears. He turned his attention back to an aggravated and unhappy Red. Nigel smiled back and said, "First light, right?"

Red turned around to look out the window. Then he turned around and said, "Bitch. You're late!"

Nigel drove his truck out on the beach using the Lee Street access and turned right toward the cape. He wanted to check the waters off Money Bayou first. It's often a hot bed of mullet activity. He pulled down by the water and eased the truck along the coast as he watched for jumpers or swirls between the breaking waves.

Red was more interested in the number of people that were already out on the beach. There was more than usual, but they weren't there for the spectacular sunrise. They were turtle patrol volunteers. Red looked out the passenger-side window; a team of volunteers surrounded a nest. He turned back to Nigel and said, "I guess the news of those poachers has the patrol a little paranoid. Looks like they are out in full force, checking every nest."

Nigel said, "Speaking of the news."

He reached behind the seat and pulled out a fresh edition of *The Star*. The print hadn't been dry long. Nigel gave the front page a quick look, dropped the paper into Red's lap, and said, "Really?"

Red picked up the paper and looked at the front-page picture and headline. He chuckled as he read it to himself. **New Super Hero Captures Poachers for Authorities**. Underneath the headline was a big picture of the captured van showcasing, not the iced-down meat and eggs, or the shells, but the secret message scribbled on the side. The caption for the picture read, *Who is this Red Devil? And where did he come from?*

Red chuckled. Nigel didn't.

There was no sign of mullet at Money Bayou, but that didn't mean they weren't there. They could be bottom-crawling the trough just beyond the first sandbar. Nigel stopped and put the truck in park. "Let's try a few blind throws."

Red said, "You go ahead. I prefer not to waste my time. Ain't nothing out there."

"Suit yourself."

Nigel shuffled his feet through the sand and surf as he made his way to the first sandbar. Unbeknownst to him, two stingrays and a large flounder gave him a wide berth. He made up his net and was ready to throw at a moment's notice. Still and patient, he watched the surface of the water. Nothing.

After a few minutes, he looked back toward the truck to see if Red was going to join him. He wasn't. A golf cart had stopped at the truck and Red was playing Chatty Kathy from the front seat. Then something caught Nigel's eye. *Movement*. He turned to pay attention. His head and eyes moved from side to side. It surfaced again. Another predator had joined the hunt. A large dorsal fin sliced the surface of the water about fifteen yards away. Nigel smiled. A bull shark had moved in for a little breakfast. He was confident he wasn't on the menu, but he kept one eye on the shark and the other out for mullet.

To his left, the surface of the water boiled with swirls. It was what he was waiting for. He made a quick check for the position of the shark, but the fin was gone. He twisted his body to the right, the windup. Then he swung and uncoiled the weights of the net around back to the left. He released the net and launched it in the direction of the swirls. It was a pancake throw hitting the water directly over his target. He let the weights sink to the bottom. Nigel spoke to himself in a whisper as he started to bring in the net, "Mullet. Mullet. Mullet. Mullet. Mullet."

The second the retrieval line went taunt, he felt his catch's futile efforts to escape the net. As he brought the net closer, the fight within the net grew. Then Nigel remembered he wasn't alone. The shark. As hungry as Nigel was to land these fish, the shark was probably hungrier, and nothing rings a shark's dinner-bell like struggling fish.

Getting himself and his catch to the beach was priority one, so he began to high-step toward the shore. He never looked back, and the beach seemed a mile away. The net lagged behind. The fight of the catch and the weight of the net dragging on the seafloor made progress seem slow. The second he was on the sand he turned toward the water and started to bring in the net hand over hand.

He thought to himself *Damn. What a catch*. The dorsal fin then appeared in the surf about two breakers beyond his net. It was heading toward shore and the net. If he were to make it to the net, it wouldn't be pretty. Backing up the beach and pulling harder, he said, "Oh, shit!"

The horn of the ten-foot net was just exiting the surf and the shark was now only one breaker away and accelerating. He yanked and yanked, and with the net now a few feet up on the beach, the shark drove itself up on the bottom of the shallow surf. It thrashed back and forth until it could back out and turn for deeper water. Nigel watched the impressive beast head back to sea. It was much larger than his previous estimate, maybe five-and-a-half or six feet long. He was out of breath with excitement, his hands were on his knees, and his skin vibrated from the adrenaline. As Nigel watched the impressive beast head out to sea he provided some parting words, "My mullet, bitch. Mine."

When he caught his wind, he stood up and looked back toward the truck. Everyone was still talking. Neither Red nor anyone in the golf cart had been paying any attention to the events in the water. He thought *Why, son of a bitch*.

He collected his net and observed the catch that was still looking for any possible escape. He smiled at his good work and picked up the net and catch and walked back to the truck. He recognized the two ladies in the golf cart. They were Sally and Tina, the turtle patrol gals he met the day before at the raw bar. Red and the gals were so deep in conversation they never noticed Nigel walk up to the truck. He got their immediate attention, though, when he swung the net and landed the catch on the hood of his truck. A baker's dozen of mullet and a stingray the size of a garbage can lid flipped and flopped a tune of panic on the hood.

Red's eyes were the size of coffee saucers as he realized what had been placed before him. From the front of the truck and through the windshield Nigel looked at Red and said, "Don't tell me there ain't nothing out there. Who's wasting time now?"

Red said nothing and answered with a grin.

"So, you gonna get your ass out of the truck and help me bleed these, or are you going to sit there like a stump?"

After extracting the stingray from the net, he showed it to Ms. Tina. He gave her a quick tour. He grabbed the tail and exposed the infamous barbed stinger. As she touched its smooth skin she said, "We don't have these in the mountains either."

"Well," Nigel said, "if we don't get him back in the water soon, we won't have this one around here either. It is time to pardon him."

As Red was bleeding out the mullet, Tina and Sally walked down to the surf with Nigel. He eased the ray back into the gulf and sat it on the bottom. It was still, getting used to being back in the water. After about thirty seconds, Nigel took his foot and gave it a little nudge and said, "Now get!"

Its wings exploded in flutter and it took flight across the sandy bottom. In a flash, the stingray was gone.

The sun was well above the horizon and the turtle gals had long since resumed their patrol duties. Red, Nigel, and the bull shark continued to work the mullet that were schooled up off the beach at

Money Bayou until they disappeared. Most of the catches were singles. On two separate throws, Red netted two fish.

They continued to throw until they became bored and frustrated with catching nothing but pesky baitfish and stingrays, both always a pain in the ass to get out of the net. After one last throw that yielded nothing, Nigel said, "I think we have more than enough for a fish-fry."

There was no protest from Red as they both made their way back to the truck. When they started cleaning the fish, they had landed an additional ten. That made for forty-six filets and twenty-three backs and gizzards. Red loves some mullet gizzards. Nigel had no plans on trying them.

With the mullet cleaned and on ice, Red reached down in the cooler past the fish and dug up two Coors Light from the bottom. He tossed one to Nigel who looked at his watch. It was 1010, a green light for personal consumption.

They sat on the tailgate to enjoy their morning beers. Red was on the phone with Trixie making plans for a huge fish-fry on the beach. "Gather the usual suspects and then some. We have plenty!" As Red discussed the expanded guest list, Nigel stared off down the beach toward St. Vincent Island and Indian Pass. Something looked out of place, or in place in a strange and awkward way. He cracked the tab on a fresh beer and hopped off the tailgate. He stood staring. What was missing? He looked down the beach in the other direction, toward the horn of Cape San Blas. The sensation was the same.

As Nigel took a sip of beer, movement caught his eye. A young, good-looking family appeared in the dunes. Tourists no doubt emerging from their beach house rental. There were a couple and two kids: a boy looking to be about ten or eleven and a girl that was maybe half her brother's age. Each of them, even the little girl, had a handful of beach gear. That's when it hit him.

Nigel looked back down the beach. *That's it!* He turned around to look the other way. *Yes!* The beaches were virtually clean of left-over tourist beach gear. A few beach camps were sprinkled here and there, but it was nothing like it had been. The beaches resembled the off-season more so than the middle of summer vacation.

Nigel made his way back to the tailgate and waited as Red was finishing up his call with Trixie. "When you're at the Pig, pick up some extra Crystal hot sauce too. We're getting low." Red looked at

Nigel and held out his beer upside-down. It was empty. Nigel got him a fresh one. "Okay," Red finished. "Call me later. I'm starting to catch my second wind." And he ended the call as Nigel handed him a cold one. "Thanks, brother."

Nigel asked, "Have you noticed the beaches, Red? They're virtually clear of all the normal shit this morning."

"Uh huh. Sally and I were talking about that earlier while you were throwing. She said she was astonished at the improvement from one morning to the next."

Nigel gazed up and down the beach and commented, "Yeah. A little too much improvement, I would say."

Red said, "Come on. Let's ride down toward the horn of the cape. We might fall into another gaggle of fish."

"Don't you think we have enough?"

Red said nothing but gave Nigel a look that said *Don't be an idiot*.

As they eased down the beach, Red kept an eye on the water. Nigel, with piqued curiosity, was appreciating the renewed condition of the morning beach. Ahead, Nigel saw two guys that were obviously upset. It looked as if they were arguing, but, as it would turn out, they were sharing in each other's frustration. When the truck reached the two guys, Nigel slowed the truck and came to a stop. Red looked up and asked, "What's going on? Did you see something?"

"Isn't this where we came across the turtle that was stuck in all the tourist shit? The one that ended up as a false crawl?"

Red looked around and said, "Hell. I don't know. It was somewhere around here. It was so damn dark."

Red saw the two guys and said, "Damn. They don't look too happy."

Nigel rolled down the passenger side window and called out across Red, "Hey guys ... what's going on?"

One guy took off running toward the beach house, the other approached the truck. He leaned in and said. "Somebody stole all our stuff last night. My buddy has gone to call the police."

Red and Nigel looked at each other, as the guy continued to speak. They were both thinking the same thing, but neither spoke a word. They turned their attention back to the guy when he said, "Everything. They took everything. Tents, chairs, coolers..."

"Wait! Your coolers?" Red interrupted. "Holy shit. Did they have beer in them?"

"Ah... yeah. Like probably at least a case or two. Plus, they took my fishing kayak."

Beneath a half-grin, Red mumbled, "Scandalous."

The guy continued, "And it isn't just us either. The people that were set up on either side of us had all their stuff stolen too." Pointing and waving his finger down the beach he said, "The guy over there had his fishing kayak stolen too."

Red said, "You can't have stolen what you abandon and leave behind."

The guy tilted his head and gave Red a puzzled look. That's when Nigel gave Red a gentle nudge with his elbow and said, "Enough, Red."

Red bent over and chuckled as if he'd been tickled. Nigel leaned over and spoke through the passenger-side window, "Sorry for your misfortune, dude. Good luck with the deputies."

Nigel eased on down the beach. After about a tenth of a mile Nigel and Red looked at each other and said, "Bucky," in unison.

Nigel said, "There is no way he did all this by himself."

"Bucky," Red replied, "never does anything by himself."

This was true. And there was no need discussing who else was involved.

Nigel motored on and Red leaned his head back for a little five-minute nap. With his eyes closed, Red said, "Let's try marker 305. There's bound to be fish there."

"Sounds like a plan." Nigel looked through the rearview mirror at the beach and shoreline behind him. What once looked like a tent city for the homeless now looked like an inviting beach for the imagination. He said, "The beach does look good."

With his eyes still closed, Red said, "Yup. The boys did good."

The plot thickened as Nigel pulled off the beach and onto the Cape Road at Salinas Park. He was about to turn left and head to Red's house, but, to the right, the flashing blue lights of two squad cars caught his attention.

The Cape Road, or County Road 30E, begins as a road off County Road 30A and dead-ends into the gate of the Saint Joseph Peninsula State Park. At the intersection of 30A and 30E there is a spot off the side of the road, a super-wide shoulder. Locals often use this spot to peddle goods and services to the tourist crowd. One day it might be firewood for the beach, another it might be Tupelo Honey from Wewa, boiled peanuts, or fresh, head-on shrimp by the pound.

Today it was none of those things. The side of the road looked like the camping section of a big-box department store. Tents, umbrellas, chairs, coolers, a couple of portable propane grills, and just about anything else you might need for a day at the beach. A four-by-eight sheet of plywood was painted dark blue. *For Sale* was written on the side with orange spray paint.

Bucky, Sammy, and Blair were talking to two deputies while three other guys stood by their cars and watched. Red chuckled and said, "Good morning K-Mart shoppers. We have a Blue Light Special on aisle ten."

Nigel parked his truck by the other three cars. He noticed the tags: North Carolina, Nebraska, and Texas. *Tourists.* He and Red got out. Red went straight to browse through the merchandise. Always frugal ... no, *cheap* is more like it, Red always keeps an eye out for a value. Nigel stepped over to talk to the out-of-towners.

All three of them wore angry faces and were planted to the dirt with a defiant stance, arms crossed tight across their chests. Nigel got in line and joined them, imitating their deportment. The guy closest to Nigel noticed him and asked, "Did you have all your shit stolen off the beach last night, too?"

"Naw. I carried my shit off the beach and back to the house like I was supposed to."

The guy didn't catch the verbal jab and said nothing, so Nigel continued, "So that's what this is all about? These three stole your gear off the beach?"

One of the other guys said, "We didn't actually see them do it. They did it in the middle of the night. But that's some of my stuff right there." He used his fingers to point in a general direction.

The guy on the far end yelled at Red in his thick Texan accent, "Hey, Fella! Hands off that Yeti cooler. It belongs to me!"

Nigel looked down the row at Tex and asked, "You left a Yeti cooler on the beach? Now that was dumb."

Tex gave Nigel a go-to-hell stare, then turned his attention back to Red who was ignoring Tex and proceeding to open the cooler. "Did you not hear me? Leave the Yeti alone!"

Red reached in and grabbed a cold beer, popped the top and yelled toward the squad car, "Hey Bucky! How much for the Yeti?"

Bucky cupped his fingers around his mouth and yelled back, "Fifty bucks!"

Red slammed the cooler shut and yelled back, "Highway Robbery, Buck. Too damn high."

Bucky yelled back, "It's a three-hundred-and-fifty-dollar cooler if you bought it new. The price is fifty. Take it or leave it."

Tex exclaimed, "It's not for sale, goddammit!"

Nigel yelled at Red, "How much beer is in there?"

Red opened the Yeti and riffled through the ice and cans. He stood up and called back, "About a case and a half."

Nigel pulled out his wallet and hollered at Bucky, "Hell, I'll give you fifty for it, but the beer stays with the cooler."

Sammy entered the negotiations, "The beer is free, Mr. Logan. We can't sell alcohol; we don't have a permit."

The guy standing next to Nigel said, "I can't believe this shit!"

The deputy conducting the interview turned and said, "Would all of you just shut up for a minute?"

Tex asked, "How much longer is this going to take?"

"As long as we want it to," replied the other deputy.

The three men waited with much impatience and nervousness as the deputies finished up their discussions and as Red continued to riffle through the merchandise. Other folks, some locals and some tourists, had stopped to look at the stuff as well.

Red came across a pair of Sperry Top-Sider flip-flops on the table. They were well broken in, but in excellent condition. He dropped them to the ground and slipped his feet into them. A perfect fit. He didn't want to disturb the deputies again, so he pulled out his wallet and three dollars. He felt that was fair enough and left it on the table before continuing to browse.

The meeting at the squad car broke and the deputies approached Nigel and the three other guys. As they got closer, the guy next to Nigel asked, "Why aren't those little thieves cuffed and in the backseat of your car?"

Nigel said, "You're about to find out."

One deputy did all the talking. "The guys admit to taking the stuff off the beach after midnight. Does that sound about correct?"

The three men looked at each other. They shrugged their shoulders and Tex spoke, "So they've confessed to stealing our stuff? Book them!"

"That's not exactly what I said. I said, 'taking the stuff off the beach,' not stealing."

The guy in the middle that hadn't said anything to this point asked, "What's the difference?"

"The question of ownership," said the deputy. "You see, we have a *Leave No Trace* ordinance here which makes it unlawful for folks to stage their gear on the beach all night." Using his thumb to point over his shoulder at Bucky and the gang, he continued, "The kids there argue that possession is ninety-nine percent of the law and when you walked away at the end of the day, you were abandoning your gear, making it available for picking and ... *crap*. What did he call it?"

The deputy had to think. The phrase had escaped him. He looked at the other deputy for help. The other deputy smiled back and that was enough to restart his memory. "...Profitable repurposing. Yeah, that's what they called it. Profitable repurposing. I wonder where they heard that?" And the deputy gave his head a slow turn to cut a glance at Nigel.

One of the tourist asked, "But what about our stuff?"

The deputy maintained eye contact with Nigel and answered, "The guys have agreed to sell the stuff back to you at deep discounts."

"You got to be shitting me," said Tex.

"Another tourist asked, "So, they ain't going to jail?"

"No. They ain't going to jail. And you can bet the farm they'll be back out on the beach tonight."

Nigel pursed his lips and held his breath as he felt his eyebrows lift. "Well," said Nigel. "I guess that settles that. I better collect my partner and get going." Nigel walked away calling out, "Hey Bucky! Let's settle up on that Yeti cooler!"

TOM AND THE PYGMY

Nigel was enjoying a deep, coma-like sleep until the depth of his slumber was shallowed by the distant sound of a rattlesnake. *Where was it?* It didn't seem to matter. All of a sudden, he was lying in the weeds, listening. He sat up and looked around. An image began to materialize. It was of a skinny, black fella in dreadlocks. He looked familiar, a past enemy perhaps. They were in a swamp. The black guy was standing by the water's edge; the sound of the rattler got louder and louder. Nigel squinted for a better look, but it didn't help. Then, sounding like a scared woman, the dark fella spoke in a quiet, panicked tone. "Nigel ... Nigel ... Please Nigel. Wake up, Nigel. Help me."

Thinking first of a snake bite, Nigel jerked and his eyes sprung open the second he felt something grab his arm. He stared at the ceiling to gather his wits, panting, allowing his eyes to adjust. But the sound of the rattler continued and the grip around his arm drew tighter as he heard Candice plead, "Honey. Please, get it off of me."

Nigel was waking up fast. He turned his head to look at his best girl and couldn't believe what he was seeing. "Don't move. You hear me?"

"Don't worry. I'm not going anywhere."

"Just stay perfectly still. He doesn't mean anything by it. He's just showing off. I'm going to turn on the lamp so I can see."

Nigel reached over toward the nightstand and said, "Close your eyes." *Click.* The room filled with light.

Sitting proudly on Candice's stomach and looking her in the eye was Tom, Nigel's cat. He was eager to share yet another trophy. Most often, it is a dead rodent of some sort left on the back steps. This time though, Tom brought his good work into the house alive. He looked to be smiling as he held the pygmy rattler between his teeth. He gently held the snake right behind its head, the rest of its body trailed along looking to escape, wrapping itself around Tom's neck and always flicking its tail.

Tom turned his head to look at Nigel. "Whatcha got there, boy?" Then he gave out a slight chuckle and followed by saying, "Don't answer that. You might drop it."

"This isn't funny, dammit," Candice added, her eyes still closed.

Nigel got up and walked around to Candice's side of the bed. Tom looked up at him, with tail wagging. There was just enough space behind the puffy cheeks of the snake that Nigel could get a grip. He reached down and petted Tom on top of his head. Tom pressed back against his fingers. "Now, let me have the snake, Tom."

Candice said, "What are you doing? Why is this taking so long?"

"Shush, dammit. I'm working here. Just keep still and your eyes closed."

Nigel was slow and careful as he took hold of the rattler. Once he was sure he had a good grip, he used his free hand to scratch underneath Tom's neck to coax him to let it go. "Thank you, buddy. Good job. Now, let me have it." Nigel gave a slight pull and Tom opened his mouth.

The second Nigel had the snake, he stood back and said, "Okay. I got it."

Candice opened her eyes and wiggled. Tom jumped off, and she rolled to the other side of the bed jumping to the floor. She danced and pranced around. She shook her fingers while she made a slight growling sound. Then she took her hands and attempted to smooth her crawling skin as she turned around and around. Body, face, head, arms, legs, her palms worked fast to rub away the creepiness that seemed to encase her entire body.

Nigel couldn't help but chuckle, but made a point of not letting her catch him. That wouldn't earn him any points. He ducked away into the utility room so she couldn't see him and asked, "Are you going to be alright?"

"Hell no, I'm not going to be alright. That son of a bitch'n cat!"

Nigel smiled as he found a spare pillow case and deposited the snake into the bottom and closed the top with a twist and a knot. The snake went quiet. He walked back out into the room and said, "Don't be sore at Tom. He loves you. It was a gift. He didn't mean no harm."

Candice studied Nigel's face and her emotions shifted. "You bastard," she said. "You've been laughing. You think this shit is funny."

"No, baby," He said with a thin smile. "It was a serious situation at the time, but we're past it now. You know what they say, 'we will laugh about this later.'"

"Well, it's not later enough, goddammit."

Nigel put the pillowcase on the floor and approached her naked body. He was grinning. She wasn't. She gave him a half-hearted punch in the chest and said, "Stop that, now. Just stop."

Tom sat on the corner of the bed and divided his attention between his humans and the squirming pillowcase on the floor. Nigel took her in his arms and hugged her, rocked her back and forth to comfort her. It took a while, but she stopped shaking. He backed off to look at her pretty face. He kissed her on the lips, then said, "You're okay. Everything is fine."

"You're still an asshole," she said with a smile and hit him in the chest again.

He smiled back and said, "It's one of my finer qualities." And they both began to laugh.

She shook one last time and said, "I can't believe this shit. A damn snake."

He kissed her again on the forehead, then her cheek and neck. He kissed her on the mouth and she welcomed him in. They broke away and she whispered in his ear, "Come on. Get back in bed."

"Hell. I'm wide awake now," said Nigel. "I couldn't go back to sleep if I wanted too."

She backed away with a raised eyebrow and bit her bottom lip. Then she moved in closer and said, "My sweet hero. Who said anything about sleep?" She kissed him and he responded. They stood there consumed with one another. Their body temperatures and passion were rising fast. In an abrupt motion, Candice pushed away and said, "Not so fast, lover."

Nigel was on the verge of a pant. "What? What is it?"

She moved in close to his right ear and through her clenched teeth, growled, "Get the freak'n snake out of the house."

Sleep did find its way into the bedroom, but only for Candice. After dealing with the snake and the unexpected desires of his partner, Nigel was wide awake. It was a little before five in the morning. He was on his side, head propped up with a hand so he could watch her sleep. He found her gorgeous, even in slumber. He couldn't help but notice how peaceful she looked and how her hair was framing her face. A thin smile told him she was happy. So was he.

Nigel doesn't like taking pictures of people. As subjects, they can be a pain in the ass. Before him, though, was a shot he wanted. One of her in her most peaceful state. He wanted to capture the moment for all time, which is what photography does. It freezes time on a two-dimensional plane called a snapshot.

He slipped out of bed and went into his office for a camera. He came back into the bedroom. She hadn't moved, but her right breast was exposed. He took the bed sheet and draped it over her to conceal her nipple. He stepped back to admire her again. Then he began to shoot.

At his computer, he was admiring the new images. Of the several taken, he chose five as his favorites and deleted the others. He began to edit his work. When he heard the final gurgles of the coffee pot coming from the kitchen, he got up to grab a cup. As he was pouring, he saw the notification light on his phone blinking. He took a sip of coffee and walked over to take a look. It was a text from Sherry Stone, the reporter from Tidewater, Virginia. The date stamp said it came in at 0237, over three hours ago. A text that late at night couldn't be good. He opened and read the message: *Call me ASAP. We may have a situation here*.

What the hell was that supposed to mean? He took another sip of coffee and decided he would call her back during normal working hours. He went back to his office to finish editing the pictures of Candice. He liked each of the five shots he kept, but there was one he loved best. He converted it to black and white and worked the brightness, highlights, and contrast. When it reached his satisfaction, he raised his hands off the mouse and keyboard and spoke to the monitor. "Stop. No more."

He sat back with his coffee and studied her beautiful face on the screen. It made him happy. He was sure she would love the picture, too. But as happy as the shot made him, there was one distraction that was consuming his brain and ruining the moment. That damn text message.

He did his best to ignore it, at least for now, but he couldn't. The hidden meaning between the lines were too powerful and worrisome. He picked up the phone to read it again. *Call me ASAP*. When someone sends a text after midnight and wants a call back as soon as possible, chances are it isn't good news. *We may have a situation here.* Those words, coupled with the others, are a tidy way of spelling trouble.

He got up to refresh his cup of coffee and walked out on the front porch. He went through the screen door and sat on the front steps. He looked at his phone and scrolled through his contacts until he found her. He looked at his phone, staring at the name and number thinking *Dammit! I don't want to do this.* But, he did.

She answered in two rings and sounded alert, but groggy, like she had been sleeping with one eye open. Her first words were spoken through a dry mouth and a throat that hadn't been cleared yet. "What took you so long to call me?"

"What's going on?"

She sat up in bed and began to tell him what she knew. She didn't have all the details yet, but the source was too credible. Nigel was speechless. He took a deep breath and mumbled, "Son of a bitch," as he listened and looked to the heavens. Then he interrupted her. "When? When did this happen?"

"Two days ago. Unexpected and out of the blue. Totally blindsided."

He said nothing and there was silence on the phone.

"Nigel? Are you still..."

"Yeah. I'm here. I'm thinking."

"What are we going to do?"

"We?" Nigel asked. "What do you mean, we?"

There was an awkward silence on the phone before Stone said, "Don't be an ass. You're going to need help. Help that is on your side."

Nigel said nothing.

"It's part of the reason I called to begin with. Now … what are we going to do?"

"Do me a favor," he said. "Start from the beginning and tell me everything."

She did.

He stood in the doorway and watched her sleep. She looked so peaceful and totally relaxed. She held a slight smile. Her hands were open, no sleeping fists of tension. He tried to count her easy steady breathing, but she was so relaxed it was impossible to catch the rising and lowering of her chest. He didn't want to disturb her, not now, so he leaned up against the door jam and waited.

When her eyes began to flutter, it got Nigel's attention. He stood straighter at the door. When her eyes opened, she was looking at the wall. Then she turned her head and found Nigel watching her. She offered a good-morning smile.

He walked over to her side of the bed and she scooted over to make room. He sat on the edge. He offered a feigned smile, but it only fooled her for a few seconds. She began to catch the worry in his eyes. She reached up and touched the side of his face and returned her own look of worry. She said nothing.

Nigel leaned in and kissed her on the lips. He sat back up and said, "I have to go to Virginia."
She sat up in bed. His fake smile was gone and his expression matched his eyes. She could tell there was a problem, and, in that moment, she wasn't looking for details. She only wanted to cry, and she did after she grabbed him around the neck. He held her tight and close and rocked her back and forth. After a while, he said, "Everything is going to be alright." She took this as a lie, to protect her from the truth, and tightened her grip around his neck.

Sissy Marks

He packed light, except for the cash. He crammed a couple changes of clothes and some toiletries into a large backpack. Then he went into the living room and moved his TV stand away from the wall. He removed the section of the tongue-and-groove wall that covered the old fireplace. He got down on his knees and pulled his safe out of the hearth. He opened it and grabbed two stacks of hundred-dollar bills, each strapped with a mustard-colored band. Then he took the cell phone he obtained during his night in Tate's Hell along with the charger he had bought for it. Everything went into his bag.

He wasn't sure what he would encounter once he got back to Virginia, but figured if he needed anything, he would just buy it. If he couldn't do what he needed to do with two straps, he was in trouble. He put the safe, the wall, and the TV stand back in place. He grabbed the bag, which now contained a dangerous amount of cash. Before zipping up the backpack, Nigel thought *Only a fool would walk around with this much money.* Then he chuckled and said aloud to himself, "Only a bigger fool would try and take it."

He said his goodbyes to Candice the night before. She was strong while they were together. On her front porch, she smiled when he kissed her and said, "I'll be back in a few days." She didn't believe him. She knew better and fell apart the second she went back into her house.

Nigel did believe it. He knew in the back of his mind that things could go to shit and his stay extended, but he refused to let that seep into his mind and control his expectations. He was coming back, dammit, if it was the last thing he ever did. Remaining in Virginia wasn't an option, or so he thought.

Nigel got to the airport in Tallahassee with plenty of time to spare. It was a busy travel weekend, and he wasn't about to fall victim to the inadequacies and inefficiencies of the TSA. The Transportation Security Administration had saturated the news lately because of problems all across the nation. Over the past several

113

weeks, airport security had not made any new friends. In a recent U.S. congressional subcommittee hearing, American Airlines alone reported that 70,000 of their own customers had missed flights and 40,000 bags had been lost, delayed, or misrouted due to security checkpoint bottlenecks. *Damn!*

Even as a member of TSA's PreCheck program, which moves travelers through an express lane, Nigel wasn't going to take any chances. But he zipped through security, and, with two hours to spare before his flight, he decided to spend his idle time at the bar to help keep his mind off Virginia. He knew of a number 17 stool that awaited his arrival, and a Jamaican bartender named Rendall that whips up a mean Bloody Mary.

Nigel walked in and smiled. Rendall greeted him with a laugh and said, "Ha! It's Nigel, right, mon?"

"That's right. You remembered. Good man."

"Fifth time da charm, mon. The usual?"

"No. No. Too early for bourbon, but you can make me an extra special B.M."

"No problem, mon."

Rendall spun around and went to work. He grabbed an extra tall glass that looked two stories tall and placed it on the bar. He ignored the bottle of vodka in the well and grabbed the Grey Goose. When he was done, he set the drink in front of Nigel with a big down-island smile. With all the veggies added in, it was as much a meal as it was a cocktail. If you used it to wash down a Fred Flintstone vitamin, all your daily nutritional requirements could be met.

"Now dat's a Bloody Mary, mon. We off to a regatta today?"

"Not today, Rendall. Heading to Virginia for some personal business."

"Ah. Very good."

Rendall went back to work.

Nigel looked at the piece of beverage art and almost didn't want to disturb it. He grabbed his cell phone and took a picture. Rendall caught him and laughed. "Ah! Dat's very Facebook of you, Mistah Nigel."

"Ah, shut up, Rendall." Nigel put his finger in the drink then sucked on his knuckles. *Damn that's good.* Then he pulled out one of the long green beans, popped it in his mouth, and washed it down with a generous sip. *Yummy!*

Nigel spotted a newspaper on the back counter. He got Rendall's attention. "Is that today's *Democrat?*"

"Ya, mon. You want to take a look?"

"Please."

Nigel flipped through the sections and stopped when he came across a familiar face, one he'd seen hundreds of times. He didn't know the person, but the face was framed in a shot like all the rest, including his own. It was of a young sailor. She looked smart and squared-away in her service dress blues. Her single National Defense ribbon was positioned perfectly. Her eyes were full of the pride she was feeling at the time. Above everything else, she was a beautiful young woman.

No doubt, it was the traditional mugshot captured while attending Navy boot camp. Everybody got one. Nigel thought of his own and cringed. It was awful, and, to his satisfaction, nobody has ever seen it. But it's still around, rolled up with his navigational charts aboard his sailboat, *MisChief*. He thought of tearing it up and throwing it away a few times, but something always stopped him.

Nigel realized the picture wasn't part of a newspaper article, but a Letter to the Editor. The title of the letter was *Welcoming our Sissy Home*. Nigel stopped, returned to the picture, and studied it. He pulled a long drink of his B.M. before continuing.

It was a letter written for Lisa "Sissy" Marks. It started: *Our Sissy is coming home for the last time. It will be good to have her home. More so, it hurts knowing she has left her life in the Middle East. Her life and return will forever give us special cause to stop and reflect on those holidays which honor all veterans, both living and deceased.*

Under his breath, Nigel said, "Fuck," and took another deep drink and continued to read. The letter was actually from the sailor's mother. Sissy, otherwise known as Petty Officer Marks to her chiefs and shipmates, had been assigned as an Individual Augmentee with the United States Army in Afghanistan. She was killed in action when the Humvee she was riding in ran over an IED.

Nigel continued to read with the slow and methodical purpose the letter warranted. This mother, who had just recently lost her daughter to the savages of Islamic extremism and a war on terror, had decided to turn her mourning into a delicate love letter. There was no anger in her words, just sorrow, pain, and immense pride. The mother of Petty Officer Marks did an incredible job of harnessing her energy to write a piece that steered away from the easy path of blame and concentrated on lifting up her daughter's heroic life. In her closing remarks, she warned others not to feel pity or to view her daughter's death as being in vain. In a single line that packed a punch, she said the following: *Join us in mourning our loss, join us in celebrating her life, join us in honoring her courage, but show no pity; few of us will ever perish with more meaning and purpose.*

Nigel folded the paper and set it down on the bar so the face of Petty Officer Marks was facing up. He worked on his Bloody Mary with a little more meaning now. He gazed into the eyes of Petty Officer Marks and found a glimmer of her strength he didn't see before. He would have liked her; he could tell.

He looked up and found Rendall, "Another one, please."

"Yeah, mon. Com'n up."

Nigel picked up the paper and asked, "Are you done with this? Can I take it?"

"Yeah, mon. Everything but da sports section. Leave dat behind."

A few minutes later, Rendall delivered the fresh drink. In exchange, Nigel gave him the sports section and a hundred-dollar bill and said, "Thanks for everything. That will be all for now."

Nigel got to his designated gate ten minutes before the scheduled boarding announcement. He had a Bloody Mary glow about him but not enough to thicken his tongue. He was still able to speak without too much difficulty. He practiced a few times as he walked from the bar.

The nametag said Barbara. She was working the check-in counter at the gate and handling inquiries from waiting passengers. She was pleasant and helpful, but all business with her reading glasses down on her nose. She had a supervisor's air about her that Nigel liked, and there was no question, her word would be the last one. When it was Nigel's turn, he showed her his ticket.

With a big smile, Barbara said, "Good morning, Mr. Logan. We start boarding in just a few minutes."

"Yeah, I know." Nigel started to feel his words slip. "I'll be sitting right over there. Don't leave without me. I like to be the last one on the plane."

"But you are in first class, Mr. Logan. We'll be boarding your group first."

Nigel winked and said, "They're not my group. I'll be right over there. Please, don't leave without me." Nigel always flies first class--at least when he can, not because he is a big shot, or because he doesn't mind spending too much for the extra peanuts and free booze. No ... Nigel grits his teeth and pays the extra required ransom for the leg room. At six foot three inches and two hundred thirty pounds, there's no airline in the world that gives him enough space in coach.

He often tries to secure an emergency exit row seat. Those are perfect. But more times than not, if he is successful at getting one, he becomes annoyed sitting there.

The emergency exit row seat is reserved for those that can assist in the event of an emergency. Logan fits that description; many that sit there do not. The last time Logan secured an emergency exit row seat, he sat down next to a fat, pudgy teenager wearing headphones. Next to him was his sister; they looked too much alike not to be. Logan shook his head.

As the rest of the passengers filed in, another large strapping fella inched by. He gave the seats next to Logan a look and grimaced. Nigel knew what was going through his mind. He looked at Logan and shook his head. Then Nigel said, "Don't worry pal. In a squeeze, Twiddle Dee and Twiddle Dumb here have got your back."

He rolled his eyes and continued down the aisle.

The bottom line is, if airlines were so damned concerned with safety, they would cherry-pick their emergency exit row detail. Those seats should not be for sale on the open market. Once passengers begin to arrive, the flight attendants could identify passengers they would best like to depend upon in an actual emergency. Once the detail is full, the newly available seats can go to those on standby. And there are always folks on standby.

Nigel had been asleep for close to fifteen minutes. But it only seemed like seconds when he felt the gentle touch of fingers on his shoulder. His eyes focused and found the smiling face of Ms. Barbara. She said, "It's time, Mr. Logan. We're about to close the doors."

Nigel opened his eyes wide and took a deep breath to help himself wake up. He grabbed his bag and newspaper, stood, and said, "Thank you. And call me Nigel."

He ducked his head and stepped aboard the plane. He did his quick glance into the cockpit to look at the instruments. He saw the radar image; rain was coming, lots of it. He strolled into the cabin to find someone sitting in his aisle seat. It was a young man, and he and Logan exchanged glances. The young fella said, "Oh ... This must be your seat. I'm sorry. I was hoping..." The young man was embarrassed and continued. "It doesn't matter. I'm sorry, let me move to the window."

The young guy reached across the aisle and kissed the pretty young lady on the other side and said, "Love you, baby."

Logan put his hand on the young guy's shoulder and said, "Whoa ... y'all flying together?"

The little gal nodded and said, "Yes. I'm his wife."

"Oh hell," Logan said. "Keep the seat, buddy. I'll take the window."

She grabbed Logan's hand and said, "Thank you, so much. Flying makes me nervous."

Logan gave her a smile and a wink.

Nigel settled into his big, comfortable seat. All the window shades were pulled down to help keep the cabin cool. A pretty flight attendant asked Nigel if he needed anything. Her nametag said Cindy. Still feeling the warm glow of the two Bloody Marys, he said, "Coffee would be good, extra cream. Thank you, Cindy."

Behind Logan and in the aisle seat sat a woman. She was dressed to the nines. Logan caught her wince and turn up her nose as he squeezed by to his window seat wearing a ball cap, a T-shirt from the raw bar, some khaki shorts, and his favorite worn out Sperry Top-Sider boat shoes. She, on the other hand, was dressed to impress. Her hair was done, and her make-up was as perfect as any war paint job Logan had ever seen. She wore a diamond ring on her finger that she liked to wiggle and flash around. She was on the phone. Everyone in the cabin heard one side of the conversation, but it was obvious that she was bitching about nothing important.

Cindy brought Logan his coffee. As she leaned in to serve him, the princess covered her phone and demanded, "Where is my vodka tonic, dear? I ordered it like hours ago." As she handed Logan his coffee, he caught her eye and said, "Isn't she just a darling, Cindy? Perhaps she would be more comfortable in the cargo hold?"

Cindy snickered as she backed away.

Logan sipped his coffee. It was good, and he felt its immediate effect as it worked against his earlier cocktails. He sat back and closed his eyes in search of quiet. He didn't find it. The drama queen was still on the phone. She was throwing her hair dresser under a bus. Nigel turned his head and watched her in hopes that making eye contact would send a silent message. He eavesdropped as he waited.

"...Yes, girl. That's what I told her. I said, 'You cut it too short, dammit. What am I supposed to do with this?' It looks just hideous, Carol. I'm so glad you're not here to see it. I don't know what to do. And the color is just awful. I told her, 'I'm not paying a dime for this color job. It isn't anything like I asked for.' Carol, when I get back, you have to help me find a new girl. You just must."

It took her a bit, but she turned her head and caught a glimpse of Logan's indifferent stare. When she stared back with scrunched eyebrows, Nigel said, "I see what you're saying. I, personally, would not have left the house. You're brave going out in public looking like that."

Nigel turned his head forward, smiled, and tried his best to ignore the rest of the phone conversation. It was tough, though, especially when he heard her say, "Carol. Did you hear what that man just said to me? O! M! G! I can't believe it." She continued to talk into the phone, but she was now speaking to Logan, "You sir are incredibly rude. I can't believe you would say such a thing."

Logan continued to keep his eyes closed, but said, "Believe it, lady. And you're catching me on a good day."

The lady went on talking about Logan, but only for a short while. Cindy came by and told her, "Ma'am, the captain has already announced that all phones and electronic devices must be turned off or placed in airplane mode. Please end the call now."

She ended the call and Logan said, "Thank you, Jesus." He was relaxing, eyes shut, settling in and ready for some peace and quiet. But even after ending the call, she continued to talk. She didn't seem to be traveling with anyone, so who was she talking to? Logan figured she was annoying the person next to her, but, when he opened his eyes and turned for a look, she was talking to herself as she riffled through her purse.

Logan shook his head and mumbled, "Son of a bitch," as he flipped up the window shade. It had started to rain. A huge, black rain cloud had settled above, blocking the sun. He watched as the ground crew worked to load the last of the luggage in the hold. As the luggage vehicle pulled away, he followed it with his eyes. Then he saw something that made him gasp and his body go rigid. He removed his cap.

Across the tarmac and down on the flight line of the next terminal was a white-hat sailor. He stood at attention with a hand salute drawn tight as the downpour drenched his coat. A container was being unloaded; a fallen shipmate was coming home.

Logan felt the lunge of his own plane as it began to back away from its gate. As his plane backed away, he could see the shipping container descend from the other aircraft. The container was special, with only one purpose. The U.S. flag was painted on the top and the emblems of each of the services were displayed on the side. He craned his head around so he could continue to see, and when the container was offloaded and placed on a cart, the white-hat sailor dropped his salute. Sailors don't salute out of uniform, they don't salute while indoors, and certainly not while uncovered, but Logan didn't care. He didn't have to play by those rules anymore. He rendered a salute to the fallen and held it until the container disappeared from sight.

Logan fell back into his seat and remembered the newspaper article. He pulled it out of the seat pocket and turned to the page. He stared at the picture of Petty Officer Marks, Sissy as she was known by her loved ones. Logan looked out the window, and under his breath said, "Welcome home, Petty Officer Marks."

Logan sat back and returned to the article. He tried to re-read it but couldn't. The princess drama queen was still in full complaint mode. He gave up and tried to block out what was being said behind him. This time she was talking to the person on the other side of the aisle. She had moved on from her hairdresser; now she was dissing her sister in Newport News. There was obvious disapproval of the sister's fiancé and how she was about to marry a bum.

The plane was finishing its taxi out to the runway and started its final turn to begin its takeoff. Logan grabbed the newspaper again and looked at Petty Officer Marks' face. Then he turned to look at Ms. Bitchy and said, "Hey, you! Lady."

She turned her attention toward Nigel, but said nothing.

"Remember earlier when I said, '...you caught me on a good day?' Well, it just got worse. Would you please do us all a favor and just shut the fuck up!"

She replied in protest, but as the whine and roar of the engines rushed the plane to speed, her words were drowned out. As the plane started its climb, he heard nothing, but his mind was back on the tarmac. *Fair Winds, Sissy*.

IN VIRGINIA

Unlike huge airports like Atlanta's Hartsfield-Jackson, or Chicago's O'Hare, the number of people waiting to greet the arrivals of friends, family, and business colleagues at Norfolk International was a small and cozy crowd. They were gathered in small packs here and there.

You can identify the friends and families waiting for loved ones over those that are there strictly for business reasons. Families look anxious, happy, and excited all at the same time. Their heads are in constant movement as their eyes focus around and past the slow migration of emerging strangers in search of their loved ones.

Friends, for the most part, would rather be somewhere else. That's not meant to be mean. It's just a fact. There is always something better to do than sit around an airport and pick someone up. And, if by chance a flight becomes delayed, it is only by some sense of duty or loyalty that they stick around and surrender more of their time.

Those picking up business folks are easy enough to spot. They all seem to mill about together in the same general area and position themselves so they are front and center. They hold their little signs and facial expressions to portray a certain *we're more important than the rest of you* look.

As Nigel stepped out of the crowd, he scanned the wide-open space until he saw her. She was off by herself, leaning against the back wall. She had already spotted him, and when their eyes met, Nigel saw her look of worry and concern shift to a welcoming smile. She was gorgeous, but he knew she would be. He took a deep breath and walked over to her. When he got close enough, Sherry Stone took a couple steps forward, slipped her arms around his waist and embraced him in a hug.

It felt awkward. He stood there as she held on tight. When it was obvious she wasn't going to loosen her grip, he dropped his large canvas backpack to the floor and wrapped his arms around her. They held each other tight for several beats until she squeezed him hard one last time and loosened her grip. He did the same. Then she leaned in on her tippy-toes and gave him a soft, friendly kiss. He let her. Then he said, "Thanks for agreeing to pick me up."

They broke from tight quarters and Nigel picked up his gear.

"Any checked luggage?" she asked.

"Nope. This is it."

"Well, come on then," she said. "Follow me."

They walked in silence to Sherry's car, a new model Toyota FJ. She opened the back hatch and Nigel dropped his gear inside. They jumped in the vehicle. The interior still had that showroom aroma. She started the car and asked, "Where to?"

He changed the subject.

"There's something that's been nagging at me. Why did she call you? Why didn't she call me first?"

Stone shut down the vehicle and turned to look at Logan. She took a deep breath, let out a huff, and said, "Don't take this the wrong way. It's not a jab, but you haven't exactly been around the past few years. You up and disappeared."

"Only because I thought it best to get out of the picture. I did it for their good, not mine. Do you think I wanted to leave? Up and leave everything behind?"

"Well, from all appearances, it certainly didn't take you long to adjust to a new life."

"Go straight to hell. You hear me?" Nigel turned his head to look out the passenger-side window. "You have no idea what you are talking about. Those people saved me from myself."

"Nigel," Stone called. "Nigel. Look at me please."

He did and waited.

"I'm sorry. Like I said, 'Don't take it the wrong way.' I didn't mean anything by it. It's just one of the two facts that answer to your question."

Still full of aggravation Logan said, "Yeah ... what's the other?"

Stone started the vehicle again. She threw the shifter into reverse, started to back out, but stood on the brakes jerking the vehicle to a stop. She looked forward, out the windshield and said, "When two women are raped by the same man, a special bond and trust is created. A bond you will never understand." She turned her head to look at Logan and said, "She is scared. She needs you."

"Did she ask you to call me?"

"She didn't have to. She knew I would."

An uncomfortable silence filled the cab. Stone broke the ice-cold quiet by repeating herself. "Where to?"

"First," he said. "I need a newspaper. Then take me to the Matthews place. The address is..."

Throwing a hand up, Stone interrupted, "I know where they live."

Not a word was spoken as they left the airport parking lot. They continued to ignore each other until Stone pulled into a convenience store and stopped in front of a couple of newspaper boxes. Nigel got out and Stone watched as Logan inserted the two quarters and opened the box. He shuffled through several pages and pulled out a single sheet from the classifieds. He folded the page, stuffed it in his pocket, and trashed the rest of the paper.

When he got back to the passenger-side door, he grabbed the door handle and stopped to think. Stone watched him step away and walked around to the driver's side window. Stone rolled down the window as he approached.

"Listen," he started, "if you just want to leave me here, I wouldn't blame you. I shouldn't have said what I said. You're just trying to help. I'm sorry."

"It's okay. Emotions are running a little high right now."

"Yeah, I guess you could say that." He took her hand through the window. "Truth is ... I will need your help, even if it's just having your ear."

Stone smiled and asked, "Is this where we kiss and make up?"

She closed her eyes and puckered up. He leaned in and kissed her on the cheek, at the edge of her lips. Her eyes opened with disappointment. When she looked at him, he lied, "Did I mention that Candice wanted me to say hello?"

Stone shook her head and said, "Just get in the truck."

Stone parked the Toyota on the curb directly across the street from the Matthews place. Logan had to duck down and look at the place from across Stone's lap. The house looked quiet.

"Do you think he's home?" she asked.

"Yeah, he's there. That's his Lexus there backed in the drive. The one with the buggered up right front quarter panel." Logan laughed to himself. *Son of a bitch. The cheap bastard hadn't fixed that yet.*

"What's so funny?"

"Ah, nothing. Thanks for the ride. I'll be in touch."

Logan reached for the door handle and Stone reached for his arm.

"Where're you planning to stay tonight?" she asked.

"Don't know yet. I'll probably get a room. Charlie will insist I stay here, but I won't. I don't think it would be smart."

"I think you are right," she added. "You can stay with me at my place."

"I appreciate it, but I don't think that is a good idea either."

"I promise to behave. Promise."

"I don't know..."

"Well, at least let me know where you end up, so I'll know how to get in touch with you."

Logan leaned over and kissed her again on the cheek and said, "Thank you. Thank you for everything."

He pulled a Port St. Joe ballcap and a pair of sunglasses out of his backpack, put them on, and stepped out to the curb. Stone drove away, leaving him to look at the house. He looked both ways and crossed the street. He walked up the front steps and stood quiet at the front door. He tilted his head to bring his ear closer to the door. He could hear Charlie's wife talking about something. He couldn't make out what, but it didn't matter. He was just happy to be this close to his old friends. When he couldn't stand it anymore, he rang the doorbell.

Nigel heard Charlie say, "Who is it?"

Through the door, he heard footsteps approach the door along with an announcement. She said, "Keep your seat, dear. I got it."

Nigel watched the doorknob. He saw it turn and the door swung wide open. She had a huge smile on her face when she said, "Yes. May I help you?"

With the hat pulled down tight, the sunglasses, and the longer hair, it took her a few beats to understand and recognize what she was seeing. Her lips began to tremble and her eyes started to fill with tears. She quickly brought her fingers up to cover her mouth when Nigel said, "Hello, Caroline. It's been a long time."

She said under her breath, "Oh my God. I can't believe it." And she rushed to hug him. He dropped his bag and hugged her back. She kept saying, "Oh my God. Oh my God."

From somewhere in the house, Nigel heard footsteps and Charlie asking, "What is it, honey? What's wrong?"

Charlie entered the foyer to find his crying wife clutched to a man on their front porch. He asked again, "What's going on? What's wrong?"

She released Nigel and kissed him on the lips. Then she stepped away, turned toward her husband and said, "Absolutely nothing. Nothing is wrong."

At first Charlie stood looking at the stranger before him. He said nothing. Caroline ran to stand beside her husband. Then she hugged him and said, "He's home."

Captain Matthews, always sure and confident, wanted to believe what he was seeing, but he wasn't sure. Then Nigel took off the glasses and hat and said, "Do you have any bourbon, Charlie? I sure could use a drink about now."

They both took a couple of steps toward each other and then rushed to a hug. They held their embrace and patted each other hard on the back like guys are supposed to do when hugging. They didn't stop until Nigel said, "If you don't, we can always drink that Famous Grouse shit. I know there's no shortage of that."

They both held each other's shoulders and looked at each other.

Nigel said, "Sorry to drop in unannounced like this."

"Don't be an idiot."

The door slammed and they all three disappeared behind the door.

It only took Nigel about three minutes to realize that neither Charlie nor Caroline knew anything about what was going on. They were too happy. He wasn't about to say anything, not yet anyway. Until he knew more himself. It wouldn't be proper.

"Booker's, Blanton's, Maker's, Knob Creek," announced Charlie from the bar, "take your pick."

From the living room sofa, Nigel replied, "The Knob Creek sounds fine."

He poured a neat, long pour for Nigel and the same of scotch for himself. He joined Nigel by sitting in the big chair. Caroline emerged from the kitchen with a white wine and sat next to Nigel. She put down her wine and hugged him once more and whispered, "It is so good to see you."

He hugged back and said, "I'm sorry I've been away so long."

She released him, wiped a tear from her eye, and said, "You just hush."

The next moments became awkward for Charlie; the right words didn't seem to come. Given past circumstances, starting a dialogue was difficult. None of the usual ice breakers seemed right. For some reason the standards *How have you been? What have you been up to? How have you been keeping yourself?* all felt disingenuous and fake, especially when his senses told him that something was wrong. With Nigel's sudden appearance, there seemed to be only one proper question: *Why are you here?* Charlie didn't want to start the visit in that manner either.

Caroline broke the ice.

"So, are you still in Florida? Port St. Joe, right? I looked it up on the Google map. It looks lovely."

Nigel gave her a questioning look. *How did you know?*

"The article," she said. "We read the Sherry Stone article."

"Ah..." And the light came on.

It was Sherry Stone and her newspaper article that had announced to the world Nigel's whereabouts in Florida. In the article, she questioned the accusation that Nigel had indeed been the murderer of Terrance Lundsford, a local, wannabe rapper and thug. That he had done so to avenge the brutal rape of Charlie and Caroline's daughter. Stone also revealed that many years earlier, she too had been raped by Lundsford and that his untimely death also avenged her own brutal attack.

In her own subtle way, Caroline had done them all a favor. By mentioning the article, she had opened the room to the past without directly bringing up the subject. The eight-hundred-pound gorilla was no longer in the room. Everyone felt some relief.

Nigel asked, "How is Grace?"

Her mother answered, "She is doing great. She took some time off from school, but she is back in the saddle trying to finish up her last few classes."

That confirmed it. They knew nothing.

"That's great," Nigel replied.

Charlie said, "She's at the library. She'll be home before long. She will be so happy to see you."

Nigel didn't want to comment, so he said nothing and smiled.

The conversation turned light and joyful. They did what folks should do after extended separation; they focused on the good times. The booze was flowing and laughter filled the room as one story led to another.

They were all slurring their words. Charlie said, "No. No. No. That was nothing. Remember that port visit in Naples? We rented a car and went to Sorrento."

"Oh ... you mean when we almost got thrown in jail because you decided to assault those Italians with a lug wrench?" Nigel turned to Caroline, "Has he told you about this?"

"I'm not so sure I want to know," she replied.

"Well," Nigel started. "We rented this little P.O.S. Fiat for the day and went to Sorrento. We wanted to get away from fleet-landing, the knuckleheaded crew, and the gut. We had a great day..."

"Too great, if memory serves," Charlie interrupted.

"Yeah," Nigel continued. "I can't remember who was driving, but we were headed back to the ship. Neither one of us was in any condition to drive."

"It was you. You were driving and I remember the hangover," Charlie added. "Son of a bitch!"

"Oh ... don't remind me. I think I puked for three days."

Concerned, Caroline said, "Stay on track. Y'all beat someone with a lug wrench?"

"No! No! Let me finish," replied Nigel.

Nigel stopped to put together the details best he could. Then he started to laugh and said, "Now I got it. We were headed back to the ship. We were still in town on those skinny-ass streets when we came across a disabled car in the middle of the road. They were blocking traffic."

Charlie made a peace sign and said, "Two American nuns had a flat tire. They were from Kansas, if memory serves."

"Hell, I can't remember. Anyway, they were having a time with changing the tire, so we got out to help. Despite being hammered, everything was going just fine until a bunch of impatient Italians started laying on their horns and yelling whatever Italians yell. Well, with all the commotion, the nuns were getting nervous, I was having a hard time concentrating on lining up the spare tire, and Charlie was losing his temper. Next thing I know, Charlie heads over to the

Italians with the lug wrench in his hand and goes into an F-Bomb dropping rage."

"In front of the nuns?" asked his wife.

"It was a moment of passion," Charlie added.

"Well," Nigel continued, "It got worse when the Italians wouldn't shut up. So, he decides to start popping the hood of the car with the lug wrench, calling them assholes, and telling them to shut the F up."

"Charlie!" said Caroline.

Charlie shrugged his shoulders.

Nigel said laughing, "Anyway, I grab and pull Charlie and the lug wrench away from the Italians. He's mad as a hornet and keeps trying to go over there, which makes changing a tire and managing his temper a real chore. As I'm finishing the tire change, he's begging for forgiveness from the nuns, slurring and dropping additional, unintended F-Bombs along the way. 'I'm, so F-ing sorry, sister. I feel like an F-ing boob.' That's when we heard the sirens..."

Caroline was giving her husband a stern look of disapproval when the story was interrupted by the sound of the front door opening and closing. All three stopped and turned their attention toward the hallway. They were quiet for a few beats then Caroline said, "Come here, honey. In the living room; someone is here."

As Grace Matthews entered the room, Nigel stood up. She stopped and stood still in quiet disbelief as a smile developed, then tears. Nigel stepped around the couch to meet her. She remained anchored to the floor as he approached. He reached for her and took her in his arms. "Now ... now ... now, pumpkin. You just stop that."

They held each other in a long hug. Grace couldn't stop the tears and Caroline was now crying, too. Charlie didn't watch in fear of crying himself. There was so much emotion in the room you could cut it with a knife.

Grace said, "I can't believe you are here."

"Believe it, pumpkin," said Nigel. Then he whispered in her ear, "You haven't said anything to them?"

He felt a subtle shake of her head. *No.* Then she whispered back, "We need to talk."

The phone rang and rang. No answer. Before it went to voicemail, Nigel ended the call and tossed the phone in front of him on the bar.

"How are we doing?" asked the bartender. "Another round?"

"Why not?"

As his shot glass was being filled, Nigel's phone rang. He looked at the name on the screen, then answered. "Did I wake you up?"

Trying not to sound groggy, Candice lied and said, "No."

Nigel laughed and slurred, "Bullshit!" They both got quiet on the phone and Nigel did his best to sound at least half-sober. He wasn't very good at it. "I just wanted to talk to you. I miss you."

"Where are you?"

"Stool 17."

"That much I can tell. Where?"

"One of my old hangouts. It really doesn't matter. I just called to say goodnight and that I love you."

"What's wrong, Nigel?"

"Just remember that, okay?"

"Sure," replied Candice. "I love you too. But..."

"Get some rest," said Nigel. "I'll be alright. Don't worry."

He ended the call. She heard the line go dead. Asking her not to worry was like telling her not to breathe. It was impossible. She scrunched down into her pillow and held tight to her sheets as she pulled them close to her chin.

Nigel dialed another number. It rang twice and an alert voice answered. "Where are you?"

"The Fifth National Bank. Do you know it?"

The Fifth National Bank was a honky-tonk that was just outside the gate of the Little Creek Amphibious Naval Base. It was as he remembered: a smoke-filled joint, with cheap drinks and plenty of drunk sailors. He was one of them.

"Do you want me to come get you?"

"Does your offer still stand?"

"Stay put," she said. "I'll be there in fifteen minutes."

Nigel took his knuckles and rapped on the bar to get the bartender's attention. "Let's settle up."

When they got to Stone's house, she showed him to the shower. "Clean up and scrub that cigarette smoke off your ass."

He did and he came out of the bathroom wearing a towel. He saw Stone working on her laptop. He looked at his watch. It was 0155. She looked up to see him. "You feel better?"

"Where are my clothes?"

"In the laundry. They smelled worse than you."

"What are you doing up so late?" he asked, as he stumbled to the couch.

"Writing," she replied. "That's what reporters do. What's on your agenda tomorrow?"

"I'm meeting Grace for breakfast."

"How did things go at the house with the Matthews?"

Nigel didn't answer.

She went back to work. As she typed she explained how she was working on a new piece about the case. She wanted the public to re-familiarize themselves with the details. Plus, there had been several other developments to materialize since her last article. The she stopped and said, "You know. I called that Detective Anderson and asked if he was reopening the case? He refused to comment."

Nigel said nothing.

"Logan. Did you hear me?"

She got up and walked around to check on him. He was out cold. She smiled and got him a blanket. She tucked him in and stole a kiss off his lips before heading back to her laptop to work.

Five days earlier, Grace was exiting a lecture hall on campus when she was ambushed by Detective Anderson. He had been leaning up against a wall, waiting just outside the auditorium doors. "Miss Matthews." He flashed his badge. "Could I have a word?"

Grace clutched at her books, said nothing, but stood still. Anderson approached. "Do you remember me?"

"Can I see those credentials again?"

He showed his badge and she read the name off the identification. "Detective Anderson. Yes, I do remember you. Is this going to take long? I have somewhere to be," she lied.

Sounding conciliatory, Anderson said, "By all means, head that way. I'll walk with. I just have a few questions."

She said nothing and decided on a direction to walk.

"So, if you recall," said the detective, "during the Terrance Lundsford murder investigation, I interviewed you. Do you remember?"

"It was a long time ago, but how would someone forget such a thing?"

"Of course, excuse me," he said. "Anyway ... I was going through the transcript of our interview the other day and I just can't help but think..."

Grace interrupted him, "What is this all about? Why are you here? I thought this matter was over with." Grace continued to walk and picked up her pace, a subliminal effort to get away from the detective. She was practically running.

"Yes. You see, that's just it," said the detective. "The matter is not done. I still have a victim and an unsolved murdered."

Grace stopped dead in her tracks and turned toward the detective. "Don't you ever refer to that piece of..." She refrained from the profanity that was resting on the tip of her tongue and rephrased her demand. "Don't ever refer to him as a victim again, not in my presence. Do you understand me?"

The detective stopped, too, and his tone changed. It was no longer friendly and casual. He told her straight up. "These things don't *just* go away. I'm just trying to see if I've missed something. That's all. Maybe you missed something too."

"What do you want?" asked Grace.

"Just the truth. That's all. What happened that night?"

"Why are you asking me? I've already told you. I was home in bed."

The detective smiled and said, "Yes. You were in bed at the time of the murder. I found that in our interview. But..." The detective shook his head in disappointment and continued, "stupid me, it seems I failed to ask where you had been earlier in the evening."

Grace said nothing.

"Do you remember?"

Grace said, "We are done here!"

The detective watched as Grace's breathing increased. Her body started to tremble and she no longer maintained eye contact. She clutched her books even tighter and walked away saying, "Goodbye, detective."

"Goodbye, Ms. Matthews. Don't leave town. I'm sure we'll be talking again real soon."

"Yes, please." Nigel moved the cup closer to the edge of the table and the waitress topped off his coffee. He thanked her with a smile and watched her walk away. He added some cream from the tin cow and asked, "What else did he say? Anything else?"

"No, sir," replied Grace. "That's everything that happened. What's going on? Why did he just show up like that after all this time?"

"I'm not sure, sweetheart. But one thing is for sure, he hasn't given up. Good for him. I admire persistence."

Grace looked at her plate of half-eaten omelet and said, "I'm scared. What do I do?"

"The first thing you have got to do is tell your parents. They need to know before Anderson drops in to ask questions. Tell them everything. They don't need to be blindsided."

"What else?" she asked.

He took a sip of coffee and said, "Cooperate. And above everything else, you tell the truth."

"But..."

"But nothing. The truth is on your side. *Use it*. Just remember to never give them more than what they ask. That's what I expect, nothing less."

"And what about you?" she asked as she gathered her bookbag and things.

"Don't worry about me," Nigel assured. "You just worry about finishing your classes and the semester. I'll be just fine."

He came to his feet as she stood and met her for a hug. "Love you, pumpkin," he said as he gave her one more tight squeeze and a kiss on the cheek.

"Love you, too."

He remained standing until she walked out the door. He sat back down and took a pull off his coffee. He reached into his pocket and pulled out a page of newspaper, the one he collected the day he got into town, a page of classifieds. He spread it out on the table and put on a cheap pair of Dollar Store reading glasses, the left lens poked out because he doesn't need it.

He borrowed a ballpoint pen from the waitress and ran his fingers down each column. He circled a few possibilities, and then he came across an ad that momentarily removed his current worries. It brought about a child-like excitement. Instead of circling the ad, he carefully outlined the block that surrounded the text. He went over it several times until the ad was blocked off with a bold perimeter. He grabbed his phone and called the number.

"Hello. I'm calling about your classified ad. Is it still available?"

He listened to the reply and said, "Perfect. When can I see it?"

The guy told Nigel he had received several calls and three other people were already scheduled to see it. He thought about that for a second and asked, "How are you on the asking price?"

"The price is negotiable," said the seller.

"Don't negotiate," said Nigel. "If it shows as advertised and I like it, I will give you what you are asking."

This made the seller think. He had priced it high since he knew any asking price, regardless of how reasonable, was going to be countered. He wanted some wiggle room to haggle down.

Over the phone, Nigel could almost hear the mental wheels turning in the guy's head. He let it cook for a bit before adding, "And, if you will move me to the head of the line, I will give you a one-hundred-dollar bill whether I buy it or not."

"How soon can you be here?"

Nigel ended the call with a smile. Feeling like a goofy kid, he laughed at himself. Then he looked out the window and saw something that reminded him that this was no pleasure trip. He knew it would happen eventually, but he had hoped to have some more time. He dialed for a cab and, as he listened to the phone ring, he said, "Oh, well. It is what it is."

The cabbie stopped in front of the house and asked, "Do I need to wait?"

Nigel was satisfied with what he saw in the front yard, so he paid the fare and tipped the guy with a ten-spot. "No thanks. You've been great."

Nigel stood on the sidewalk looking at the vehicle. Then he walked up on the grass and took the liberty of looking it over before heading up to ring the doorbell. He walked around it. The body was very straight. He kicked a tire, because it was customary, then he peeked inside. It was very clean. So far, he was happy with what he saw, and again, for just a little while, his troubles were distant. The feeling wouldn't last.

Nigel turned his head and smiled as the front door of the house opened and a young fella walked out to meet him on the lawn. Nigel didn't hesitate. He met him halfway. As they were approaching each other, the guy asked, "Are you the fella I spoke with on the phone? I didn't catch your name."

Nigel produced a C-note from his front shirt pocket and handed it to him as he extended a hand. "Does this answer your question? The name is Ben Franklin. Nice to meet you."

The guy took the bill and they shook hands. The young guy said, "Thompson. Scott Thompson."

"Nice to meet you. My name is Nigel Logan."

Thompson's eyebrows came together in thought. Then he asked, "Did I hear you say, 'Nigel Logan' as in *the* Nigel Logan? Chief Logan?"

Nigel said nothing. He wasn't expecting to have his name recognized. He felt stupid and careless for not thinking of the possibility. Any relief or escape he was feeling had now vanished. It was written all over his face.

"I'm sorry," said Thompson. "I upset you. I didn't mean to sound..."

Nigel raised a hand to stop him. "It's okay. Really. Forget about it." Then he turned toward the vehicle and said, "Let's talk about your Bronco here. She looks great."

Still a little starstruck, Thompson said, "Sure."

Thompson gave Nigel the tour. It was a full-size Bronco, 1993 model, black with a beige top. It had a lift kit installed to help accommodate the oversized tires. Nigel sat behind the wheel and rubbed his hand across the dash. It was perfect.

"How many miles?"

"A hundred and twenty-seven thou."

"That's it? Nice. Does everything work?"

"Yup. I bought it about five years ago. I had been looking for one, and it was the only one I could find. So, I grabbed it. It's been great. It's never been wrecked, and it doesn't leak any fluids. She does burn a little oil, though. He handed Nigel the keys and said, "Fire it up."

Nigel inserted the key and gave it a twist. The engine roared to life and idled. The guy raised his voice over the engine, "Glasspacks! You won't be able to sneak up on anybody."

Nigel liked what he was hearing. He turned the engine off and said, "So why are you selling?"

The guy motioned with his head for Nigel to follow, so he did. The guy reached through the grill and popped and lifted the hood. "I wouldn't tell most folks this, but ... you being who you are and all. But..." Pointing to the engine he said, "You see that? It's the 351 Windsor, the large block, one thirsty son of a bitch. I can't afford the gas anymore and ... the wife is expecting. It's not doing me any good just sitting."

"Oh, congratulations."

"Thanks."

Nigel looked the engine over and checked the oil. It was about a half-quart low, but looked good. It wasn't burnt. "Very clean. I'm impressed." Nigel pulled out a small flashlight from his bag and crawled underneath. While he was inspecting the undercarriage, a car pulled into the drive. Nigel watched two guys get out and approach the Bronco. He crawled out from underneath and brushed the grass off his clothes. "No rust. She looks perfect." Nigel looked at the two guys that were walking toward them and said, "It's sold, fellas. You're too late."

The two guys threw their hands up in the air and grumbled as they turned to leave. The guy looked at Nigel and said, "Don't you want to test drive it?"

"Do I need to?"

"Well, no. I guess not, but..."

"Shut up then and go get the title."

The guy disappeared into the house as Nigel walked around and admired his new ride. As far back as he could remember, he always wanted a big, full-size Bronco. He could have gotten one years ago, but it always got put on a back burner. Now, with so much uncertainty in his life, he might never get another opportunity. He wasn't going to let this one slip by.

Nigel sat with his back against a front wheel and opened his bag. He counted out eight-thousand five hundred dollars in one-hundred-dollar bills and stacked them in the grass. He thought about the price. In his opinion, it wasn't too high. He felt like he was getting a deal.

When the guy emerged from the house, Nigel stood up. The guy was carrying the title in one hand and a skinny, ornate, wooden box in the other. Nigel recognized it immediately. It put a smile on his face. The guy handed Nigel the title. He glanced at the back, it was already signed away. Then he looked at the guy and said, "You're a fucking SLUG? Or do they even use that term for you slimy bastards anymore?"

SLUG is the acronym for Selectee Learning Under Guidance. It is the title earned by a Petty Officer First Class, but only after being tested and selected. If everything goes as planned, he would later be known as *Chief.* When you *put on the hat*, it's a big deal. The world of the Navy Chief is far different than the rest of the enlisted ranks, or at least it used to be. There is plenty of Navy brass trying their best to muddy the waters and fuck that distinction up. It still pisses Nigel off to think about it.

Thompson said, "The chiefs..." He saw Logan's eyes raise in displeasure. "Excuse me, the genuine chiefs that have been around a long time still call us SLUGs, but the others just call us Selectees."

Nigel said, "Listen, pay attention, especially to the old guys. There will be hidden lessons in what they tell you. Who is your sponsor?"

"Genuine Senior Chief, Jethro Bear."

Nigel busted out laughing. He collected himself and said, "You got Max as a sponsor. You got a good one. He'll teach you right."

The SLUG asked, "You know the Genuine Senior Chief?"

"Yeah. You can say that. Max Bear and I went through initiation together. He's a bad ass. One tough, crusty fucker. You pay close attention to what he does and tells you. He's like me, he doesn't like all this watered-down transition shit. He likes the old lessons. He will teach you good."

The SLUG said, "I've noticed that he doesn't exactly follow the CPO transition guidance from the MCPON."

"That's because he knows better."

The MCPON, the Master Chief Petty Officer of the Navy, is the Navy's most senior enlisted and serves as advisor to the CNO, the Chief Naval Officer. The further you get away from the fleet, and the closer you get to the top, the less chiefly and more polished you become. It's understandable to a certain degree.

Each year the MCPON comes out with that year's "CPO Transition Guidance," the blueprint for successfully absorbing a two-tone blue, white-hat petty officer into the khaki ranks of Chief! None of the guidance approves of the *old ways*, but that's okay, the old salts view the guidance more as mere suggestions anyway. Certain parts of the MCPON's recommendations are ignored. Max was that kind of salty.

It's funny how things can get turned around. Nigel came to this house as a silly villain, just a guy looking to buy a Bronco. Now, in a flash, his deportment had changed. The Bronco no longer mattered. He was back in the Navy, wearing the hat.

"So," said Logan, "I guess you want me to sign your fucking charge book?"

The SLUG went into a very well-rehearsed response. Nigel, who was now playing Chief Logan, smiled as he listened to the SLUG grovel the very words he too had often repeated. "Oh great, all knowing, most honorable fountain of wisdom, excuse my slovenly appearance and accept my most humble apologies for encroaching on your most valuable time. I most humbly beseech you..."

Chief Logan raised a hand. He was satisfied the SLUG knew the words. Max had been teaching him well. "That's enough. You're boring me. Tell me. How many in your class know those words?"

"Not many. Just a couple of us, Genuine Chief Logan."

"Consider yourself lucky. Now did you prepare a page for me in your book?"

"Yes. I did. While I was in the house. That's what took me so long. I dedicated a page just for you. It's the last page in the back, but ... I don't know what page number to give you."

"The last page? In the back? What the fuck?"

The SLUG looked embarrassed, not knowing what to say. He had no idea he would come across Chief Logan. All the other pages toward the front of the book were already dedicated for the other chiefs on active duty. He stood there looking dumb, not knowing what to say.

"Jesus, SLUG! Can't you do anything, right? Seventeen! Make it seventeen, then give me the book, goddammit. You're wasting my fucking time."

Chief Logan snickered as he watched the SLUG pull the old green logbook out of the wooden box and open it to his page. After marking the page number, he opened the book wide and handed it to him.

"Is there a particular color pen you wish to use?" asked the SLUG.

In the old days, Chief Logan wouldn't have cared. But the mention of color caused him to think about his newest, old friend in Port St. Joe and said, "Make it red."

Chief Logan was about to write in the book, then he stopped. He looked at the SLUG and said, "Before I do this, I have one more test for you."

The SLUG said nothing.

"Tell me, SLUG. How long have you been in the Navy?"

"It will be fifteen years this January."

Chief Logan was not pleased. He said nothing, but his anger showed all over his face. SLUG Thompson immediately caught his mistake and started to back-pedal.

"Excuse me, Honorable Genuine Chief Logan ... if I may have another go at it.

"Do they even teach this stuff anymore?" asked Chief Logan.

"*They* don't ... but Genuine Senior Chief Bear does. He said others would ask. Not all, but others."

"Well, SLUG. From now on you consider me to be one of the *others*. So, I'll ask you one more time, but before I do, I will tell you this: Never once, ever, when asked, did your sponsor or I do anything but put our entire heart and soul into answering. It's not about the words, it's about the attitude. Do you understand me?"

The SLUG said nothing and nodded his head.

Logan raised his voice, "Is that supposed to be some kind of fucking answer you piece of shit? I asked you a question. I want a fucking answer."

The SLUG sprang to attention and said, "Yes, Genuine Chief Logan. I understand."

"Then tell me SLUG, how long have you been in my Navy?"

The SLUG began to move slowly, in a crouch. He closed one eye, as if in need of a patch. One shoulder began to rise, creating a hump on his back. He tilted his head and began to growl through the side of his mouth.

Logan feigned impatience and yelled, "Tell me, dammit. Tell me now, How long...?"

The SLUG interrupted Logan, "All me blooming life, Chief! Me mudder was a mermaid. Me fodder was King Neptune. I was born on the crest of a wave and rocked in the cradle of the deep. Barnacles and kelp is me clothes. Seaweed is me hair. Every tooth in me head's

139

a marlin spike. Every bone in me body's a spar. And when's I spit..."
The SLUG hawked up a mouthful of sputum and spat it in the grass.
"I spits tar! I am hard, I is, I am, I are."

Logan showed no emotion. He looked at the SLUG with neither
approval nor displeasure. Then he turned away, placed the charge
book on the hood of the Bronco, and began to write.

On the bottom right corner of the page was a note to the
SLUG's sponsor.

*Max, by what chance of fabulous misfortune did you end up with this shit-
bird as a SLUG? Did you piss in the Master Chief's Wheaties again? Damn,
you are one unlucky bastard. Remind me to never fly or ride in a car with you
again. Peace, brother.*

Using the rest of the page, he wrote his note to SLUG
Thompson.

*SLUG, You will probably get a lot of advice until your pinning day. Most
of it will be good, some of it will be shit. A favorite phrase is "Take care of your
sailors." Personally, I think that's stupid. Your sponsor would agree. It's a safe,
emotional, happy, over-simplification and totally inaccurate description of your
duties as CHIEF. Momma and Papa take care of their children. Sailors are not
your offspring and it isn't your job to make them your friends.*

I would say, by whatever method necessary, TEACH.

*Teach the new sailors how to take care of themselves. Most, probably not
unlike yourself, will never have been truly held accountable for anything. Their
joining the Navy is their wake-up call. Hold them accountable for everything.
Give them nothing. Except! ... <u>every opportunity to make mistakes and excel</u>.*

*When they make mistakes, be sure there are consequences that fit the
circumstances. Consequences that send a clear message: <u>Don't do that again</u>. Then
turn around and show a caring side. <u>TEACH them the right way</u>. Show them
the error of their ways and how not to make the same mistake twice. It is always
in your best interest to have effective sailors.*

*When they excel, tell them in a public and fitting manner. And just like
consequences, make sure the rewards fit the achievement. Even small achievements
deserve a reward, even if it's just a "Bravo Zulu" at the morning muster.
TEACH them there are rewards for being effective and earning your respect.
These are lessons that will serve them well, long after they have left the fleet.*

*As your sailors advance as petty officers, build an army of teachers.
TEACH them to TEACH others. Having a deep bench of effective petty
officers is invaluable. Use and TEACH them well to one day fill your shoes.*

You may have also heard the idea that there's no such thing as a worthless sailor. I agree, as long as we're talking about sailors. A recruit takes on the title the day he or she joins. <u>Welcome to the Navy, sailor!</u> This, however, doesn't make them an actual sailor. Becoming a sailor is easy. All one has to do is accept and embrace the life, even if that means faking it. Point is, not everyone is cut out for the life of a sailor. Bootcamp will weed many of them out, but a few will fall through the cracks. They will disrupt harmony, resist authority, and be unproductive. Above all else, they will be unreliable when the shit hits the fan. The World's most powerful Navy doesn't have room for bugs like that. Document your efforts and TEACH them to find the door.

I know this is a lengthy entry. It will likely be the only book I sign this season, maybe the last ever, so I wanted to make it count. To that end, I will leave you with these final thoughts.

Don't be a tyrant, even though there will be times your sailors will think you are one. "Let them." Some days they will hate you: "So fucking what? Let them." If you do it right, you will create sailors that will want to be just like you, and they will follow you down into the depths of hell, which, God forbid, is part of a sailor's job description.

Good luck, CHIEF!

Then Logan signed it at the bottom

From Stool 17, Nigel Logan, QMC(SW), USN (Ret.)

The remarks covered the better part of two pages. He looked them over one last time, then snapped the book shut. He turned around to find SLUG Thompson holding two frosty beers. Somewhere along the way he had slipped away to get them. He set them on the hood as Logan handed him the charge book and the money for the Bronco. Thompson put the money in his pocket and stowed the book in its box.

"Aren't you going to count that?" asked Logan.

"Do I have to?"

Logan smiled. They grabbed their beers and clanked the bottles together. "I think you're going to be just fine."

They made small talk about the Navy and life in general. Nothing too serious. Logan wanted it that way, nice and simple, while it could last. He was enjoying his beer and talk of the service. It made him happy, but he knew it was temporary. He knew, all too soon, things were about to change. Changes were coming, no doubt, with outcomes he would have little control over.

After finishing his beer, Nigel handed Thompson his bottle. "Thanks. That hit the spot."

"My pleasure."

"So, before I take off, does Max have you bring him coffee every morning along with a..."

Thompson chimed in to helped Logan finish his question. They both laughed after they both said in unison, "...bear claw."

Logan kicked at the grass with the tip of his shoe and said, "It was a dumb question."

"No such thing as a dumb question, Chief."

"That's bullshit and never forget it."

There was some awkward silence. They had run out of things to say. Logan couldn't procrastinate any longer. It was time to go.

As Logan opened the door to the Bronco he said, "I have one last order for you, and it must be done without fail. Do you understand me? There's no ignoring this. It's important."

"Sure. Just name it."

Logan rolled down the window and gave SLUG Thompson the meticulous details of his marching orders.

Thompson said, "He'll kill me dead."

"Yes, he will. But you'll live through it. I promise." And with that, Nigel stuck his hand out the window and said, "Scott. It's been a real pleasure doing business with you."

Nigel fired up the Bronco. He liked the way it sounded. He ran his hands over the steering wheel. He liked the way it felt. He fiddled with the radio and out of habit dialed in 100.5 FM, but found only static. He laughed at himself and watched through the rearview mirror as Thompson walked up his front porch steps.

Then Logan stopped smiling. It was great while it lasted, but the fun was over. Logan turned his attention to the black Crown Vic that was parked across the street and down two houses. It had been there the entire time. It followed him from the diner where he and Grace met for breakfast.

The driver of the Vic was watching and snapping pictures through the driver's side window. The camera zoomed in tight to Logan's face. It looked angry, mean, and irritated. The driver was startled when suddenly they were making eye contact through the lens. Logan was looking right down the barrel of the lens and into the driver's soul. A slight gasp was made, when there was erratic movement and everything was out of focus.

The driver lowered the camera to see the Bronco on the move. It was charging across the lawn. It was still accelerating when it jumped the curb. The Bronco was headed right toward the Crown Vic. At the last moment, Logan stood on its brakes, the wheels stopped turning and the tires squealed as it came to a stop inches from the Crown Vic. He blocked the Vic from moving forward. As Logan jumped out of the Bronco, the driver pulled her service weapon and held it in her lap.

With a brisk pace, Logan approached the driver clearly showing his open palms: unarmed. When he reached the window, Logan grabbed the car door with both hands. "Who are you: Moe, Shemp, or Curly?" He noticed the Glock in the detective's lap. "What do you plan to do with that? Shoot an innocent unarmed man?"

The detective said nothing. She was under strict orders to observe only and not to engage the suspect.

"I'll give you the benefit of the doubt and call you, Moe. Moe, I need for you to pass along a message to Larry."

"Larry? Larry Anderson?"

"Keep playing stupid and I'll start calling you Curly. Got it?"

Moe said nothing.

"Tell Larry to leave the girl alone and to do it now."

The detective maintained eye contact and placed the Glock on the passenger seat and felt around until she found her cell phone. She brought it to her ear and said, "Did you hear that?"

The voice on the other end said, "Put him on."

The detective handed the phone to Logan and said, "Tell him yourself."

Logan took the phone. "Thanks, Moe."

He stepped away from the Vic for some privacy. Not that it mattered; he knew the conversation was being recorded. "Larry. I don't know what kind of shit you are trying to pull, but leave Grace Matthews alone. Do you hear me?"

"Is that a threat, Mr. Logan?"

"It's a goddamn demand, asshole."

"Oh, I hear you … but I don't think I can acquiesce. You see, I have good reason to believe Ms. Matthews knows more about the

Lundsford murder than she lets on. I can't even rule out her being an accomplice. Hell, she may even be the killer."

"That, Larry, is impossible."

"No, it's not. None of it is. She was there, Logan. She was definitely there at the bar the night he was murdered. She was one of the last people to see him alive and she failed to mention that during our interviews with her."

"Leave her alone, detective. She had nothing to do with this."

"You seem mighty sure of yourself. Why is that, Chief?"

Logan said nothing.

"That's what I thought."

"Leave her alone. I'm telling you. I swear, if you don't..."

"Nice touch, but I can't do it, Logan. She was there. She had motive. She's a suspect now. I have to bring her in for more questioning. That's all there is to it."

"Detective, you're playing games. I hate games. You and I both know..." Logan let the rest fall away.

"We both know what?"

"We both know ... you're bluffing."

"Don't bet on it, Logan."

If District Attorney James needed something new, then Detective Anderson wasn't going to hesitate. As soon as he got back to his desk he pulled that old familiar file. Scanned over the old material again, like he has so often before, but this time thinking *New ... Something new.* What am I missing? With a green light to pursue Logan, he did so with renewed energy. Another detective, a rookie named Sammy Lott, was assigned to assist. The same detective that would later get caught tailing Logan to a morning meeting with Grace Matthews and then later to the location of one full-sized Bronco.

Detective Lott was small, but tough. She was also smart, which Anderson appreciated. Her serious, business-like deportment hid the fact that she was much prettier than she appeared. She is single and lives alone with her brown Labrador named Butch and a stray cat she hasn't named yet.

While Anderson poured over the notes from the investigation, he had Lott review all the surveillance video that had been captured as part of the original investigation. This is where her smarts and savvy with technology proved beneficial.

She began with the video that captured everyone as they entered the nightclub. She let the video run in real time. The bottom right corner of the video displayed the time of day that the footage was captured. She began reviewing the footage about an hour prior to when the club opened its doors. It would be hours of coverage, but she was prepared. She sipped on a Monster energy drink and sat back to watch the screen.

Scattered about his desk, Anderson had various reports and transcripts staring up at him. In his hand was the initial interview with Logan; he was reading it, again for probably the hundredth time. His eyes were always drawn to Logan's final words. Anderson had underlined them with pens and pencils several times over the years. He would underline them again on this day. *I did nothing wrong.*

He put the transcript down and pulled the police report where Logan had reported his weapon stolen. The report was dated six weeks before the same weapon was used to take the life of Terrance "T-Daddy" Lundsford. It detailed the events leading up to the discovery of the theft from Logan's pickup truck at a local thrift store parking lot.

The report showed and confirmed that Logan had checked his handgun out of the base armory for range shooting at a private gun club in Virginia Beach. The firing range records and eyewitness accounts verified Logan's arrival and use of the facility.

During Logan's drive back to the base, he stopped at a large chain sporting goods store on Military Highway where receipts confirmed the purchase of two boxes of 9mm ammunition and one bottle of gun oil. He later met a female companion (Kim Tillman) for dinner at a popular Mexican restaurant called Fat Sombrero. Due to the crowded parking lot, Logan parked his truck next door at Karen's Consignments, a local thrift store that was closed at the time.

Upon returning to his truck, Logan noticed the glove box open, papers scattered about, and the weapon and ammunition missing, along with an unknown amount of small bills and change from the center console. He called the authorities immediately. The thrift store had no security cameras and those from the restaurant did not cover the adjacent parking lots.

Anderson slung the report down on the desk and said aloud to himself, "It means nothing."

"What means nothing?"

Anderson looked up to find Lott standing at his cubicle. He grabbed the report again, held it up, and said, "This!"

"That might not mean anything," said Lott, "but what I found might mean everything in the world."

In an instant, she had his full attention.

Anderson stood behind Lott and watched over her shoulder as she sat at the terminal. She said, "This is footage of folks coming and going from the night club."

"I see that," Anderson replied in an impatient tone. "Get on with it. What do you have?"

She rolled the footage and pointed to someone approaching the bouncer at the door checking identification. When the person got close enough, Lott stopped the footage. The person's face was framed in a green square with a caption underneath identifying the face. Anderson said, "Son of a bitch. Look what we have here." He laughed and pumped a fist. "Yes!"

Lott said, "Hello, Miss Matthews."

"Why wasn't this found before?" asked Anderson.

"You probably weren't even using facial recognition then," said Lott. "And, if you were, it would have been limited in its effectiveness. Thanks to social media and the wide availability of photos online, the FBI has been able to expand and update its availability of profiles in its database."

"This is awesome," he said. "Are there any more?"

"This is it, so far. I haven't even started with the footage inside and what was captured by other surrounding cameras."

Anderson patted her on the back and said, "Great work, Sam. Keep looking."

District Attorney Patrick James was enjoying his morning coffee and reading the paper. He liked starting with the sports section and working his way to the more serious front-page stuff. The local community section he skipped altogether as it mostly contained human interest stories with little to no relevant news value. Plus, there were all those recipes he would never use and the church announcements he felt he didn't need. The commentary section he saved for last.

There would always be at least two guest contributors with substantive content and the Letters to the Editor could prove to be pointless or informative, either of which created some level of entertainment value. He felt it was a good way to end his morning reading ritual.

James poured what was left of his pot of coffee into his cup and sat back down to the paper. He turned the page and waved the paper in the air and folding the section back on itself. There were only two guest columnists today.

One article served as a congratulatory message to the leadership within the City of Norfolk. It had to do with their decision to move forward with a rehabilitation and revitalization of the Waterside District, the festival market along the Elizabeth River waterfront. It was written by a prior city commissioner who had played a role in the original development of the community project.

In its heyday, it was quite the attraction. It was marked by good places to eat, fun places to shop, plenty of slippage for transient cruisers, and a large green space with an amphitheater stage for musical acts and the occasional movie on the lawn. It was fun and family-friendly, until it was discovered by the city's undesirables.

A new element moved in and used the place as a hangout, creating an alternate vibe that was counterproductive for the Waterside merchants and its visitors. Before long, the anchor retailers and cornerstone restaurants vacated their spaces. Some were backfilled with new vendors, others not at all. In short, the place was ruined and no longer had the magnetic appeal that once drew huge crowds. Now, it's with great hope that the city's renewed interest in the waterfront parcel will see it restored to its previous state as a crown jewel of the town.

The other article was titled *My Story ... Their Story*. It was written by Sherry Stone, television news reporter and occasional contributor to the newspaper. James was trying to decide if he wanted to read it. He was out of coffee and would soon need to jump in the shower and get ready for work. He glanced over the words in the article looking for anything that might pique his interest. His eyes grew to the width of golf balls when he was drawn to a couple of words typed on the page, the name: Nigel Logan.

He spread the paper out on the kitchen table and started to read the piece. Three or four paragraphs in he stopped and said, "Shit!"

Over the course of my career as a newsperson, I have reported on some very significant events, from groundbreaking medical advances that have profound benefits for the world, to uncovering corrupt politicians that take advantage of their power, position, and constituents. I have had the misfortune of being shouldered with the immense responsibility of reporting local tragedies. Those that involve small children are the worst. And, of course, I get to report the happier side, such as the heartwarming homecomings of our sailors as they return home from harm's way.

Most news is a one-way street. We deliver. You receive. There is very little reciprocating feedback when it comes to delivering the news. You have a need, or a perceived need, to know, and we have a responsibility to inform. As long as we get it right and tell the story straight, all is good. We don't hear a peep. But, if we get it wrong, you can bet your bottom dollar our switchboards will light up like a Christmas tree. It is the nature of the business and we wouldn't have it any other way. Luckily, we look at no news as good news, so I guess we are doing it right.

We tell the stories of others. We are a conduit of information and detail. One that is removed from the influence of emotion and feeling, at least that is what some of us strive for. That all changes when the story you are telling is your own. It is impossible to report the events of your own life and not let the passion show up in the spoken or written words.

Several months ago, I wrote a piece called Who really killed Terrance Lundsford? It centered on the unsolved murder investigation and prime suspect, retired Navy Chief Petty Officer, Nigel Logan.

For those of you unfamiliar with the case, the cornerstone details are this. Lundsford was accused of the brutal rape of a young girl, Grace Matthews. The DNA evidence that would have proved his guilt was mishandled during the chain of custody and the case was thrown out.

Logan is close to the victim's father and family, and it is suspected he murdered Lundsford to avenge the rape of Matthews. Although it was a bullet from Logan's own gun that took Lundsford's life, the Grand Jury failed to bring down an indictment. Logan is still a free man.

In my article, I let everyone in on a personal, deep, dark secret. I too had been raped by Lundsford. In the article, I admit to being glad Logan did what he did, if he did it.

Some may think, as a newsperson, I shouldn't report such personal opinions. To that I would agree, but as I have already established, this isn't a news story. It's my story, and I was happy to share it. As it turns out, it is also the story of several others.

In the days and weeks after that article was published, I received phone calls from five other women that alleged being raped by Lundsford. As a newsperson, I know to be skeptical of such contact. Not everyone that responds to such an article is going to be genuine and truthful. I, however, have good reason to believe these ladies speak no lies.

I have personally met with each. We shared our stories and experiences. It is uncanny how similar they all are. However, some have dealt with their version of history better than others. For this reason alone, it's important that we found each other. At the recommendation of one of the women, all six of us got together. I coordinated the event and we had a wonderful lunch. Six women of varying backgrounds and personal lives, but with one common bond: Nigel Logan.

Despite our horrific experiences, we found that it wasn't Lundsford that brought us together, but the man, Nigel Logan. It was because of Nigel Logan that I wrote that article. And that article, in turn, allowed the six of us to find each other. Together, we find that a blessing, as we support and help each other heal. But our real blessing is Nigel Logan, for it was he who destroyed the monster of our past, that creature that always seemed to live under our beds. Lundsford is dead, and we take great comfort in that.

"So much for discretion," said the DA. He finished his cup of coffee and shook his head. The last thing he wanted was pro-Logan publicity floating around in the news. And the timing of the article didn't come without suspicion. Had Stone thought it newsworthy to mention these other five women, why hadn't she done it before? *Why now?* He concluded she knows about the investigation, and the new article was no coincidence. It was a strategic measure to remind the public that Terrance "T-Daddy" Lundsford was a genuine piece of shit. *Damn!*

Detective Anderson was driving to the station when his cell phone rang. He looked at the screen. It was the station calling. He answered, "Anderson." The next thing he heard was the voice of his boss.

"The DA isn't very happy this morning. Have you seen the paper?"

Anderson didn't care too much and said, "The DA isn't happy, because he hasn't spoken to me yet. He wanted something new. I got it."

149

Anderson rolled his own eyes back into his sockets, embarrassed to himself that he sounded like he was taking all the credit. Then he added, "Lott found something in the surveillance video footage. I'll be there in fifteen mikes."

At 0400 Nigel's eyes opened wide. He felt well rested as he continued to lie on the couch. Stone's couch was actually very comfortable. The room was dark except for the subtle nightlights that glowed here and there.

He had been dreaming. He couldn't piece together about what, but he knew it contained Candice. She was the first thing to pop into his mind after his eyes opened. He missed her. And while thoughts of her made him happy, the thoughts of never seeing her again weighed heavy on his heart. He reached for the coffee table and found his phone. He texted a quick message: *Love and miss you!*

Nigel had no idea what the coming days, or even hours, would bring. All he knew was, he needed time to think, and he couldn't do that under the same roof with Sherry Stone. She was too much of a distraction, a pleasant but unproductive distraction. He needed a drive or a beach, or better ... both.

He put a lid on a huge Tervis tumbler he borrowed from Stone's cabinet after filling it with fresh coffee and headed for the door. He slipped out while Stone clutched at her pillow as she dreamt of him. Her eyes drew tighter, then opened briefly as the roar of the Bronco fired up on the street. She smiled and closed her eyes in hopes of picking up her dream where it left off.

Nigel knew just where he wanted to go. He wanted a sunrise off a North Carolina shore. With empty streets and a press on the accelerator, he just might make it to the Outer Banks in time. The Bronco rumbled through and out of town. Soon after crossing into Carolina, his phone bonged and the screen lit up. He grabbed his phone. It was a text from Candice. He opened the screen and smiled at the single emoticon, a red heart.

As Nigel crossed the Wright Memorial Bridge on Highway 158, he could see the sky warming as the day over the Atlantic worked its way west. As he rolled into Kitty Hawk, he had to make a choice: Stay on Highway 158 and roll south toward Nags Head, or head north on State Road 12 toward Duck and Corolla. Staying in Kitty Hawk wasn't an option. He wanted to drive on the beach and there was no beach access in Kitty Hawk. He didn't hesitate and made a left toward Corolla.

The beach access at Corolla is pretty easy to find, you just keep driving and the State Road 12 pavement will end. If you keep driving, you'll plow right into the waves.

As the asphalt gave way to sand, the night gave way to the sun. He made it. He drove down the beach and found a quick place to park. He got out of the Bronco to watch. The sky was clear and free of clouds. The big star had not yet breached the horizon, but its influence caused the sea to boil red. In the moments before showing itself, the water closest to the sun will seem to catch fire. This is known as civil twilight. Nigel's favorite phase. It moved as slow as a clock, but Nigel didn't mind. He didn't want it to end. *Take your time now. There is no hurry*.

He was quiet and thought of nothing but the fireball as it rose into the sky and broke free of the horizon. There was a slight chill in the air that he hadn't noticed until then, so he got back in the Bronco. He was alone, or he thought he was. He looked down at his phone to find the notification light blinking. He turned the phone off and cussed it as he tossed it on the dash. "Leave me alone, dammit! Son of a bitch'n thing."

He stayed on the beach for hours trying to think of everything that needed to be done or handled. Once the list started to outgrow his memory, he dug around the glove box until he found a pencil and an old envelope to scratch notes on. There was simply so much to do. When he got tired of thinking, he looked at the notes. He was sure he was forgetting something, but he didn't care. He felt spent. He tossed the list and pencil next to his phone and sat back to watch the surf.

His eyelids began to get heavy and he was just allowing himself to succumb to the idea of a nap when an old familiar sight caught his eye offshore. He smiled as he opened his eyes wide to focus on the water. His patience paid off. Not 100 yards offshore, a humpback whale surfaced and sprayed the ceiling of the sky with seawater. He watched the surface of the water anticipating where the next blow might occur. He got it right. The massive animal emerged with grace and reported. A beautiful sight. It made him think of his friend. Red would have loved to see this. Tons of nature, all in one package.

It was a little early in the season, he thought, to catch a whale in the surf. This one must have wanted a little head start on the others. November through January is when whales are usually expected to be seen during their southern migration. In the spring, many of the females can be found escorting their newborn pups back north.

He watched the whale make its slow progress down the beach. He kept an eye on it for as long as his tired body allowed. At some point, his eyes shut and sleep took hold.

Nigel woke to the clanking sound of a high school class ring tapping on the driver's side window. It gave Nigel a quick start. He opened his eyes and turned his head. It was a deputy motioning for Nigel to roll down his window.

He did.

The name tag on the young deputy said Morris. This was probably his first real job away from mowing the tiny, sandy lawns of little old ladies, or the labors of finishing high school. He was a good-looking kid. He had a firm, healthy build and a square chin. A crewcut polished off his look. He was polite and professional. While he wasn't yet old enough to have earned any respect, the uniform did.

"Your permit. Where is your beach permit?"

"I'm sorry, sir," said Nigel. "I don't have one."

The deputy tilted his head and gritted his teeth as he listened.

"To be honest, I forgot that I needed one. I've been out of town for a few years and it didn't even cross my mind."

"Where are you from?"

"I'm from Florida." Those words felt a little foreign coming out of his mouth, but they felt good on his lips. Never before had he ever uttered them. And it made him even happier to say, "Port Saint Joe."

"License and registration, please."

Nigel reached for his wallet and then the glove box as he explained. "There is no registration. I just bought this Ford. Here's the signed title and Bill of Sale."

The deputy looked over the documents and stepped back to gaze over the old Bronco. Under his breath he said, "Shweet."

He handed the documents back to Nigel and said, "I'm sorry, Mr. Logan, but you will have to leave."

"You need not apologize, sir. I'm the one at fault. I just wanted to see one last sunset from a Carolina shore."

With a little sarcasm in his voice, the deputy smiled and said, "You know. Rumor has it. There will be another one tomorrow morning."

Nigel appreciated the jab, thanked the young deputy for his understanding, and started the Bronco. It rumbled over the sand as did his stomach. He looked at his watch. It was 1115. He did a little math in his head. It had been over eighteen hours since he had last eaten.

Nigel rolled down the window and called out to the deputy as he was walking back to his truck. "Deputy Morris!" The deputy turned around. "Is Mama Easley's still a good place to eat?"

"Yes, sir."

"You hungry?"

When they walked into the tiny restaurant they were able to find a table with no problem. There were lucky. It can almost be damn impossible to find a table. The number of mouths fed each day far exceeds the number of asses that are fortunate enough to find a seat. Take out and eat on the beach is the ticket.

"I probably shouldn't allow you to do this, Mr. Logan. It doesn't seem right. And besides, I should tell you ... I already eat free at the Grub Hut. With the uniform and all."

"Don't be ridiculous. Let me ask you a question. What's the difference between a genuinely grateful citizen that buys you lunch and a restaurant that lets you eat free?"

The deputy shrugged his shoulders.

"An ulterior motive."

The deputy said nothing.

"And I don't have one. After today, you will probably never see me again. Order what you like."

They had a nice lunch and spoke of nothing of great importance. Nigel spoke of his time in the Navy and Port Saint Joe. Deputy Timmy Morris spoke of his limited experiences. Mainly growing up as a local boy: fishing, surfing, and girls. Nigel was just happy to have the stress-free company. After lunch, Morris excused himself to get back to work.

Alone again, Nigel ordered a beer. He wanted one with lunch, but didn't want to put Morris in an awkward position. He pulled out the envelope with his notes and went over the list. For some of the things, he would need help; others could be accomplished online. All he needed was a computer, so he went to the public library.

He worked to the hum of silence from a corner computer. He sent a series of emails. He closed some online accounts. He logged into his Navy Federal account and made some changes there, too. Then he opened the word processor and began a letter to Red.

Dear Red,

I'm so sorry for leaving town without saying goodbye. Things have gotten complicated. Please extend my apologies to Trixie and everyone else. Simply tell folks that something came up and that it looks like I may be away for a while. No sense in them knowing the truth.

By now you have probably talked with Candice and have figured out that I'm back in Virginia. There is, as you know, much unfinished business here. Unfortunately, I must attend to it. I'd much rather be on the beach drinking beer and throwing nets with you.

I hope you don't mind if I impose on our friendship and request you handle a few things on my behalf. I have unfinished business in Port St. Joe as well. It would give me great comfort if I knew those things were settled, too.

Nigel wrote out his list of wishes in bullet format. Some would be easy, like: Go to the house and clean out the beer in the fridge and the bourbon. There were other things too. His truck was at the airport. His boats. The house he was renting. Tom, the cat. All these things would become complicated if ... and he hated to think about it, if he wasn't coming home. The last thing on the list was a simple request: Make sure Candice knows how much I love her.

He worked on his letter to Red until it was finished. Then he went over it again to clean up the first shitty draft. He found several mistakes and remembered a few items he had forgotten. When he was satisfied with the outcome, he printed out the letter folded it and stuffed it in his shirt pocket.

Nigel sat back and rubbed his eyes. He glanced at his watch. It was 1533. "Damn!" He said, in a not-so-library voice. An elderly woman who was sitting close by cut him a stare of condemnation. "Sorry," Nigel whispered to the old lady, but it did little to find forgiveness. She maintained a pencil-thin smirk as she cut her eyes back to her Sudoku puzzle.

Nigel stood up to leave. As he went to collect his things, he noticed his phone was still turned off. "Oh, shit," he said in a soft whisper. He powered up the cell phone and cut his eyes to the old lady. She seemed to not hear a thing. He smiled, but the smile gave way to panic and humiliation. As soon as the phone finished booting-up, it found the nearest cell tower and started to download everything missed over the past several hours. Every noise a cell phone can make echoed off the walls with each notification. *Ping* ... *ping* ... *ping* ... *ping* ... *ping* ... *ping* ... *ping* came the voicemails and missed calls. *Bong* ... *bong* ... *bong* ... *bong* ... *bong* came the text messages.

With frantic embarrassment, he tried to get the notifications to stop but couldn't. His phone sounded like a pinball machine awarding bonus points and free games. He looked up and found a death stare coming from the old lady. Her eyes were squinting and her lips were drawn tight, pulling all the wrinkles around her mouth to a point. As her eyes and mouth closed in on each other, her nose pulled back into her face.

Nigel shrugged his shoulders, threw his hands in the air and said, "Sorry. What else can I say?"

The little old lady said nothing.

He finished collecting his things and before heading to the door he looked at the old, grumpy lady and said, "You know. That isn't a very good look for you. Not at all."

The old lady wasn't fazed by anything he said. She maintained her eyes on Nigel until he disappeared around a row of bookshelves.

By the time he was sitting in the Bronco, he had forgotten all about the old lady. He was too concerned with why his phone had exploded the way it did. He looked at the text messages first. Two were from Charlie Matthews, two were from Sherry Stone, one was from Candice. There was another one from a number he didn't recognize. He read the ones from Charlie first: *Call me. They have Grace downtown*.

Nigel tossed the phone and rubbed his face and head. He was pulling at his hair when he yelled, "FUCK!"

He gave the other messages a passing glance. Most of them had a similar message of urgency: *Where are you? Call me, ASAP*. One of the messages from Stone gave him a special number to call.

His mind was reeling and he was out of breath from the rush of adrenaline. He sat with his face in his hands trying to think of what to do next. He pulled his fingers down below his eyes and looked at his phone. He picked it up and pulled up the message from Candice: *Come home. We'll take the boat. We'll disappear. I love you.* It was a fine idea that produced a small but sad smile. *I wish*.

He fired up the Bronco, revved the engine, and backed out of the space. The tires squealed as he entered the highway. When traffic wasn't holding him back, he was passing cars and hauling ass down the road. He was doing around ninety when he passed Deputy Morris who was tucked away behind a billboard.

Nigel saw the blue lights in his rearview and took his foot off the gas. "Son of a bitch!" He dropped his speed back down to fifty-five and let the deputy's truck close in fast. He found a place to pull over and the deputy followed and parked behind.

They sat there for several minutes and Morris never got out of his truck. Nigel watched the deputy in his rearview. He didn't seem to be doing anything. Morris locked eyes with Nigel in the mirror. This continued long enough that Nigel was becoming impatient. After another few minutes the deputy put the truck into drive and pulled up next to Nigel. They exchanged a quick look or two before the deputy motioned with his head for Nigel to get moving. He did.

For the next couple of miles, Morris kept his blue lights flashing. To keep from drawing additional attention, he shut them down but maintained a tight position behind the Bronco. When Nigel crossed the Currituck County line, he saw the deputy slow down and pull over. Nigel made his brake lights flash three times as he watched in the rearview mirror. The blue lights of the truck cycled on for a short piece.

Nigel looked ahead and pressed on.

He grabbed his phone and tried to call the number left by Stone. She didn't answer. Based on the outgoing message, it must have been her office number. He ended the call without leaving a message. Then he tried her cell and she answered on the first ring. "Where are you?" she answered.

"In North Carolina. Heading that way. What is going on?"

"All I know is Grace has been picked up by Anderson and taken in for questioning. By the sounds of it, more like an interrogation."

"How do you know this?" asked Nigel.

"I'm a news reporter. I have my share of little birds within the P.D. to feed me inside leads."

"Can you get over there and try to find out what's going on?"

"I'm already on my way, baby. Full news crew in tow," she said.

He ended the call and dialed Charlie. "Nigel. They have Grace. Where are you?"

"Heading that way but it's going to take me a while to get there. How long have they had her?"

"I don't know," said Charlie, "Maybe two hours. What's this all about?"

The first thing that popped into Nigel's head was ... she still hadn't told them anything. "The bastards are trying to implicate her in T-Daddy's murder."

"What! That is ridiculous. On what basis? She was home that night."

Nigel said nothing. A strange and uncomfortable silence grew louder on the phone.

"Nigel? What is it? What's going on?"

The only thing Nigel could think to say wasn't that comforting to the ears of a worried father. "It's complicated, Charlie."

"Complicated! What the hell is that supposed to mean?"

The panic in his voice was undeniable. So Nigel shifted the conversation a bit "Everything is going to be alright, Charlie. It's me they want, not her. They are using her to get to me. Now, listen. Does she have an attorney with her?"

"I called a personal friend, but he practices civil rights and military law. I hope he's there by now."

"Okay ... good. Charlie, take a deep breath. Everything is going to be just fine. I'm rolling that way."

Nigel ended the call and sent a text to Sherry Stone: *Is she still there?*

It only took about five seconds to receive a reply as the phone rang.

"What's the scoop?" asked Nigel.

"Yeah. She's still here and so is every other news channel in town."

"What the fuck!"

"Hey," said Stone, "I'm sorry. I'm not the only person with someone on the inside."

Nigel said nothing and banged his fist into the steering wheel.

"What do you want me to do?"

"Find out what you can, obviously. And protect her good name best you can, if you find yourself needing to broadcast anything."

"And what are you going to do?" asked Stone.

There was silence on the line as Nigel thought and rubbed his head. Then he said, "I'll talk to you later. I got to go."

Stone said, "Nigel. Wait..." But it was too late. He had ended the call. She thought about calling him back, but she knew he wouldn't answer.

Nigel scrolled through the contact list on his phone. When he found the one he wanted, his thumb pressed the dial button.

The man sitting behind the desk had four days of stubble crawling out of his face and an unfiltered Camel burning between his lips. He was reading the Wall Street Journal. His feet were on the corner of the desk. His legs were crossed and the left heel of his weathered cordovan Bass penny loafers rested comfortably in its dedicated divot worn by years of consistent placement.

When the phone rang, he jerked the paper down so he could look at it. It's an old-school office phone. The clapper rang the bell as one of the buttons along the bottom flashed to indicate which line carried the incoming call. He decided to ignore it and went back to reading his paper. Without voicemail, he knew the caller would eventually give up, but the caller didn't give up. He jerked the paper down again and looked at the phone. The light kept flashing and the bell kept ringing. He folded the paper, threw it on the desk, grabbed the receiver, and pushed the flashing button. "Hawkins," he barked through his teeth as the cigarette bounced along, stuck to his bottom lip.

His eyes drew wide as he listened to the voice on the other end of the line. He jerked his feet off the desk and sat up straighter. He took one last draw off his cigarette and crushed it in his ashtray, already overflowing with ash and old butt ends. Then he said, "Well, well. Look who has come out of the woodwork. You son of a bitch, you."

Detective Anderson came into the interview room and flopped a thick manila folder on the table in front of Grace. Already nervous as hell, it made her jump in her seat. He also produced a small plastic ashtray and put it on the table. A pack of Marlboro Lights came out of his shirt pocket and he asked, "Smoke?"

"I don't smoke, thank you."

Neither did Anderson, but he lit one anyway. He puffed on it a couple of times without inhaling to get it hot then placed it in the ashtray to burn. He knew she would find the smoke annoying. He then began to pace about the room in a quick, confident manner asking a barrage of questions. What she could answer with absolute truth, she did, but with minimal details. Other questions, she replied to with silence. Smart girl. She thought of Nigel's advice. *Tell the truth, but nothing more.*

The case folder on the table also served as a distraction, a means by which to intimidate Grace. This is what we have on you. It worked. Her eyes were drawn to the folder, her name printed in bold letters across the front. She was scared, but tried to stay focused. When the detective turned his back, she pushed the ashtray as far away from her as she could. Then she grabbed the folder and opened it. The detective's head snapped around to watch. He smiled as he turned back around and said, "Yes. Can you see what we have there?"

Grace sat in amazement as she looked at a blown-up picture of herself. It was fuzzy in the details, but it was her, no doubt. She looked at the next picture. It was the one they used to zoom in on her face; only a few feet away from her was Terrance "T-Daddy" Lundsford. She was looking right at him.

"Do you know when these were taken?" asked the detective.

She said nothing as she looked at several other photos of herself in the night club. Many of them also had Lundsford in the frame.

"They were taken just a few hours before he was killed. The night of his murder." He let that rest in her mind before asking, "So, what were you doing there that night, Miss Matthews?"

The door of the interviewing room swung opened and a well-groomed man stepped in and said, "Don't say another word, Grace." He walked around the table and took up a spot next to Grace. He placed his briefcase on the table, handed Anderson his card, and said, "Tim Johnson. Attorney for the Matthews family." He looked at Grace and asked, "How are you, dear?"

She smiled and said, "I feel better now. Did Daddy send you?"

He smiled back then looked at the detective. "So, why is Grace here? Are you bringing charges against her?"

"There is reason to believe Miss Matthews hasn't been exactly forthcoming with her whereabouts the night Terrance Lundsford was murdered. She failed to disclose originally that she was with him the night he was murdered."

"I was not with him!" Grace replied.

"That's enough," replied the attorney as he looked at his client. "Please, not another word. Okay, Grace?"

She nodded her head and the detective continued, "We also have reason to believe she may be involved somehow."

The attorney said, "That's nonsense. Her presence at the nightclub bears no weight on any involvement. Look at the pictures, detective. There are a lot of people in the club. Based on your rationale, any one of those people could be involved."

"Yeah, but there is only one problem. Miss Matthews is the only one in the club with an actual motive."

"Preposterous!"

"Oh, is it?" asked the detective.

Anderson took the folder and shuffled through a few shots until he found the one he was looking for. It was of Grace, outside the nightclub. She was in the street looking back over her shoulder. He placed the picture on the table and slid it in front of her. She looked at it and began to shake. Her breathing became short and shallow. Both the detective and the attorney could see that she found the picture disturbing. She focused on her face and the expression she held.

"So ... Miss Matthews. Is there anything you would like to share regarding this photo? What are you looking at? Or better still, who are you looking at?"

She said nothing and slid the photo to her attorney. Anderson lit another cigarette and placed it in the ashtray. "The attorney slid the photo back toward the detective and said, "This means nothing."

"By itself, maybe not," said Anderson. He walked over to the mirrored one-way window and tapped on the glass with his knuckles. Moments later someone came in and handed him an iPad. When they were alone again, the detective said, "You see that picture was taken from a surveillance video feed from the bank across the street. Have a look."

Grace and her attorney watched as the detective began his narration as the video began. "There you are leaving the club. You seem in a hurry. As you are crossing the street something gets your attention." The video continued to run and the detective said, "Right there! Did you see that, counselor?" And he stopped the video. "It looks like someone flashed a light at her. Headlamps, maybe. Did you see that? Let's watch it again."

Sure enough, as the video showed Grace crossing the street, there is a light that flashes and gets her attention. She stopped in the middle of the street to take a look. "Now ... watch and see what happens next," said the detective.

By now, Grace is no longer viewing the video. The detective takes notice as she began to stare off into the distance. He asked, "Don't you want to watch, Miss Matthews?"

She didn't have to watch. She knew what the video would show. It showed her stopping in the street, then turning to walk in the direction of the flashing light. The video ran until she walked out of the frame.

Detective Anderson stopped the footage and asked, "Help me out here. What did you see? Where are you going?"

She said nothing.

"That's okay," he said and grabbed the folder and shuffled through a few more photos. "Ah, here it is." Again, he slid the photo in front of her.

She gave the picture a glance, then looked away. Her attorney studied the photo close, then turned to his client and asked, "Grace?"

"It was taken from another video feed from down the street," added the detective. "I can't believe we missed this during the original investigation."

It was a picture of Grace outside a white unmarked van. She was bent over talking with someone through the driver's side window. Based on her closeness to the window, it was apparent she was comfortable and familiar with whoever she was speaking with.

Anderson tried to get Grace's attention, but she wouldn't look at him. He pointed to the license plate on the back of the van. He spoke to her attorney. "See that. That tag isn't registered to this van. It actually belongs to a Toyota Corolla over in Portsmouth. Very suspicious, wouldn't you say?"

Detective Anderson looked at Grace, who was looking at the wall, and asked, "Who are you talking to, Grace? It's Nigel Logan, isn't it?"

She wasn't going to reply, but it didn't matter. The question was interrupted by the same guy that brought in the iPad. He stuck his head inside the door and said, "Detective Anderson. There is someone else here claiming to represent Ms. Matthews."

Before Anderson could ask who, the door swung wide open and in entered someone familiar only to Detective Anderson. He walked across the floor and stuck his hand out toward the detective. "Detective Anderson. It has been a long, long time."

Anderson refused to take his hand. "Ah hell. You're still not sore, are you? Are you going to introduce me?"

Anderson said nothing.

"I'll do it myself, then." He turned to Grace and gave an honest, soft smile. "Hello, Grace. We've never met, but it's like I've known you for years. I'm here to represent you."

Attorney Johnson piped up and said, "Ms. Matthews already has representation. Who are you?"

The guy looked down at the table and saw the ashtray with what was left of a smoldering cigarette. "Oh!" he said. He turned to Detective Anderson who was looking frustrated and said, "Larry. You must have fucking known I was coming." In less than a second, a cigarette was lit and burning hot between his fingers. With his other hand, he reached toward the other attorney and said, "Hawkins. Jacob Hawkins."

Johnson took his hand and they shook. Detective Anderson looked at Johnson and said, "You're going to want to wash your hands, counselor."

Jacob Hawkins ... Johnson knew the name, but they had never met. To his own pleasure, Hawkins wasn't part of the normal social circles frequented by other attorneys. He was considered a mystery to many, but, in a matter of seconds, Hawkins was living up to all the rumors of his being an unconventional criminal lawyer. He was loud, abrasive, unkempt, and unprofessional with a foul mouth. It was also known that he was quite successful and good at what he does.

Then a light came on in Johnson's head. He snapped his fingers and pointed at Hawkins. "You represented Logan. I remember you now."

Hawkins pulled hard on his cigarette, then spread his palms out, tilted his head, and as he exhaled, said, "The one and only." He looked around and spoke to everyone in the room when he said, "You know. I never even got a thank-you card from that son of a bitch. I called him up in that hotel room and gave him the news about the Grand Jury decision..." He stopped, looked at Anderson, and said, "Sorry, Larry. Didn't mean to bring that up. Water under the bridge, right? We're still pals, aren't we?"

Anderson said, "Go to hell."

"Anyway," Hawkins continued, "I call him up. Give him the good news and the bastard doesn't say anything: No thank you, go to hell, or nothing. He just hangs up on me. Can you believe that? He pays his bills, though. Cash money. I guess that's one way of saying thanks."

He took another pull from his cigarette and exhaled up in the air. He gave Grace a sincere look, and with a wink said, "Everything is going to be alright, pumpkin."

And, for the first time all day long, she believed it. She knew it was a message from her Uncle Nigel. She smiled back.

"Very good!" said Hawkins. He opened his briefcase, looked at Johnson, and said, "Thank you so very much for being here. Your services are no longer required. How much do we owe you for your time, counselor?"

Johnson said, "I think I need to speak with Captain Matthews first."

"That is quite alright. Please do," said Hawkins. "But I would remind you, Captain Matthews isn't the one needing representation." He nodded toward Grace and continued, "And Ms. Matthews here is an intelligent adult, capable of making her own decisions."

Grace looked up at Hawkins and said, "But I don't have any money to pay you."

"You don't have to worry about that, pumpkin."

It was another message from Nigel. She said, "I can't let him do this."

"Sweetheart. He already has."

She turned toward the family attorney and said, "It's okay, Mr. Johnson. Thank you, but I'll be fine now. Really."

After putting out his cigarette and peeling off several hundred-dollar bills, which he handed to Johnson, Hawkins said, "Now ... if everyone would be so kind and allow me to confer with my client in private, please."

Nigel found a post office and mailed his letter to Red. He spoke to the envelope as it disappeared through the slot. "Take care, my friend." Then he continued his roll toward town. He was making all this up as he went along. His primary objective was to protect Grace from unnecessary manipulation. He grabbed his phone off the seat next to him and called Sherry Stone.

"Where are you?" she asked.

"Just now rolling through Deep Creek. Where are we?"

"We saw Jacob Hawkins go in a while ago. We asked him for comment and he said, 'Smoking Camels and an ice-cold Mountain Dew makes the best breakfast.'"

Nigel chuckled, "That doesn't surprise me. The guy is a damn loon."

"Nigel," she said, "the other stations are broadcasting that Grace is the newest suspect in the investigation. That she is somehow involved with the murder."

"She's done nothing wrong."

"I've heard that line before, my friend. It doesn't exactly instill a lot of confidence."

"You know what I mean," he said. "She had absolutely nothing to do with anything. The only thing she is guilty of is being at the wrong place at the wrong time."

"Listen," she said, "I'm going to have to start broadcasting something to keep up with the competition."

"I understand. Just spin it in a different way. Make it sound like she is assisting in the investigation and not being interrogated."

"What are you going to do?"

The phone line got quiet for a few beats as Nigel was thinking. "I don't know just yet. If you think of something, let me know." He ended the call and dialed Hawkins's cell phone.

"Where are we, Hawk?" asked Nigel.

Hawkins looked over at Grace, who was still sobbing in the palms of her hands. "She's upset, but it's done. She told them everything. It about killed her. She loves you something awful. I don't know what she sees in you."

Detective Anderson demanded, "Who are you talking to?"

Hawkins continued to listen as he shifted his eyes to the detective, and, with much love and affection, presented his middle finger.

"Who was that, Hawk? Larry?"

"Yup."

"Are they still looking at her as an accomplice?" asked Nigel.

"No. They agreed to that up front in exchange for her testimony. Not that it would have done them any good. They never had a case, plus I would have eaten them alive in court." Hawkins gave Anderson a little wink.

"Let me talk to her," said Nigel.

Hawkins tapped Grace on the shoulder with the phone and said, "Hey, pumpkin. Somebody wants to talk to you."

She tried her best to stifle her tears and runny nose, but it didn't help much. She put the phone to her ear and said, "I'm so sorry. They made me do it."

"Now you just stop. You did the right thing. You told the truth. More so, you told the truth when doing so hurt the most. Do you know how much courage that takes?"

"But what about you?"

"How many times do I have to tell you? Don't worry about me." Nigel laughed and said, "I'll be fine. It will be a new adventure."

In the background, Nigel could hear Anderson speaking to him again. "It's over, Logan. Turn yourself in."

Nigel said, "Grace. Do me a favor?"

She listened to her crazy Uncle and her tears and sadness were temporarily replaced with laughter. She pulled herself together just a touch and looked up at the detective and said with a chuckle, "Uncle Nigel said, 'Go screw yourself, Larry.'"

"That's my girl. I love you. Now give the phone back to Hawk."

Speaking through her overwhelming emotions, she replied with an unintelligible, "Love you, too." And she gave the phone back to her attorney.

"It's me," said Hawkins.

"Jacob. There is no way I can let her testify against me. The guilt would destroy her. She's been through enough."

Hawkins said nothing.

"Hand the phone to Anderson."

165

Shifting to a caring and helpful tone, Anderson said, "Make this easy on yourself. Come on in, Chief. It's over."

"She's a sweet girl, Larry. She's done nothing. Promise me you will leave her alone."

"That's already been taken care of, Chief. Where are you? We'll come pick you up."

"That won't be necessary. I'll come in on my own. I don't need a babysitter."

"Come on," said Anderson. "Just tell me..." He pulled the phone away from his ear and looked at the screen. He handed the phone back to Hawkins and said, "He better have his ass in here within the hour." Hawkins closed his briefcase and looked at Grace. "I think we are done here." He looked at Anderson and asked, "Detective?"

Anderson said nothing.

"Thanks, Larry." He put his hand on Grace's back and said, "Come on, sweetheart. It's time for you to go home."

Her mother and father were waiting for her in the lobby of the station. She broke free and ran into her father's arms. Then she hugged her mom. They all three held each other tight. As they consoled each other, Captain Matthews looked up to see Hawkins walking their way. Hawkins stopped and said, "She has a few things to tell you, but everything is going to be alright. No, worries, sir."

"Thank you, Master Chief. I was relieved when Johnson told me you were in there."

"There was nothing to it, really. It was easy. Now, Logan's plea deal ... that's another matter altogether. Wish me luck, Skip."

Hawkins took a fresh Camel out of his pocket and stuck it in his mouth. He winked at the Matthews family, took a deep breath, and turned around. He shrugged his shoulders and walked back into the station. "Hey! Which of you fuckers stole my Zippo? I need a light." As he walked toward the reception desk, he patted his coat until he found it in his breast pocket. He pulled it out and snapped it between his fingers and the blue flame rose high above the steel case. He lit his cigarette, snapped shut the Zippo, and said, "Hey Larry! Get the DA over here. It's time to play *Let's Make a Deal.*"

As the Matthews family broke their embrace, they watched Hawkins disrupt the entire police department. Despite the overwhelming admonishment for his smoking and bad language,

Hawkins commanded attention and controlled the room. Anderson reached up and snatched the lit cigarette from his lips and escorted him to an office. Before he entered, Hawkins cut a look back at the Matthews family and smiled. Then he made short work of lighting another cigarette as he disappeared behind the door. As the door was being shut, they could hear Hawkins say, "Larry ... this is bullshit now..."

"Who is he?" asked Grace.

"That, honey," answered her daddy, "is retired Master Chief Jacob Hawkins. The nastiest, smelliest, most unkempt and unprofessional attorney in town, probably the world if you want to get right down to it." He paused a bit and finished, "He's also the last guy you want to get in an argument with. In my entire life, I've never seen anyone twist a conversation or debate around like that guy can. He'll make your head hurt." Charlie Matthews looked at his wife Caroline and said, "If I ever get into real trouble. Just remember, that's the guy."

Nigel was hurrying, seven miles over the speed limit. Fast enough to move along at a nice pace, but not so fast as to draw attention. He held the wheel tight. The reality of what he was driving toward began to weigh in. And as his thoughts drifted toward what he was leaving behind in Port St. Joe, he took his foot off the pedal, pulled over to the side of the road, and coasted to a stop. He sat in quiet meditation contemplating his options.

He was on the very outskirts of downtown Portsmouth on Effingham Street. Ahead of him stood an interchange of no return. Once he made a decision, there would be no going back. He could either take the ramp for I-264 West to work his way out of town and remain a fugitive, or he could take the same and head east toward the downtown tunnel and emerge on the other side of the Elizabeth River a man destined to face a lifetime's worth of consequences. As he sat there, the thoughts and memories of one person flooded his mind. He picked up his phone and dialed the number.

Candice was behind the bar. With the exception of the little sleep she got at home, she hadn't left the bar since Nigel left town. She was using work to distract her mind from the uncertainty that flooded her thoughts. She was pulling a draft beer for her only customer when Kenny Chesney's *She Thinks my Tractor's Sexy* started playing on her phone. It was her favorite ringtone, dedicated for the incoming calls of only one person. Distracted, she turned her head and stared at the phone as the beer began to overflow the mug. She let go of everything, dropping the beer, and allowing it to bounce off the floor. She grabbed a towel to quickly dry her hands and she grabbed her phone.

After hearing her voice, he said, "Have I told you lately that I love you?"

She began to cry in silence. She could tell by the tone of his voice he wasn't calling with good news. She did her best to hide her tears when, after a few moments, she said, "Well, no." She looked to the ceiling, to take a deep breath and collect herself, then in a rush of tears continued, "But I guess you just did. You're not coming home, are you?"

"It doesn't look that way."

She wanted to make another plea for escaping on the boat, to disappear from eyes over a night's horizon, but she knew better. Instead they talked about each other and everything they have been through together, like that first afternoon they met and he beat up her third ex-husband, to more recent memories, like when Tom the cat presented her with a pygmy rattler. There were laughs and tears of happiness, but when everything had been discussed, and tears were all that was left of the conversation, Candice tried her best to be convincing and lied, "Listen, I got to go. The bar is filling up with thirsty bastards. I love you and I'll see ya soon." And she ended the call before he had a chance to say goodbye. She wouldn't have handled that well at all.

Her one customer could tell the call was distressing. And it didn't take him long to figure out who she was on the phone with. Candice never realized it, but he had gotten off his bar stool and walked around the bar to be near her when the call ended. He watched her tense up and make a fist. She was looking down at the bar, all her emotions surfacing. She was about to drink and bust every bottle of booze in the joint. Then she noticed him. But instead of going down a path of destruction, she cried and said, "He's not coming back. He's gone." He opened his arms and she fell into them. He said, "Godspeed, brother." Then Luke McKenzie held her there for more than an hour as she cried.

Nigel sat on the side of the road for another few minutes before putting the Bronco into drive and heading toward the downtown tunnel. As usual, traffic was backed up bumper-to-bumper and moving at a snail's pace as everyone worked their way under the river. He needed a distraction, so he pulled up some music on his phone, Merle Haggard. He turned the volume up to ten, which sounded like shit, but that was the least of his worries.

Unbeknownst to Nigel, Stone was trying to contact him. She sent a text that wasn't going to get delivered while he was in the tunnel. The message floated in cellular cyberspace until sometime after he emerged on the other side. Unfortunately, he was singing along to *The Fighting Side of Me* when the text message from Stone came through. He mistook the interruption of melody as a blip in the music and kept singing.

Nigel parked down and across the street from the police department. He could see the front door and all the news trucks set up out front. They were little clusters of technology reporting in real time to anyone that would listen. It didn't take long to find Sherry Stone. She was speaking into her microphone and looking into the lens of the camera, gazing into the eyes of the viewers she couldn't see. He watched as she gave the microphone to the cameraman then paced along the sidewalk. She often checked her phone. Then he watched her walk away from everyone else to be alone. She pulled out her phone, dialed a number, and put the phone to her ear.

Four and a half seconds later Nigel found it no coincidence that his phone began to ring.

"Where are you?" she asked.

Nigel said nothing.

"Okay ... what are you planning to do?"

"There's not much I can do," he said. "If I don't turn myself in, this will turn into a massive manhunt, and I don't care to waste that much time and energy hiding. Plus, I don't run from anything. And the longer I do things on my terms, the longer I maintain what freedom I still have left."

"So that's it? That's all you got? You are going to walk onto their playing field and instantly lose your voice? Because you will, you know? Once those doors close behind you, your story will become their story."

He said nothing.

"Do you want that?"

There was a long pause before he said, "What do you propose?"

"That you confess to me. Me and the rest of the world. That way you can tell your story. It can be documented while you control the narrative."

"I'm still listening."

She told him her plan. "We'll meet somewhere private and quiet. We'll find a hotel room. Film the whole thing from there with my crew and broadcast it to the world. That way, they can make their own decisions, come to their own conclusions."

Nigel said, "It also sounds like a good news story."

"That would be bullshit, Nigel Logan. It is a *great* news story ... for both of us."

Nigel said nothing as he thought.

"Plus," she added. "You owe me. I wasn't going to bring this up, but..."

"But ... you are anyway."

"But ... you left me once to a painfully long cold shower. Do you remember that?"

"My shower wasn't exactly warm," he added. Then he chuckled and said, "I can't believe you would bring that up. You are amazing. You know that, right?"

"It's too bad you will never find out just how amazing I am."

Nigel said, "Arrange for a room. Then meet me at 1900 in the parking lot of my favorite bank. You copy?"

"Got it."

"Oh, before I go," Nigel said. "That red dress is awesome. It's smoking hot on you. Please, do me a favor and change before coming to the hotel tonight." And he ended the call.

Sherry Stone was confused for only a split second. She looked down at her dress. Then she heard the nearby rumble of a vehicle starting up with a little attitude. She turned her head and found the Bronco. When Stone found Nigel's eyes, he revved up the engine one more time. After a U-turn in the street, she was watching his taillights brake, then make a right turn.

Under her breath, Stone said, "Kiss my ass, Nigel Logan. Me and my dress will be right on time."

After he was a few blocks away from the police department, Nigel picked up his phone and called Jacob Hawkins. As much as those in the room tried to ignore his obnoxious presence, the second his phone rang, he became the center of attention. He answered, "It's me."

He listened for a couple of minutes. He never said a word until he reached out to hand the phone to Detective Anderson. "It's for you."

Anderson snatched the phone out of his hand. "Logan! Where are you?"

"Change of plans, Larry. I'm still coming in. You have my word on that, just not right now. There is something I need to do."

Anderson was furious. "Logan! If your ass isn't in here in the next ten minutes, we will come for you. Do you understand me?"

"That won't be necessary, Larry. But do whatever you need to do. I'll be in touch soon enough. My word is my bond."

"Logan, dammit..."

However, Nigel had ended the call. He handed the phone back to Hawkins and demanded, "Where is he, dammit?"

Hawkins said, "I have no idea." Then gave him the middle finger and continued, "Scout's honor."

Anderson hollered, "I want an APB out on Nigel Logan right now. Find his ass and bring him in pronto." Anderson paced about the room for a second, then slammed his palm on a desk. "Son of a bitch!"

Stone and her crew waited and continued to report occasional updates on air. As bad as she wanted to up and leave, she couldn't. Everyone in the local news business understood the Stone-Logan connection. If she just packed-up and left with her crew, the other stations would get suspicious. No, she had to wait, but not for long. All the stations got their calls from the people inside the station. An APB had been issued. He wasn't coming in.

As her crew began to break down their gear, they did so under Stone's order, "Be lazy about it." She didn't want to give off the impression they were in any hurry. In the meanwhile, she began making telephone calls.

She and her trusted cameraman rolled into the parking lot. She was driving her Toyota FJ. They had ditched the news van across the street in the Walmart parking lot. It didn't take long to find the

Bronco. It was empty. She went inside. He was tucked away in a dark, corner booth, away from everyone else. She slid in next to him.

"I'm not so sure trying to do this here in town is such a good idea," he said nodding toward the big screens on the wall. "My face has been splattered all over the television."

"We got this, but we've got to get moving," said Stone. "Stan, my cameraman, has a suite reserved at the Marriott Courtyard on Atlantic. I have everything we need in my vehicle. When we get settled, I'll text you. Then you drive and park on the south side of the hotel. Text me back when you are there. Stan will come down and let you in the side entrance."

The room was big and comfortable. It overlooked the Atlantic. As soon as Nigel entered the room, he walked right past Stone and two other women and went straight for the big picture window to have a look. The sun, having already set, brought darkness on the water. The only things to indicate something other than a huge, infinite, black mass were the running lights of the shipping that moved about the horizon. Nigel wished he was out there. He gazed upon the water until Stone interrupted.

"Nigel," she started, "I would like to introduce you to some folks."

He turned around and smiled. He introduced himself, "Hi. I'm Nigel Logan." He stuck his hand out and the first woman took it and said, "We know who you are. I'm Jessica Bates." She released his hand and said, "And this is ..."

The other woman took Nigel's hand with a smile and said, "I'm Octavia Minor."

Nigel cut Stone a *What is this* look as he said, "Well, it's a pleasure to meet the both of you."

Then Ms. Minor said, "I'm afraid the pleasure is all ours."

Before Nigel had a chance to ask, Stone said. "These are victims, Nigel. Like me, they were both raped or assaulted by Terrance Lundsford. Like you, they are here to tell their story. We are waiting on one more to arrive. Then we can get started.

A few minutes later, there was a knock on the door. Stan looked through the peephole, turned and said, "She's here." He opened the door and Grace Matthews slipped into the room. As soon as she saw Nigel, she ran across the room and threw her arms around him. She began to cry. He hugged her tight. She released him so she could look at him through her tears. "I am so, sorry. I told them everything. I had no choice."

The other ladies looked on as Nigel smiled and pulled Grace into another hug. "It's okay, pumpkin. It's okay. I expected nothing less and you know it." Her head was buried into his chest and he could feel her nodding in the affirmative.

When they released their hold, they looked about the room. The other ladies, except Stone, were crying. Stone broke up the emotion by saying, "We need to get started. It's going to be a long night."

The two ladies went first. They sat together as Stone interviewed them. Each one told her own story as Nigel and Grace looked on. Their experiences were very similar to that of Stone. Both had been invited to an after-show party and things had gotten out of hand. They both admitted their stupidity for putting themselves in that position. But T-Daddy wouldn't take "No" for an answer. Their shame kept them from reporting the incidents.

While Grace's story is also full of youthful stupidity, it was very different from the others. She was drunk and passed out in the back seat of her girlfriend's car. While they were lost on a bad side of town, Lundsford carjacked the vehicle and drove off with Grace in the back. She was later found beaten and raped.

The case was going to trial. The prosecution had the DNA to put Lundsford away, but the evidence was thrown out of court. The defense had effectively illustrated its mishandling and the judge ruled it inadmissible. Lundsford walked.

All three ladies told their stories. Each taping ended the same way, with a heartfelt appreciation for Nigel Logan. The two painted him as their own personal hero. Someone who had come along and helped erase a bad memory. Someone who had delivered what the justice system couldn't … closure.

Grace's comments on Logan were more emotional and meaningful. He was family. His being a part of her life is one of her earliest memories. He has always been there. As far as she could remember, Nigel Logan has been in the picture. And now, she was devastated. To think that her own testimony would help seal his fate and remove him from her life, was more than she could bear. She became so overwrought with emotion that she got up and walked away from the camera.

When all three ladies had said their piece, they were thanked and asked to leave. They wouldn't be allowed to sit in on Nigel's confession. Grace begged to stay, but Nigel told her no. It was bad enough that Grace would see the video later, the last thing he wanted was for her to witness the words coming out of his mouth. In the end, he still wanted to protect her in whatever manner he could.

The camera kept rolling as a final rally of thanks and hugs were exchanged at the door. All three ladies were now overcome with tears as the inevitable was starting to sink in. Even Stone, the tough and professional newsperson, had to hold back the tears. Stone looked at her watch. It was getting late, so she showed everyone to the door.

When the door closed, an eerie quiet overcame the room. Only Logan, Stone, and Stan remained. Stone and Logan studied each other's faces. Nigel looked tired. He was ready to get it over with, so he could get on with whatever the rest of his life had in store. Stone was having regrets. As much as she wanted this story, she also wanted Logan to run, to hit the road. She broke the silence and said, "We don't have to do this. You know that, right? You're much smarter than those looking for you. You could take off right now and keep your freedom."

Nigel said nothing at first. He returned an appreciative smile, then said, "And what kind of freedom would that be? Always having to look over my shoulder. Always having to be ready to move at a moment's notice. Always wondering."

"But you wouldn't be in prison."

"I would be trading one type of prison for another, a mental incarceration."

He reached in and kissed her on the cheek. "Come on. Let's do this."

Nigel sat in the easy chair while Stone sat on the sofa adjacent to him. When Stan was happy with the lighting, he looked at Stone and said, "We're rolling, Sherry."

She nodded her head and looked into the camera to speak to her audience. "Hello. I'm Sherry Stone. I'm fortunate this evening to have with me a special guest. Retired Navy Chief Nigel Logan. He is currently wanted by the authorities for the murder of local rapper and entertainer, Terrance "T-Daddy" Lundsford.

"As we have illustrated, Lundsford was no stranger to trouble, violence, and crimes against women. You already know my story. And in addition to that, three brave women have come forward to share their own harrowing experiences. One of those women was Grace Matthews. It is suspected that the rape and beating of Matthews is what caused Logan to target Lundsford.

"Mr. Logan has indicated his plans to turn himself into the authorities." She turned toward Logan and confirmed, "That is correct, is it not, Mr. Logan?"

"We've been here before. When will you learn? I'm not a mister. And to answer your question, yes. I'll be turning myself in. Call me Chief."

They both exchanged knowing smiles.

The camera continued to roll, but Stone spoke conversationally and off-the-record to comment. "That will work great. Just perfect. So, are you ready?"

Nigel shrugged his shoulders. "As ready as ever, I guess."

Stone straightened out her dress and posed for the camera. Nigel interrupted her preparation by saying, "I think you should show a little more leg."

"Given the circumstances, you sure are being a little lighthearted."

"Lighthearted," Nigel laughed. "Hell, I'm serious. I'm going to jail. Yours might be the last great set of legs I ever get to see."

"Could we get serious here?"

Nigel nodded.

Stone resettled in her seat and hiked her dress up a few inches in the process. She turned to Nigel and said, "Chief, I'm not sure where we should start. Perhaps you should just tell us your story."

Nigel didn't know where to start either. He sat thinking for a while. Stone encouraged him. "Take your time. We have all night."

Nigel looked at the camera and said, "If..." and stopped.

"'If,' ... what, Chief?" asked Stone.

"If they had just done their job. If they hadn't screwed everything up, we wouldn't be here."

"You're speaking of the rape case, correct? The rape that victimized Grace Matthews?"

Nigel nodded his head. "They screwed everything up. They just let him go. Just like that." Nigel paused for a beat or two and

175

continued, "He beat and raped Grace, and he walked. We were ready for justice. But justice failed us. It failed Grace. She deserved better."

"You realize, of course, the system would have never delivered a death penalty. You know that, right?"

Nigel's face hardened. His jaw muscles tightened. His eyes looked at Stone through the narrow slits made by his lids. The veins in his neck bulged as he spoke through clenched teeth. In an icy tone, he said, "You're right. The system wouldn't have delivered. But..."

Stone quivered at the sound of his voice but whipped herself back into shape. "But, what?"

"But ... I could."

"So," she said, "you admit to murdering Terrance Lundsford."

"Murder is an awful crime. Murder involves an innocent victim. Murder steals something from civil harmony. Murder creates a void where there was once love. Murder is one of the foulest crimes toward humanity. That is something I am incapable of. No, I didn't murder Terrance Lundsford."

"What exactly happened?"

Nigel sat back in the chair and thought for a minute. Always think before speaking. He collected his delivery and leaned in toward Stone. "Let me tell you a story."

Stone nodded.

"When I was a little boy, I can't remember how old, another kid was viciously attacked and mauled by a neighborhood dog that jumped its fence. I don't know what kind of dog. That doesn't matter. All I remember is my mother would not allow me to play outside after school. She feared for my safety, because this dog was allowed to roam free. It jumped the fence all the time. There were no leash laws back then. Those were different times. Had that happened today, the owner of the dog would have been charged, convicted, and in the lockup.

"My father and several other neighborhood dads tried to talk to the owner about the dog, but the owner said his backyard fence worked just fine.

"Gosh ... I haven't thought of this in forever, but now, I remember it like it happened yesterday. I was playing with my Lincoln Log set on the living room floor. It was after school. I was in the second grade. That would have made me what, seven or eight years old? My dad came home from work and he sat down and helped me complete the roof. You know, those little green slats of wood. Did you ever have a Lincoln Log set?"

"I am a girl, Chief, if you haven't noticed. It was more Barbies and the Mystery Date Game for me."

"Anyway, after helping me with the roof, he told me to go to my room so he could talk with my mom. I was on my bed organizing my GI Joe foot locker when a loud explosion occurred outside the house. It scared me to death and my GI Joe gear flew everywhere. I was afraid to move. I was frozen on the bed. My mom came in and sat with me. I remember asking, 'What was that?', but she never answered. Then there was another explosion and I grabbed my mother tight. All she would say is, 'Everything is fine. You don't have anything to worry about.'

"She comforted me, rubbing my head and back while she rocked me back and forth. It seemed like forever, but after a few minutes my dad came in the room. I asked, 'What was that, daddy? That loud noise?' He returned a comforting laugh that told me everything was just fine. 'Fireworks. That's all. They sure were loud, huh?' I nodded my head with a smile.

"My dad looked around my room and said, 'Why don't you clean up this mess in here, then go outside and play while there is still daylight?' I looked at my mom and asked, 'What about the dog?' My dad answered by saying, 'It's okay, sport. He's gone. He won't hurt anybody, ever again.'"

Stone said nothing. Thoughtful quiet filled the room.

Nigel shrugged his shoulders. He was looking toward the floor, between his knees. He said, "We never talked about it. The dog and what happened that day. It took years for me to figure it out on my own. I never realized he had a gun until I was much older."

"Your dad killed the dog?"

The hardened features and coldness in his voice returned. Nigel eased his head up and looked at Stone. He tilted his head and said, "Exterminated. When you kill something dangerous for the greater good, it's extermination."

Stone nodded her head and turned toward Stan, her cameraman, and asked, "Please tell me you are getting this?"

"Dumb question," replied Stan.

"So, Chief. You didn't murder Lundsford, you exterminated him?"

177

"There's a difference. Wouldn't you say?"

"Based on my personal history," said Stone, "I would have to say, 'yes'. Go on. Tell us what happened."

Stone woke him with a cup of coffee. It was almost 1030. They had filmed all night, until about 0400. When they were done, Nigel crawled on a bed and looked at the ceiling. His last thought was of Candice as he closed his eyes and fell asleep. Stone was able to steal about an hour and a half of sleep after spending the early morning editing her piece. Nigel looked around the room. The cameraman, Stan, was still passed out on the sofa. He looked at Stone and whispered, "Good morning."

"Listen to me for a minute," said Stone as Nigel sat up in bed. I have a proposition. If you are against it, I'll understand. No problem."

She told him her plan. He listened to the whole thing. He didn't like what he was hearing. When she was done, he said nothing.

She broke the silence and said, "Forget about it. It's selfish on my part, I know. Just drop it. I'm sorry I said anything."

"It sounds humiliating."

"I know. Just forget it."

Nigel thought for a beat or two and said, "Maybe a dose of humility will do me some good."

He swung his feet to the floor and walked around to where she stood. He hugged her and they held each other tight. He whispered in her ear. "You're better than a great friend. You've done nothing but try to help me. Thank you, for everything. The answer is, yes. You have a green light."

They broke their embrace and she kissed him on the cheek. He looked at his watch and said, "We better get moving."

Stone threw a pillow at her cameraman and said, "Let's go, Stan. We go live in about 90 minutes."

Deputy Timmy Morris was back at Mama Easley's having a little lunch. He paid little attention to the television on the wall that was showing the noon news out of Tidewater. Then a casual glance led to his full attention. "Hey! Turn that up!"

Morris read the "Breaking News" caption at the bottom of the screen: "Suspected Murderer Nigel Logan Surrenders." He watched the sidewalk scene as the camera zoomed in on the face of a man stepping out of a vehicle. It was the same man that a day earlier had bought his lunch. "Dang! Look, Mama. That's the guy that I had lunch with yesterday. We sat right over there."

Morris continued to watch as the camera rolled on Logan who was talking on the phone. Stone provided the narrative. As Mama turned up the volume, he heard Stone say, "He's on the phone with Detective Anderson as you are watching this. As promised, he's turning himself into the authorities."

As Stone was telling everyone about her exclusive interview with Logan the night before, Nigel ended the call and handed her his phone. He took a few steps toward the building and bent down on his knees and placed his hands behind his head, interlocking his fingers.

His wait wasn't long. The camera showed every available uniform in the building rush out with weapons drawn. Anderson stood at the top of the stairs that led to the front doors of the station. Despite Logan being cooperative, he was still taken down hard. Logan grimaced as his face was driven into the sidewalk pavement. He continued to cooperate as a knee was placed on the back of his neck. His only protest was toward Stone. As they were cuffing his hands behind his back he shifted his eyes up at Stone and said, "Thanks, sugar. This was a grand idea."

Stoned mouthed the words *I'm sorry* as he was jerked to his feet and rushed up the stairs. The camera followed and the uniforms stopped Logan in front of Anderson. Nigel said, "Hello, Larry."

Anderson chuckled and pointed to the red, strawberry abrasion dripping blood under Logan's eye. Anderson asked, "What happened here?"

Logan said, "I fell down."

They stared at each other and exchanged unexpected looks of respect and admiration. Each had proven persistent. As opposite as they were, each had stuck to his values. They were both determined and results-driven. They both saw all of that in each other. The moment was lost and interrupted when an out-of-breath voice bellowed through the smoke of a freshly lit cigarette.

The camera turned to see Jacob Hawkins running up the stairs. "Easy on the goods, officers. Easy on the goods."

Hawkins asked his client, "You okay?"

179

"I've had better days. Me and Larry, here. We were just getting to know each other again."

Then Anderson ordered, "Take him inside. Stick him in interview room two."

Deputy Morris watched the television and saw Logan and the officers disappear behind the doors. The camera was on Stone and she spoke to her audience. "There you have it. Chief Logan has turned himself in and is in custody. Viewers will want to tune into the six o'clock news as we show a preview of my exclusive interview with Nigel Logan."

The noon anchorman asked, "Can you share any insight, Sherry? Did he confess to killing Terrance Lundsford?"

"I will say this. You'll have to tune in and watch to find out. From Police Headquarters in Virginia Beach, this is Sherry Stone. Channel 7, The News Voice of Tidewater."

Mama turned off the television. "Damn, Timmy," she said. "You had lunch with a killer."

"Seems so," said Morris. "And he was such a nice guy."

Mama said, "I guess it goes to show. You never really know, do you?"

The envelopes shuffled through his fingers. When he came across a plain white envelope with no return address, he stopped. He flipped it over to look at the back; a circle was drawn on the point of the envelope flap. The number seventeen was written in the middle. He stuffed the envelope in his pocket. From the other side of the house, Trixie raised her voice, "Anything good?"

Red turned his head in her direction and lied, "Just bills."

Trixie was still in the dark. There were few that knew. Only Red, Candice, and Luke McKenzie knew the truth about Nigel's whereabouts. They all agreed to keep quiet until there was more to share. The last thing they wanted is for folks to speculate.

Red knew more than the other two. He had been keeping up with the news on the Internet. He read the online news articles of Nigel's surrender and the video confession obtained by Sherry Stone. The station had planned to air the confessional piece the day Logan turned himself in but backtracked on that idea. None of the other news stations had anything as exclusive, so time was on their side and the station promoted the upcoming news segment heavily. The piece would air on the evening of his sentencing, and it was expected by everyone that Sherry Stone and the station would own the news cycle that day.

Red knew the sentencing was scheduled for next Monday, five days away. It pained him to think he would probably never see his friend again. The thing that bothered him more was that he knew he would have to bring Candice up to speed on the latest. Although she was half expecting bad news, the truth and reality of it all would destroy her.

"Whatcha got there, Red?" asked Trixie as she lit a cigarette and blew her smoke up in the air.

Red had moved to the back deck to sit in one of their tall Adirondack chairs that overlooked the water. He was just finishing Nigel's letter. He folded it back up and thought for a bit as he looked out over the Gulf of Mexico. Without looking at Trixie, he said, "It's a letter. From Nigel."

Trixie said nothing.

Red said, "You better sit down. I have something to tell you."

She didn't like the tone in his voice, so she put the cigarette out and took a seat in the big chair next to him. They both looked out over the water. Red was searching for the right words and where to start when Trixie said, "He's not coming back, is he? The fuckers finally caught him, huh?"

Red's head snapped to the left to look at his wife.

She said, "Don't look so surprised, damn you. I'm in the bail bond business for crying out loud. I check out everybody. I got dirt on just about everyone in town. Shit! I'm a regular J. Edgar Hoover."

Red said nothing.

"Son of a bitch," she said. "I was hoping this day would never come. So ... bring me up to speed. Where are we?"

They compared notes. Red told her everything he knew. Most of which she was already familiar with. He got the laptop and showed her the video of him on the sidewalk, turning himself in. She gasped when she saw how hard his face hit the pavement. "Bastards," she said under her breath.

Red closed the laptop.

"They really got him," she said. "He's really not coming home."

"He confessed," said Red. He picked up the letter and waved it. "That's what this is all about." She handed it over for her to read. He got up and said, "We need to go tell Candice. But I need a Bloody Mary first."

"Make it two and make them strong."

The five of them, if you include Maxine, decided to meet at R.I.D.D., Red's Institute for Drunk Drivers. It was after hours, quiet, and private. They could stream the newscast from there and watch the Stone-Logan interview which was scheduled to air during the station's six o'clock news hour.

At first the station executives were thinking of breaking the interview into three 10-15 minute segments. Air it over the three full hours they dedicated to news, which started at four o'clock. They wanted to keep a viewer glued to the television over the entire newscast. This would have caused much of the interview to be excluded in editing. Instead, they gave Stone the entire six o'clock news hour. She would own the entire hour. They promoted it heavily in the days before, and, on the day of, they used much smaller teaser segments during the four and five o'clock news hours.

Candice brought beer and wine for herself, Trixie, and Luke. She also threw in a couple tall boys of PBR for Maxine. Her flavor of the month. Red had more than enough Jim Beam stocked in his desk drawer. At ten minutes before the six o'clock hour, Red fired up the computer and started streaming what was left of the 5 o'clock news hour.

They scrambled around topping off beverages before gathering around the desk to get a view of the monitor. Candice tried to be strong, but she lost it as an image of Nigel sitting with Stone appeared by the anchorman's head as he announced, "Stay tuned for reporter Sherry Stone's special report. Stone takes the full hour as she reveals her exclusive interview with Nigel Logan, the confessed killer of local rapper, Terrance "T-Daddy" Lundsford. You don't want to miss it, and it all happens ... right here ... on Channel Seven, The News Voice of Tidewater. Starting at six. Don't go anywhere."

As the screen went to commercials, Trixie brought Candice hugs and a box of tissues. "Are you sure you want to do this?" asked Trixie.

Candice thought for a few seconds and nodded her head. "I'll be alright. I think." The room then fell silent as the broadcast started. They watched as Sherry Stone stood on a city sidewalk. She looked into the camera and said, "Welcome to a special edition of The News Voice of Tidewater. I am reporter Sherry Stone, and I will be your host tonight as I bring you a story of love, revenge, and justice. The story of retired Navy Chief Nigel Logan and the Terrance "T-Daddy" Lundsford murder."

The camera started moving back as she began to take a few steps toward the camera and her audience. She stopped and with her thumb she pointed behind her and said, "For me, the story starts right here, at the old River Theater in Portsmouth. The doors and windows are boarded up now, but they do nothing to conceal the things that went on inside. It was here that I, too, was raped by Terrance Lundsford."

Candice gasped and said, "Oh dear," as the camera and Stone turned to take the focus off the old dilapidated building. There was a long stretch of sidewalk behind Stone; light foot traffic passed by as she continued, "But tonight's broadcast isn't about me. My tale has been told. Tonight, three other women come together to tell their stories and to meet the man that delivered their justice. One of the women is Grace Matthews.

"Allegedly, it was the rape and beating of Matthews that caused Logan to take the law into his own hands. I had the privilege of recently sitting down with Chief Logan. In his interview, he leaves nothing to the imagination. And it all starts, right now."

The screen shifted to the normal opening credits of the broadcast, then to Sherry Stone sitting behind the news desk. The camera zoomed in on her face and she said, "Hello again, and welcome to the Channel 7 six o'clock news hour."

She gave another brief introduction and jumped right into her interviews with the other women. Red and Luke looked on as the eyes of Trixie and Candice were glued to the screen. They watched and listened as the ladies told their versions of what happened. They particularly paid attention to what Grace had to say. Her interview was especially emotional and riddled with guilt. Nigel Logan wasn't just a stranger; he was family. And it was with her own words that law enforcement now had a tougher hold on Logan.

The camera briefly showed the ladies hugging Logan and saying goodbye. The long embrace between Nigel and Grace was special and moving. The box of tissues was passed back and forth between the two women. Not even Red and Luke could hold back their alligator tears. They didn't even try; accompanied by the occasional sniffle, they let them spill over their lower lids and run free to the floor.

Now the camera was on Stone as she did her intro for the interview with Nigel. You could have heard a pin drop as they listened to Nigel tell the story of his father and the dog that was no more. Candice was wringing her hands as Trixie bit her fist knuckles. Trixie wanted a cigarette something awful, but Red wouldn't let her, not in the building.

As soon as they cut to commercials, Trixie ran to the door to light up. Candice followed her out and they paced together on the sidewalk. Trixie said, "I just can't believe this. I don't want to believe this is happening, or has happened."

Candice said, "I don't think I want to watch anymore. I don't think I can stand to watch Nigel..."

The front door opened and Luke stuck his head out the door. "It's back on, ladies."

Trixie dropped her cigarette and squashed it with the sole of her shoe and said, "Come on."

Candice hesitated. But as bad as she didn't want to watch, there was a side of her that couldn't stay away. She went back in and they all took her chairs with fresh beverages.

Stone said, "Go on. Tell us what happened."

Nigel said, "I need to do something first. I have something to say and you have to promise me you will air it. It can't be edited out. It is that important to me."

Stone smiled and said, "I promise. The floor belongs to you tonight."

The camera zoomed in on Nigel's face and he said, "I love you, Candice." As he paused, she gasped and choked. The tears were again rushing down her face. "If you are watching, it's important that you know that. I've never loved anyone like I love you. This is exactly what I didn't want to happen. I wanted to insulate you from my past. I didn't want to start something I wouldn't be able to finish."

He laughed a little and said, "I tried to resist you, but you were so damn persistent. I couldn't help myself. You probably never realized it, but I surrendered myself to you long ago. I gave you my soul. And now, I sit here empty because you are not here."

Candice never took her eyes off the screen. It was as if the others weren't even in the room. She nodded, and, through the tears, tried to make a joke of her own. She spoke to Nigel on the screen and said, "I know. I'm irresistible that way." For a brief moment, she laughed at herself but stopped when he started talking again.

"I'm sorry for putting you through this. I'm so sorry for the pain I have caused. I'm so sorry. But I'm not sorry for what I have done. I would do it all over again, because, as strange as it all sounds, it ultimately brought me to you. It didn't take long before I knew I wanted to spend the rest of my life by your side. But that isn't possible. I love you Candice. I will miss everything about you. I just wanted you to know that."

As Stone continued the interview, nobody was paying attention to the screen. All wet eyes were on Candice. They each searched their minds for the right thing to say, but came up empty. Candice was wiping her eyes and blowing her nose when she felt something nudge her lap. It was Maxine. Candice broke the tension in the room when she said, "Hello, Maxi. Are you ready for your PBR?"

She looked at Luke and said, "It's in the cooler along with a bowl. Do you mind getting it for her? I think I'm going home."

Luke said, "Sure."

Everyone rose as she stood and headed toward the door. As she reached for the handle, Red said, "If you need anything ... you know that right?"

She nodded her head. Trixie said, "We love you."

Candice smiled and disappeared out the door.

JUDGMENT DAY

There were four of them in the room: Logan, Hawkins, DA James, and one of his clerks. The DA started off pushing for life without parole. Hawkins stood up and said, "Oh shit, you got to be kidding me? That's how you want to start things? Well, screw you." Hawkins got up and looked at Nigel and said, "Get a good night's sleep, shipmate. We'll see these assholes in court."

James said, "Do you want to do that? He confessed."

"Confessed? To who?" Hawkins looked at Nigel and asked, "Have you told them anything yet?"

Nigel said nothing.

"That's what I thought," said Hawkins. Then he looked back at the DA and said, "Oh … The news reporter interview thingy. Shit, that's no confession. Hell, you don't even have a copy of it. They could have been talking needlepoint and lemon pie recipes. And even if Logan did spill a bunch of beans, it doesn't mean anything. Shit … My client is an egotistical, habitual liar when it comes to the ladies, especially when they look as hot as, umm … umm…" He was snapping his fingers trying to remember.

The DA's clerk said, "Stone. Sherry Stone."

Hawkins snapped his fingers one last time and pointed to the clerk. "That's the one. Sherry Stone."

The clerk received a scalding look from his boss as Hawkins continued, "That boy right there will literally do, or say anything, if he thinks he can work his way into some sugar britches." He stopped and turned to Nigel and asked, "By the way…," He made a pumping motion with his fist and continued, "how did that work out for you? Were you able to…"

Nigel finally broke his silence and said, "Hawk! That's enough."

The DA was able to sneak a few words in and added, "I couldn't agree more, Mr. Logan."

"Call me, Chief," said Nigel.

Hawkins dismissed his client with a wave of the hand and said, "Okay. You can tell me later." He turned his attention back to the DA and said, "It doesn't matter anyway. We're not taking your deal, which isn't exactly a deal, now is it?"

"What do you propose?" asked James.

"Second-degree murder and five years."

The DA laughed and said, "That's ridiculous."

"Almost as ridiculous as your offer, Patrick. Wouldn't you say, huh?"

"Please. Take your seat."

Stretched across the left breast of his international orange jumper was his last name; under that was 23-ZA-973. Nigel found his new digs comfortable. In the Navy, they were blue and called a Poopy Suit, an alternative to dungarees or working khakis. Nigel was sitting on his bunk reading and laughing his way through *The Man Who Invented Florida*, a Randy Wayne White novel.

Since beginning his twenty-five-year sentence, Nigel felt it would be important to stay as connected to Florida as possible. He did so vicariously through works of fiction and other books about the Sunshine State. He typed *Books about Florida by Florida Writers* into the Google search box. A host of possibilities filled the screen. He printed a list of authors and then began to search the prison library system. He found a few titles by White, as well as Carl Hiaasen, John D. MacDonald, Michael Lister, and a few others.

He started and enjoyed the John Jordan series by Lister. But Lister lives in Wewahitchka, Florida, the little town just north of Port St. Joe. And while his tales take place in a setting with fictional names, Nigel recognized too many descriptions that reminded him of home. He had to put them down, temporarily anyway.

He fell in love with the Doc Ford novels of Randy Wayne White and the wacky Skink series and other titles by Hiaasen. The problem was the selection in the library was limited, and it didn't take him long to burn through what was available. Nigel asked the librarian about obtaining more books and received laughter as an answer. Books cost money, and taxpayers didn't give a shit about the reading needs of inmates. Nigel asked, "What if I buy them and donate them to the shelf after I get through reading them?"

That's what he was reading now, one of three new titles he had purchased: Two Whites, one Hiaasen.

Nigel was deep into his reading. A smile on his face. Reading was the only comfort and enjoyment he could find in prison. He liked to exercise as well, but reading was the perfect escape from his neighbors and the concrete box he slept in each night. Each book brought endless hours of being lost in other worlds, not his own. He was thankful for being a slow reader.

His thoughts and memories, of home and Red and Trixie and everyone else, always made him smile. He especially missed Candice. He cherished every letter from her. But, unlike the books, they weren't fiction. They were real, and the realness of his circumstances always settled into a sadness that found no boundaries. And he missed his boat, *MisChief*. He often wished that he had grabbed Candice in the middle of the night and set a fast, close reach for distant horizons. They could have started another life. But he didn't.

Instead, Nigel was flipping pages, lost in the wacky discovery of Florida's hidden gem: The Fountain of Youth. Doc Ford's insane Uncle Tucker was setting out to change the face of the Sunshine State. Nigel read with a smile until a nightstick tapped on the bars. "Logan! You got a visitor."

"Who is it?"

"How the hell would I know? What do you think I am, your damn secretary or something?"

Logan was led to the visitor's room where tables were scattered about, separated enough to give the impression of privacy, but not really. The guard at the door said, "Table seventeen, Logan."

Logan gave the guard an inquisitive look.

"He requested it."

Nigel scanned the room and found a thick stream of cigarette smoke rising to the ceiling. He made his way over to the table, sat down, and said, "You should really make an appointment from now on. You never know how busy I might be."

His attorney laughed and said, "I figured I would take my chances. Jesus Christ! What happened to you?"

By instinct Nigel reached up to feel what was left of the swollen mouse under his left eye. He looked around the room to see if anyone was paying attention and said, "I fell down."

"Damn, boy. You should be more careful."

"You should tell that to the other guy. He looks like he fell off a building."

Hawkins raised up his hands and didn't say anything.

"To what do I owe the pleasure?"

Hawkins handed him an invoice for services. Logan looked it over and said, "What the hell is this?" He slung the paper back at Hawkins. "I paid you, bitch. Cash money, remember?"

"Yes ... I remember. I put in a little overtime."

Hawkins crushed his cigarette in the overflowing ashtray and reached for his pack. He offered a cigarette to Nigel, but received a *you're an idiot* look in return. As he lit his new cig, Nigel asked, "So what's this all about? Why are you here?"

Hawkins chuckled and said, "You're gonna love this shit, brother," as he reached into his briefcase and pulled out a document and placed it on the table. Nigel picked it up as it was slid toward him.

He looked it over, front and back. It was a Voter Registration Application from the Virginia Department of Elections. Then he looked at Hawkins and said, "What the hell? Is this some kind of sick joke or something?"

"In a way, yeah," said Hawkins. "It's the dumbest thing I've ever seen. It's also the most beautiful thing I've ever seen too."

"You're not making a lick of sense, Hawk."

Two more documents, letters, were produced from the briefcase. Hawkins looked them over one last time before handing them to Nigel. "Merry Christmas, Motherfucker."

"You're a few months early, aren't you?"

Nigel hesitated, but Hawkins shook the papers in his face, "Take 'em. Read 'em, you dumb shit."

He did. The first letter was from the Governor's Office. It was addressed to him, but it wasn't really a letter. It was more of a campaign pitch. He looked up at his attorney and said, "The son of a bitch is asking for my support and vote. What is he, a moron or something?"

Hawkins laughed and said, "Yeah, but don't be so quick to judge. Read carefully."

He did, but nothing made any sense. He read through the important parts again.

It gave me great pleasure to restore your status as a whole citizen of Virginia. I hope you will enjoy your new freedom and exercise your voice on election day. Please do not hesitate. You can only vote your conscience if you register. For your convenience, I have included a Virginia Voter Registration Application. It is my hope that you will use it and support my re-election.

Nigel looked over the top of the letter. Hawkins was grinning from ear to ear. Nigel said, "This guy is a moron! And that smile on your face doesn't make you look much smarter."

Hawkins kept grinning. "Look at the other letter, asshole."

Nigel shuffled the pages and began to read through the other letter. This one was from the Secretary of the Commonwealth of Virginia. He read through it three times. It didn't make any sense either. He read through it again. He was shaking his head, not believing or quite understanding what he was looking at. He looked at Hawkins and said, "What does this mean?"

Hawkins snatched the letter from Nigel's hands, slammed it on the table, and began pointing to the letter saying, "That's why you pay me the big bucks, to explain the obvious. Did you not see this part?" Hawkins pounded his index finger on the letter. "It says, 'Absolute Pardon.' What's so hard to understand? You're getting out, bitch!"

Nigel's head was spinning. *What?* It was more information than he could wrap his head around. He couldn't believe what he was hearing. Minutes earlier he was planning his reading list for what he expected to be the better part of the rest of his life, and now he was being told he was a free man. He looked at Hawkins and said, "You're not real. None of this is. It's a goddamn dream, and when I wake up, I'll be back in my cell looking at concrete and steel."

Hawkins took a long drag on his Camel and flicked the ashes in the ashtray. Then he made a swift move and tapped Nigel's bare arm with the red-hot burning end. Nigel jumped back and out of his chair. "Fuck, Hawk! What the hell are you doing?"

Hawkins took another deep pull on his cigarette and exhaled, saying, "Waking your ass up."

Nigel sat back down rubbing his arm and said, "Is this for real?" Then his mind shifted to the burn on his arm. "You asshole. That goddamn hurt."

"Yeah. Yeah. Yeah," said Hawkins. He picked up the invoice and shook it in the air. "You can thank me later."

Nigel rubbed his arm and said nothing. He listened as Hawkins explained.

"I guess when you checked out of Virginia, you really shut the door behind you, huh?"

Nigel said nothing.

"Anyway ... while you've been playing on the beach, it's been a caustic election year here in Virginia, especially with the Governor's race. The current communist administration has been an absolute nightmare." Under his breath he said, "Goddamn Democrats." And shook his head and continued. "Well, thankfully, his popularity polls have been in the tank all year. There didn't seem to be any path to re-election. There was no way to recover, so do you know what the corrupt fucker did?"

Nigel shook his head and shrugged his shoulders. "I have no idea."

"Man. You really have been living in a cave. So, check this out, with a swipe of a signature he tried to pardon and restore the voting rights to some 200,000 convicted felons that had served their time. He did this a few months back, but the State Supreme Court smacked his hand, and in so many words said, 'Hey, dipshit. You can't do that. Every pardon must be looked at individually.'

"When I heard about this, I called an old girlfriend that works in the Office of Pardons. I asked about it, and she gave me the scoop. Basically, she said the dirty bastard was trying to find any vote he could, and he wasn't giving up, even with the Supreme Court decision. She said he was initiating an auto-signature system that would allow him to sign off on every pardon individually. Doing so would legally satisfy the requirement to consider each case independently and bypass the court's admonishment."

"You got to be shitting me," said Nigel.

"I wouldn't shit you. You're my favorite turd."

"Okay then, if he did this for people that have already served their time, how does it affect me?"

"Good question." Hawkins lit another cigarette. "As the mass numbers go, it affected those that had already served. That's where he would get the biggest bang for his buck. But it could also apply to pardon applications already in the system for consideration."

Nigel thought about that for a beat or two and said, "So you..."

Hawkins cut him off. "...submitted an application for an absolute pardon. Hell, I submitted an application for every level of pardon there is. I did it the day after they locked you up."

Hawkins leaned forward and used his fingers to wave Nigel in closer. In a much lower voice he said, "Actually you don't qualify for an absolute pardon. They're quite rare. Reserved for those that pleaded not guilty and have exhausted all their other appeal rights."

Again, Nigel said, "So you..." And again, he was cut off.

"...filed it anyway. Shit ... the system is so big and clumsy. I figured I'd let them figure it out."

It still didn't seem real. Nigel refused to let himself enjoy any of the news. He would reserve that for when, or if, he stepped outside the walls and fences that contained him. He looked around the room at all the other inmates that were visiting loved ones. For a brief moment, he felt some guilt, but he decided he would reserve that until he was free. He looked back at his attorney and asked, "So when do I get out?"

"Today."

"Today?"

Hawkins lowered his voice some more. "It's an absolute pardon, Nigel. It means the system recognizes your innocence. You committed no crime. And they can't keep an innocent man behind bars."

Still in disbelief, Nigel shook his head. "Hawk? How could they screw something up so badly in my favor? How could the Governor accept and grant me such a pardon, if I don't qualify?"

Hawkins sat back up. He was grinning from ear to ear again. He started gathering up all the paperwork, except the invoice, and packed it away in his briefcase. He handed that to Nigel and said, "You said it best. He's a fucking moron!"

That was enough to bring Nigel a little bit closer to the reality of being free, and they both busted out in laughter.

Nigel never went back to his cell. There was nothing back there but bad memories and misery, both of which he quickly dismissed and no longer needed. The books were going to stay anyway.

It took a couple of hours for the system to wade through the administrative procedures to release him. Nigel thought that at any minute someone was going to realize the error and say *Now hold on one damn minute.* But they didn't, possibly because Hawkins was such an obnoxious distraction. He had the clerks and the rest of the warden's staff in a tizzy. He never shut up.

Nigel sat with his eyes closed in quiet patience. He tried his best to ignore Hawkins, but like everyone else in the room, he could not deny Hawk's presence. Nigel cringed when he heard Hawkins say, "Jesus Christ! What the hell is taking so long? Hey you ... over there. Yeah, I'm talking to you. Could you tell me why my goddamn client's civil liberties are still being violated? He's an innocent man, dammit."

The staff did their best to stay focused, but one female working behind the counter said, "If you would just shut up for a minute, we could finish here."

Hawkins looked at his client to find his eyes still closed and a thin smile on his face. "Did you hear that, Mr. Logan? What arrogance!" He turned back to the woman and asked, "Can I borrow that typewriter? And what's your name? I need to prepare a summons to bring suit against all your asses!"

Nigel almost said something. He kept his eyes closed and his mouth shut. Instead, he kept saying to himself *You're not out yet. You're not out yet. You're not out yet.* Still half expecting someone to come in and stop the proceedings, he jumped a bit when the door swung wide open and bounced off the wall. He cracked open an eye to see a guy carrying a clear plastic bag. Nigel recognized his wallet and a few other personal effects. He closed his eyes again. *You're not out yet. You're not out yet.*

The things that happened next in the office were a blur. He was in a trance-like state and remembered nothing after seeing the bag with his stuff. Perhaps he willed it all away from his memory. Maybe he didn't allow it to seep into his grey matter. In the end, it didn't matter, because as soon as the outside gate slammed closed, he snapped out of it.

He was looking out toward civilization. Then, he looked back toward institutionalization. He looked down at himself. He was in his own clothes. Out of instinct, he reached around and slapped his right pants pocket to feel for his wallet. It was there. Then he smiled and found his attorney. "I'm free, Hawk."

"No shit, Sherlock. Let's go get a whiskey."

"Where?"

"My office. Keeping you out of the public eye for a while is probably a pretty good idea. I know the governor's office is trying to keep this second round of pardons from gaining too much attention. I figure it best to extend him that one courtesy."

Nigel nodded his head in agreement.

"Hey, I know," said Hawkins as they were walking to his car. "Maybe you need to go ahead and register to vote. The deadline is only a few days away."

"Piss on his crooked ass, Hawk. Maybe I'll send him a Christmas card."

The next morning delivered a hangover from hell. Nigel's eyes felt swollen against his lids and sockets. A massive headache lurked with patience in the background. All it was waiting on was for Nigel to get up to go to the bathroom. As soon as he stands, it will hit him like a twelve-inch iron skillet.

Nigel was on the couch. He remained still, afraid to move. He opened one eye. It took a few seconds to focus, but he found the bottle of Knob Creek on the cocktail table. It had maybe two fingers left in the bottom. It was new when they started. He groaned some pathetic noise, and closed his eyes to think about what they had done. That was a mistake. Stimulating his brain to think caused it to throb against his skull. He didn't have to think. The fact he remembered so little made it all quite obvious.

Nigel brought his head up to look around. He found Hawk passed out in his desk chair. His feet were up. He was crouched over, his head hung low and his hands dangled off to the side. It looked uncomfortable as hell, but Nigel figured Hawk was no stranger to waking up like this. He wanted to chuckle, but he knew it would be a mistake. Instead, he eased himself with subtle movements to an upright position. He looked around the office as he rubbed his head. It was filthy. The last time it was really clean was probably the day Hawk signed the lease.

He was thirsty and his head was pounding. He made his way to the refrigerator. There was only beer. *I'm quite sure there's water in beer. It will have to do*, he thought. He grabbed a PBR tallboy and popped the top. It went down easy. So did the next one. He walked over to the window that looked out over the street. Cars drove by. There was a guy on the corner with a newsstand selling papers. He watched people come and go on the sidewalk. Those were his favorites. He was one of them again. He wasn't in prison. He smiled, and, all of a sudden, the hangover didn't matter.

The phone rang. Stone recognized the voice the second she heard the words *I need a lift*. She was wide-eyed as she listened in both amazement and disbelief. Nigel fed her bits and pieces of his release and all she could do was shake her head. She grabbed her keys before she even hung up the phone.

A short toot of the horn got his attention. He looked up from the park bench as Stone reached across the FJ and pushed open the passenger-side door.

After closing the door, she reached across for a hug, but backed off saying, "Whoa! You smell like..."

Nigel said, "...prison, whiskey, cigarette smoke, and beer. Some of it may be the smell of my attorney's office. Either way, I'd love to scrub this stench off me. Then maybe grab a bite to eat."

She sat outside the bathroom door and waited with his change of clothes. He was in the shower for what seemed like a month, but she didn't care. She considered joining him, but decided to behave. Her eyes shifted to the door when she heard the water stop. He came out two minutes later, a towel wrapped around his waist. She got up and handed him his clothes. "Feel better?"

"I used all your hot water. Sorry."

She closed her eyes and almost said *a cold shower might come in handy right now*, but instead said, "That's okay. Go get dressed."

As he walked through the house toward the kitchen, he was met with the smell of bacon on the stove and fresh coffee. When he came around the corner, she was cracking eggs in a bowl. She stopped when she saw him and asked, "Can I have my hug now?"

They held each other tight. It was a hug they both benefitted from. In his ear, she said, "None of this makes any sense."
They released and looked at each other. He said, "I'm still wrapping my head around it, too."

She went back to tend to the late breakfast as he poured himself a big glass of ice water. She flipped the sizzling bacon, and asked, "Does Candice know yet?"

Nigel said nothing.

Stone looked up to catch Nigel staring into his glass. She knew he heard the question. There was no way he couldn't have. "Well? Does she?"

Nigel looked up. The answer was on his face.

"You haven't told her, have you? She doesn't know, does she?"

He shook his head.

Now she was actually getting a little mad. "What the hell is wrong with you? Why doesn't she know?"

"I don't want anyone to know I'm out right now. Please don't ask."

"You sound like an idiot, Nigel Logan."

He walked over and held her shoulders. He looked her in the eye and said, "I want to call her. I almost did last night, but I didn't. I can't. Not, yet anyway." He paused a bit and continued, "I still have some things left to do."

"Nigel Logan! You are confusing and scaring me. What in hell are you talking about?"

"Please, do me a favor?" asked Nigel. "As tempting as it might be, do not report that I have been released. Report all you want on the corruption of the governor's actions to manipulate the election. Just leave me out of it."

"But, what about …"

"No, buts. Please. For me. For me and Candice. Okay?"

They sat next to each other and ate in silence until Nigel put his fork down and said, "Thank you. That was wonderful. I feel much better now." He reached over, took her hands and brought them up for him to kiss. "I better get going."

She wanted to cry, but she didn't.

They walked in the garage and she said, "There she is. Your bag and stuff. Just like you left it."

His Bronco was parked on the far side, next to her FJ. She pushed the garage door opener and daylight started to flood in as they walked around to his vehicle. He got in and took a quick inventory. He put the key in the ignition and rolled down the window. "Thank you, again. Really. I will always be indebted to you."

"Will I see you again?" she asked.

"If you do, you'll know everything is alright."

"And if I don't?"

Nigel said nothing.

"Well ... I'm going to bet that I do."

Nigel smiled and said, "Betting on Nigel Logan usually carries pretty good odds."

She reached in and grabbed his face and kissed him. He held the back of her head and kissed her back. When they parted, she said, "Perhaps ... if we had met in another place and time, huh?"

Nigel nodded with a smile and started the Bronco. It was loud in the garage and as he put it in gear, he raised his voice and said. "Take care of yourself."

She watched him roll out of the driveway. She walked and followed so she could see him go down the street. After he made a left turn and disappeared from sight, she yelled, "You better hurry back, asshole!"

It was three days before Christmas. Nigel was looking at himself in the bathroom mirror. He ran his fingers through his beard, now full after two months of growth. He hated it. It drove him crazy, and he was ready for it to be gone.

He was done with the shitty motel where he had been staying. He had registered under the name Jim Horton and told the owner he was in town for business from Sanibel Island, Florida. Nigel paid for the first four weeks, up front and with cash. He could tell the owner could care less about who he was, or where he was from. As long as he kept paying in cash, he could stay as long as he liked. That was a perfect arrangement, but it wouldn't last. After today he wouldn't be back, even though he still had two more weeks on the books. The cash cow would disappear.

He had done all his planning over the past several weeks. He knew where to go and what to expect. He had thought it through a hundred times.

He went around the room and collected everything and anything that could connect him with staying there and put it in a garbage bag. He even piled all the sheets in the floor so the owner's wife, Carla, would change the sheets when she came in to clean next. Carla liked cleaning Mr. Horton's room. Once a week, he left her a twenty-dollar bill on the dresser. On this day, he left a Ben Franklin, a little note scribbled on the bill: Merry Christmas, Carla.

He counted what cash he had left. Out of the twenty grand he started with, he had just over eleven hundred dollars left. He was getting low, but figured it would be enough. He put a rubber band around the money and put it in his bag. He picked up the Ruger Mark IV. He had bought it from a guy way out Highway 58, around Adam's Grove. He checked the magazine. It was full. In the bag it went.

On the dresser, a cell phone was charging. It was full, so he put it in his pocket. He collected everything else and packed it away. With his personal bag slung over his shoulder and the garbage bag in his hand, it was time to leave. He stood at the door and looked back around the room one last time. He liked what he saw. On his way to the Bronco, he ditched the trash bag and room key in the dumpster.

As he was getting close to his vehicle, he could hear his cell phone ringing. He crawled up in the Bronco and picked his phone up off the console. It was Sherry Stone. She tries to call him every few days. He always let it go to voicemail. He tossed the phone on the passenger seat and said, "Keep the light on for me."

He wore a full-length topcoat with a broad, faux-fur collar. The same fur brim on his hat matched his coat. He walked through the door right on time. He took a seat at his favorite table, so he could see the whole room. It was almost empty. At the bar, drinking alone, was a big guy in a dark blue hoodie. Across the room and by a window, a couple sat in a booth chatting.

As he was taking off his hat, the bartender showed up at the table with a snifter, a long pour of Cognac sloshed around in the bowl. He set it down and said, "Evening, Big Man."

"How's it been, tonight?"

"Slow, boss. Real slow."

The bartender kept talking as his boss surveyed the room. "I was think'n, boss. Since it's so slow, that maybe we could shut down early. It being Christmas Eve and all."

"That's what you get for thinking." Then he pointed at the couple and asked, "How long they been in here?"

"About an hour, I guess," replied the bartender. "They should be leaving soon. They settled their tab about five minutes before you came in."

"And what's his story?" he asked pointing toward the bar.

"I don't know. White boy. Comes in here from time to time. Doesn't say much. Drinks Jim Beam." He leaned in and lowered his tone. "I think he knows it isn't the real stuff. He never says anything though, and he always pays in cash."

They heard the shuffling of the couple scooting out of their booth. The bartender called after them, "Merry Christmas. Thanks for coming in."

The coupled waved as they headed to the door.

"So ... what do you say, boss? Close early?"

His boss tilted his head toward the bar and said, "As long as he's pay'n, you're stay'n." And that was the end of that conversation. The bartender returned to his duties.

He took a sip of his cognac and relaxed. He was decompressing after a long week and was ready for the holidays to be over. There was a library quality to the quiet that filled the bar, until his cell phone rang. He put his drink down and thought *Leave me alone,* but dug into the breast pocket of his topcoat. The phone continued to ring as he looked at the name on the phone with both shock and a haunting amazement. The screen lit up his face and revealed his unexpected nervousness. It was Jimbo Waters.

He took the call and lowered his voice. "Jimbo? It's Big Man. Is that you?"

There was quiet on the other end of the line. Then the call ended.

He tried to call him back, but it rang and rang without ever being answered. He knocked his cognac back and yelled to the bartender to bring him another. What did all this mean? Jimbo was dead, or so he thought. And that Logan guy was in prison. A million ridiculous possibilities rushed through his head. Then, as his fresh drink was placed in front of him, the phone rang again.

The bartender saw the uneasiness of his boss and left in a hurry to finish cleaning behind the bar. Big Man answered again. "Jimbo? Where are you?"

This time he could hear breathing. Somebody was playing games with his head. "Dammit! Who is this?"

Whoever was on the other end began to chuckle with amusement as Manchester Lundsford began to lose it. "Who is this, goddammit? What do you want?"

The chuckling turned to full laughter. Manchester ended the call and slammed his fist onto the table. He yelled, "Son! Of! A! Bitch!"

Big Man looked up and around the room. He found his bartender straightening the bar stools. They were alone. The barkeep asked, "Is everything alright, boss?"

Big Man said nothing. He sat back in his chair and stared at his phone that lay on the table. He waited, half expecting at any second that it would ring again, but it didn't. He didn't know what was worse. The ringing or the waiting.

After about an hour and two more cognacs, he gathered his things and left. The bartender said, "Good night, Big Man." He was hoping his boss would say to close it all down and go home. But he said nothing before heading to the back door.

He stepped out into the dark, cold alley. A stiff north wind funneled its way between the buildings and made it feel much worse. He clinched the collar of his coat as he scurried to his car. He was fumbling for his keys when the phone rang again. He clutched at his breast pocket, but quickly realized it wasn't his phone ringing. He looked around and followed the sound of the ringer. It was close. It was real close. As it rang, it also vibrated, and he found it ringing and buzzing on the hood of his car. He picked it up.

From behind him he heard someone say, "Go ahead, Manchester. Answer it."

Big Man turned around. At first, he saw nothing. Then he saw the large hooded person move toward him from out of the shadows. He went for his gun, but it was too late. The dark figure was swift and moved with accuracy. The first blow to the head was a huge hook to the jaw. Bones cracked. It sent Big Man down to one knee. He tried to get up. He clawed at his car, looking for anything to grab to help pull himself up. Then he was hit again. Another very hard hook. Big Man collapsed face down. He was down for the count, but he wasn't out. Big Man's arms and legs had some movement left in them. He felt his collar get grabbed and his head raised about a foot off the ground. Then, one last blow was delivered. This time to the back of the head, just above the base of the neck. The force drove Big Man's face into the pavement. He went still.

Logan pulled back his hoodie. He placed the roll of quarters he had clenched in his fist back in his pocket. He looked at his target and said, "I told you. You were next."

Logan rolled down the highway, his package tied up and contorted in the back. He was headed south again, to North Carolina and the Outer Banks. This time, after crossing the bridge on Highway 158, he took the easy bend at the intersection and headed south. There was no traffic to speak of. He owned the streets. He also knew he would own the attention of every squad car on the road. It was late. It was Christmas Eve. And every patrolman would be thinking *Why isn't this guy at home?*

The series of stoplights going through Nags Head were the worst. It seemed like he caught every one of them, but that was an exaggeration. What wasn't an exaggeration were the nerves he felt as a squad car pulled in close while he was stopped at a light.

The light turned green and Logan decided that acting too careful would probably draw more attention than anything else, so he got a little aggressive with the gas pedal. It wasn't a drag race, but he didn't ease his way to the speed limit. As a matter of fact, he pushed it to five miles an hour over. That was everyday normal driving. The squad car stayed close behind.

They were approaching an intersection. A choice had to be made, to continue down the coast on Highway 12, or to continue on 158, cross the sound and head toward Roanoke Island. Logan eased over in the lane for Highway 12 and began to slow for the red light. The squad car seemed to accelerate and continued on. Logan threw up a hand to offer a Christmas wave. There was no reaction from the officer, his mind clearly on something else. Nigel smiled.

As he drove on, Logan realized how dark the road seemed, even with his high beams on. The sky was blanketed by a thick overcast, not a star to be seen anywhere. He looked in his rearview and side mirrors. Everything behind him was virtually black. The surface lights of Nags Head were distant on the horizon.

The Bronco rolled on down the highway. The glass packs bellowed and the mud tires roared on the pavement. Then he felt a bump. That was followed by a grunt. Logan looked in his rearview. His package was coming around. "Don't kick my truck, asshole." Then a moan emerged from the back.

The Oregon Inlet was just ahead. The view from atop the Herbert C. Bonner Bridge is always stunning during the day. But even on a night as dark as this, with so little to see, the view was awesome. Offshore, the horizon was marked by the running lights of merchant vessels making their way up and down the coast. Some would be heading to the Chesapeake Bay, no doubt.

As he reached the top of the bridge, Nigel slowed. He rolled down the passenger side window and began to toss items out the window. One by one, items were jettisoned into the inlet. Jimbo's phone, Manchester's phone and revolver all took flight. The last item was Manchester's wallet. Logan checked its contents, but left everything intact, even the several hundred dollars that lined the billfold. *He was a lot of things; a thief wasn't one of them.* He laughed at the thought as the wallet was slung out the window.

He got back up to speed as he came down the other side; up ahead the Cape Hatteras National Seashore provided what seemed like additional darkness, if that were possible. That's what he was looking for. His thoughts were interrupted again by more movement in the back. Manchester was awake now. Logan could hear him trying to talk and move around. The movement developed into thrashing about as he tried to get free; his muffled talking had a certain panic in its tone.

Nigel demanded, "Knock it off back there, asshole!" But it didn't help, so Logan looked around and thought *This is as good as anywhere.* He pulled off onto the left side of the road and turned off his headlights. In an instant, he was reminded of just how dark it can be. He sat for a bit to let his eyes adjust. Then his phone bonged. It was a simple text from Sherry Stone: *Merry Christmas. Wherever you are.*

Logan looked at his watch. The face read 0011. He tossed the phone on the passenger seat. He looked into the rearview mirror and said, "Merry Christmas, Manchester."

He put the Bronco into four-wheel drive and placed her back into drive. He thought about how his night vision goggles would have come in handy about now as he began to navigate the Bronco. Off to his left was nothing but sand, dune, beach, and ocean. His eyes hadn't adjusted much and he felt like he was driving by braille. The headlights would draw too much attention, so he turned on the parking lights. They didn't help much either. Then he remembered his LED flashlight and pulled it from the bag.

He rolled down his window, so he could hear the surf that he couldn't yet see. The crashing waves were loud, close, out there somewhere. The wind was louder, howling out of the north, bringing a bitter cold. The extra noise was good. It helped drown out the commotion from the back of the Bronco.

Logan stuck his hand out the window and turned on the flashlight. That was much better. He shined it around and once he got his bearings, he turned the light off and eased forward. As the Bronco rolled to the top of the next dune, he could just see the breakers: faint; flashes of luminescence glowed in the dark water with every crash.

This seemed good. He was far enough off the road, and he didn't want to navigate back up another big dune if he could prevent it. He rolled down the back window so he could open the back. He left the engine running. He put his hoodie back on to help with the cold and got out, slamming the door. He walked toward the back of the Bronco and stopped to shine his light in the side window. Manchester squinted as he looked up.

Logan swung the spare tire rack to the side and opened the gate. He shined the light in the eyes of Manchester. "We're here, bitch. Get out!"

Manchester didn't move. He couldn't, not really. His legs were bound tight with a combination of zip ties and duct tape. His hands were done the same way and behind his back. Logan knew moving was near impossible, but he used his target's disobedience to get angry. Logan put the light between his teeth and reached in with both hands and dragged Manchester feet first out of the back.

Logan saw his head slam against the rear bumper before he landed on the dune. "Damn! Sorry 'bout that." Logan crouched down over Manchester and shined the light in his face and slapped his cheeks. "Stay with me, now. No more passing out. No fun killing you, if you're not awake."

Logan smiled when he saw Manchester's eyes open to look at him. "That's better. Wait here."

Logan went back to the cab and retrieved his bag. When he got back to Manchester, he said, "Roll your fat ass down the dune. I'm not dragging or carrying your ass anymore."

Manchester did nothing.

"I'll give you five seconds." Logan didn't. He kicked him hard in the ribs and said, "Move!" Then there was another shot to the ribs and Manchester began to rock back and forth. Logan put his foot on his target's hip and rolled him like a log. Manchester began to roll.

Logan applied an occasional kick to keep him motivated and moving. When they got to the bottom of the dune, Logan sat Manchester up and ripped the many layers of duct tape off his mouth.

All the panting that had been coming out his nose moved to his mouth. He gasped for more air and the flow of adrenaline helped ease the sting of the tape being torn from his lips. He took a second to catch his breath and asked, "Who are you? What do you want?"

Logan sat back on the sand across from his target. "The same thing anybody wants. Justice."

Logan began to hear a hint of panic rising in his voice. "Justice for what? How did you get Jimbo's phone? Where is he? I thought he was..."

Logan almost finished his sentence. He almost said *dead*, but he didn't. He sat and listened.

"What is this all about? Is it money? Is that it? Who the fuck are you? Who sent you?"

Logan squinted in confusion as it dawned on him; Manchester was really in the dark. He had no idea who it was. He assumed Manchester would figure it out on his own. That he might put two and two together. But he hadn't. Logan gave it some thought, and it began to make sense. Hell, nobody knew he was out of prison. Not yet anyway. That made Logan think harder. How should he play this?

Logan reached into his bag and found the Ruger, then the loose magazine. He was cold, tired, and ready for all this to be over. He worked the magazine into the bottom of the grip and slapped it in place. It was seated with that signature sound that is unmistakable. Manchester flinched, and he flinched again as Logan pulled back on the bolt and let it slam home. Logan took the LED flashlight and shined it in Big Man's eyes. He reacted by squinting and Logan said, "Give me one good reason why I shouldn't kill you right now."

Manchester raised his voice, "Give me one good reason why you should."

Logan said nothing. He kept the light in Big Man's eyes.

"Please! I can make it right. Whatever it is. No problem. You don't have to do this."

Logan was silent.

"Talk to me! What is this all about?"

Logan said, "Everything. It's about everything. Every sin. Every injustice. Every murder. Every crime against humanity. Welcome to your judgment day."

"Money," Manchester said. "You want money. I have plenty. How much? Just tell me."

Logan was insulted and angry. "Manchester, this has nothing to do with money!"

"EVERYTHING IS ABOUT MONEY!" yelled, Manchester in a panicked frenzy. In a quieter more sensible tone he said, "Every man has his price."

Logan kept the light on Manchester's face and stood up. "You're right. And every man names his form of payment." He drove the bottom of his foot onto Manchester's chest and shoved him back against the dune. Logan leaned in closer and said, "Some things are about love. Now, open your mouth."

Big Man resisted, so Logan pressed the barrel against his tight lips and yelled, "Open! Open or I'll blow a hole through your teeth!"

Manchester was shaking. Out of fear and the cold, he was shaking. Logan pressed harder and twisted the muzzle against his mouth. Manchester moaned as he relented and Logan slid the barrel deep into his mouth. Logan was done, ready, tired of his time being wasted. But as he was choking Manchester with the barrel of the Ruger, ready to pull the trigger, he became conflicted.

Logan wanted to kill him. He was capable and on the verge. No doubt. The life of Manchester Lundsford meant nothing to him. He had more respect for roadkill. But … should he let him die wondering who and why it had been done, let that horror run through his mind, or should he lean in and watch Big Man's face as he introduces himself and reminds him of Grace Matthews and the two thugs he sent to Port St. Joe.

Deep down, Logan wanted him to know. He wanted Big Man to know he had come back. That he had come back from Tate's Hell and prison, just for him. He wanted Big Man to see his face. He wanted to see Manchester's eyes the very moment he realized it was true. That it would be Nigel Logan to end it all. Logan wanted to see his face the second before the trigger was pulled. Logan wanted those moments. Each of them.

"Manchester, before you die. There's a couple things you need to know." Logan could feel Manchester's body tighten under his weight, a knee now planted in the middle of his chest. Logan leaned in. He was about to speak, but something stopped him. It was a voice in his head. It was Candice. Six simple words: *What have you become? Come home.* He closed his eyes and heard it again. It wasn't a hallucination. The voice was real, but they weren't Candice's words. He heard her voice, but the words were his own. *What have you become?* He got quiet and listened some more. He let Candice tell him. *You can't do this.*

The adrenaline running through Logan's veins was at an all-time high. He began to shake. He looked at Manchester. He began to think about what he wanted most. It was home. Home and Candice. He wanted his life back.

He panted as he spoke, "Manchester ... we're not that much different. Me and you. We've both done bad things. The difference is the reasons why we do them."

Big Man was quivering, listening. He tried to say something, but it was pointless with the muzzle in the back of his throat.

"The scars you people leave are real and painful. They affect your victims in the deepest way. They are constant reminders of the horrible things done to them. Many often wish they were dead."

Logan let that sink in for a few seconds and he said, "So, death ... tonight ... might be too good for you."

Manchester's eyes crossed as he looked at the barrel in his mouth and nodded his head.

Logan continued, "But ... you have a problem, Manchester. You don't have the emotional capacity to walk away from this with mental scars. So, the question is; what good would it be to let you live?"

Manchester looked at Logan. Said nothing.

"I just don't know. But I know you're a piece of shit and I'm tired of looking at you."

Manchester closed his eyes.

Logan moved the barrel of the Ruger to the side causing Manchester to turn his head. Logan pushed his other hand to the side of Manchester's head, pinned it down to the sand, and growled, "Merry Christmas, motherfucker."

Logan moved and pressed the muzzle around Manchester's mouth until he found fleshy cheek tissue. When he felt the sand give, he pulled the trigger. He moved the muzzle around to different spots. He fired three total rounds and burnt three small reminders in the right cheek of Manchester Lundsford.

Logan stood, panting, looking at his target. He was out cold. Logan reached down and checked his pulse. Still alive. Very alive. He grabbed his chin and turned his head to look at the damage. He used the flashlight to find that Manchester had been left with a nice pattern of exit wounds to commemorate the night. There was virtually no bleeding thanks to the muzzle blast. Logan was happy with his work.

He stepped away and used the flashlight to find his casings. Then he rolled Manchester over and dug into the sand until he retrieved the bullets. He worked quickly to clean up the rest of the scene and pack the Bronco. He walked back down to Manchester and propped him up against the dune. He put his hat back on his head, which caused a welcomed chuckle. *Stupid looking hat.* Then he used his knife to free Big Man's hands.

Logan stood over him for a bit to reflect on the night, but it was cut short by the howling wind and cold. He ran back to the Bronco. He could think about it as he drove.

THE STOOL

One of the advantages of being a good television news reporter is being asked to guest anchor the news desk when someone was on vacation. The disadvantage is that those opportunities usually only come during the holidays. Sherry Stone was driving home from the station. She had been asked to cover the Christmas morning news. She had begrudgingly accepted. Take every opportunity you can get.

She delivered a flawless performance and the producer, who was also a stand-in, was pleased. She almost screwed up one story, though. It was the classic holiday piece designed to pull at the heart strings. A cute, but lonely pooch at the humane society was wearing an ugly Christmas sweater and made to look both adorable and pathetic, desperate for a home.

She was on a commercial break, looking into the camera knowing there was nobody looking back. Who in their right mind is watching the news on Christmas morning? Nobody really. If you're watching, what does that say about your life? Then she thought of the one or two asshole dads that she imagined were out there telling their kids to *Shut the hell up. You can open your gifts after the weather. Now sit your asses down and be patient.*

She busted out in belly laughter as the cameraman started his count down, "Live in seven, six, Sherry!, four, Get it together!, two..." The second the camera was live, she was back on point and delivered like a pro.

She was thinking and laughing about that moment as she turned her FJ onto her street. She continued to laugh as she drove, but for different reasons now. Tears began to join the chuckles and she began to find it hard to breathe. A Bronco was sitting in her driveway.

She found him asleep on the couch. She kneeled on the floor next to him and brushed his hair back. His eyes opened with a start as he found her looking at him. She was looking for the right words, but he beat her to it. "Hello, friend."

Friend. She felt her heart sink a bit, but that did nothing to overshadow how happy she was to see him. She smiled and said, "Hello, friend."

"I hope you don't mind."

She shook her head and said, "That key will always be there for you." With a quick smile, she changed the subject. She reached down and ran her fingers through his beard. "What is all this scruff on your face?"

"I hate it."

"I love it. It's sexy."

"Really?" he asked.

And she changed the subject again. "I am so very happy to see you."

He said, "Me too. Merry Christmas." She started to cry again and he sat up and held her until she stopped.

When her tears were done, she squeezed him tight and asked, "Hungry?"

They parted and Nigel said, "Like a refugee."

There was no mention of or questions about where he had been or what he had been doing. She considered the worst and didn't want to know. He didn't want to talk about it either. As a matter of fact, to Nigel, it was already forgotten history. She was pouring him a cup of coffee when she asked, "So when do you go back?"

"In a few days. Could I maybe..."

"Of course you can stay here. Don't be ridiculous. I just would have thought you would be itching to get back."

"I am. Believe me. It's just the past few months have been..." He stopped. "I would just like to chill a bit. Not think of anything for a while."

She smiled. "I would like that very much."

He stayed for four days. A couple days longer than he thought he would. He knew that when he left, he would probably never be back. Not for a long while anyway.

He made time for visits with Charlie and Caroline and, of course, Grace and the boys. He came by twice. They spent quality time together and never once dwelled on the past. It was like old times and Nigel was thankful for that. As he left for the last time, Nigel asked, "You guys will come to St. Joe to visit, right?"

Charlie said, "Well, yeah." But both Nigel and Charlie knew a visit probably wouldn't happen, at least for a very long time. Now that everything was behind them, forgetting the past was best, and that would be near impossible when they were together, so … maybe … forgetting the past might include forgetting each other. That idea saddened Nigel as he said, "Goodbye, my friend."

Charlie didn't say anything. He just nodded.

She came home from work to find him finishing the last few pages of a book. When it was done, he got up laughing and tossed it on the kitchen counter. "You should read this."

She picked up the copy of *The Man Who Invented Florida* and looked over the cover. She opened it and glanced at the front matter. "You'd like it," he said. When she raised her head to look at him, she saw something different in his eyes. Two or three beats later, he came right out with it. "It's time."

He caught her off guard. She secretly hoped this day wouldn't come. She nodded her head, held back the tears, and asked. "When?"

"Tomorrow. It will take me a few days to get home. I'm going to take my time, but I got to be home by New Year's."

She nodded her head again. This time with a smile. "They will be happy to see you."

He took her by the hand and smiled. "Can a sailor buy you a drink?"

They bellied up at the bar in front of the draft beer station. The bartender came over. "What'll it be?"

"A Coors draft with a lime, for me. Your best Cosmo for the lovely lady." Nigel slid the barkeep a ten-spot and it went straight into his pocket.

"You got it!"

Nigel looked around. The place looked newly redecorated. It made him sad, bothering him more than it should. The bartender came back with the drinks and Nigel said, "The place has changed a lot since I used to come in here."

The bartender shrugged his shoulders.

Nigel asked, "Does old Mackie still manage the place?"

The bartender pointed to a picture back behind the bar. Nigel laughed and looked at Sherry, "That old fart has been here forever." He turned to the bartender and asked, "Is the old cuss here?"

"In the back."

"Go get him. I want to see him."

"I can't," he replied. "He's busy counting money."

"Screw that. I don't care what he's doing."

Both Stone and the bartender watched as Nigel reached in his pocket and pulled out a thin curved brass plaque. "Here. Take this to him. Tell him I've come for my fucking stool. And use those exact words. You hear me?"

The bartender took the plaque and hesitated until Nigel said, "Go on, dammit. Do as I say, or give me my ten-dollar bill back."

A few minutes later a large, burly man, grayed with a salty Hemingway look, emerged from the hallway that led to the offices. At six foot three, two hundred thirty pounds, Nigel was big enough. But this guy had Nigel by three, maybe four, inches and probably thirty to forty pounds. He walked up to where Nigel sat with Stone. The young bartender watched from the other end of the bar. The big guy looked at Logan, then back at the brass plate. The word seventeen was barely readable. He rubbed the plaque between his fingers.

Nigel was enjoying himself. He looked at a confused Stone and winked. Then he looked at the massive figure that stood before him and said, "Hello, Mack. It's been a long time."

Mack said nothing.

"Do you remember when you gave that to me?"

Mack looked at Nigel and said, "I thought you were in prison."

"A vicious rumor for sure. Have you been getting your news from the Internet again?"

His last night in Tidewater couldn't have been better. For hours, they sat at the bar and told stories. Stone so wished she had her tape recorder. She laughed and smiled as Mack told Nigel's bar stories. He told her everything he knew about a young seaman that would only drink from one barstool, number seventeen. He was cocky, egotistical, and obnoxious. But he was fun and everybody loved him. Then he picked up the plaque off the bar and said, "When he got orders to ship out, it just didn't seem right. So, I removed this plaque off the back of his stool and gave it to him."

211

He gave it back to Nigel, who in his drunken glow slid it back into his front pocket.

It was getting late and Stone said, "I hate to break up this little party, but I think my boy here has had enough."

Nigel reached in his pocket and pulled out his keys and dropped them on the bar. He looked at Stone and slurred, "Don't scratch the Bronco. You hear me?"

"Yeah. Yeah. Yeah. I hear you," replied Stone.

As they were getting up, Mack said, "Hold on. Let me show you something."

With a little assistance from Mack, he helped Nigel walk down a hallway. Stone brought up the rear, ready to catch him if he fell back. Mack leaned Nigel up against the wall and asked, "Are you okay? Can you stand?"

Nigel nodded his head as Mack opened a door and turned on a light saying, "It's in here somewhere."

Stone looked into the room. It was a storeroom full of old crap. She asked, "What's in here?"

Mack turned and said, "His stool. Number 17."

Nigel heard those words, and they were almost sobering. He stood up straighter. Stone grabbed his arm and was surprised he felt so steady on his feet. "Really, Mack. You still got it?"

Nigel and Stone stood at the door as Mack slung stuff every which way. After a while he came back toward them dragging an old wooden barstool. He stood it up in front of them. "See? This is where the plaque went."

Nigel reached in his pocket and pulled out the plaque. He placed it over the discolored wood, the place where it once was attached. He rubbed his hand over the wood and looked at Mack and asked, "May I?"

"Of course."

Nigel walked around and climbed up and took his seat. He felt stupid and silly, but he knew he was drunk, so he didn't care. He looked at Stone and with a childish grin said, "My stool." She looked on as tears began to fill her bottom lids. She wiped them away as Nigel turned to Mack and said, "Thanks, Mackie. This has been a great night."

The next afternoon, Stone came home from work. The Bronco was no longer waiting in the drive. She waited a while before getting out of her vehicle. She took a deep breath. They had said their goodbyes earlier that morning, but Stone decided to use the comforting tactic of denial to help her make it through the day.

As she walked through the front door, the place was quiet. A lonely quiet. He was gone. She already knew that, but it was like she had to keep reminding herself. Then she walked into the kitchen and lost it. Her hand stretched across her mouth as she gasped. The tears now came with ease. Standing next to her kitchen counter was the old wooden barstool, a note taped on the back. When she pulled it off, she cried even more. The old, brass plaque was reattached. She touched her finger to what was left of the old engraving. Then she opened and read the short note. *Thank you for everything. And if you ever need anything, you know where I'll be. Please remember that and me. I will never forget you. Nigel.*

As she read the note for the third time, the Bronco was barreling down Interstate 95. He smiled and pressed a little harder on the gas, a Brian Bowen CD was playing, but struggling to compete with the roar of glasspacks and mud tires on asphalt. He turned the volume up to ten. The Kraco speakers sounded like shit. He made a note-to-self: replace them.

As he crossed over into North Carolina, Nigel never once glanced in the rearview. There was no need to. He left everything behind for a reason. None of it would be needed anymore. The only things that mattered now were the problems awaiting him in Port St. Joe: Beach People Problems.

Happy New Year

Even on a clear night, when the moon is full and the starlight of our Milky Way stretches to the horizon, visibility at night on the beach is limited. Such darkness is a beautiful thing. Tonight, though, it was more than that, it was perfect.

Nigel looked at his watch; it was 2325, only thirty-five minutes until New Year's. He sat in his Bronco atop the dunes of the beach access at Salinas Park. He could see the glow of the bonfire down the beach. It was a beautiful sight. It was Red and Trixie's New Year's beach party, an annual event and tradition, well planned, well prepared for, and well attended.

During the week after Christmas, Red takes his Ford Explorer, pulls a trailer, and cruises the streets of Port St. Joe to go Christmas tree hunting. As the good folks in town dump them on the street, Red swoops in and tosses them on the trailer. For the last couple of years, Nigel has helped, but not this year.

Red missed having Nigel around. For one thing, Nigel always drove. That gave Red plenty of latitude to scout, navigate ... and drink beer, more beer than he would have had he been driving. Plus, Nigel was bigger and stronger and could handle the really big trees. Red was reminded of this as he was pulling an eight-and-a-half footer up on the trailer by the stump. He cussed Nigel under his breath once he got it secure. But, for the most part, Red just missed his friend.

Once Red feels he's got enough trees, he takes them to the beach in front of their place and replants them. With twelve or fifteen trees, he will create a small Christmas tree forest at the edge of the dunes. Trixie always picks the King Tree. The King is always the largest, best-looking tree of the bunch. Unlike the others, it will not be sacrificed during the night. It, and a couple others, will be decorated with solar lights, seashell ornaments, Mardi Gras beads, and a variety of Christmas bling.

As Trixie and the others decorate the trees, Red and a few helping hands dig the pit for the bonfire. Over the course of the day, they transform the beachfront into a festive New Year's beach party, complete with a low country boil. Depending on how many trees he has, as the clock ticks away toward midnight, Red will grab one of the undecorated trees and toss it in the fire. Always a favorite of the attendees. Everybody likes to witness the roaring inferno that stretches high into the sky. They like the feel of the massive heat that radiates off the engulfed evergreen. Many try to keep their seats by the pit, but the heat of the trees wins every time, pushing folks back.

That was what Nigel was waiting on. He looked at his watch again, it was 2330. He looked down the beach and waited. He wanted to see it from where he sat.

Trixie smacked Red on the arm. "What are you looking at, Red?"

Red had been gazing down the beach, looking at a set of headlights that were illuminating the tops of the dunes. "Oh ... nothing. I guess."

"Well, it's time for another tree. Folks are waiting."

He looked at his watch, "Oh, crap. It is."

Red inspected what was left of his inventory and decided on a short, fat Douglas fir. He reached in, grabbed it by the trunk, and pulled it out of the sand. He stood it up and bounced it on the ground a couple of times. He looked up at the headlights in the dunes. He watched them for a few brief moments, but, from around the bonfire, he could hear folks calling for another tree. They cheered as he came around the corner dragging the fat evergreen. They all scattered and backed up as he tossed it into the flames.

It was still fresh and green, more so than the others. It would be a slow starter. At first, everyone heard the crackle and popping of needles and branches. Then a stream of bright, green smoke worked its way out the top as the rich chlorophyll began to get hot and burn off. Then, in an exchange of roles, the flames took over and stretched high into the sky, casting heat and light for everyone to enjoy. As the flames roared, the area around the pit was lit up like daylight.

From where Nigel sat, it was an awesome spectacle. The flames seemed to stretch and touch the stars. During the brightest moments, Nigel could see the remaining trees, the people standing around, and

215

KIRK S. JOCKELL

all the trucks parked on the beach. It was a good turnout. He smiled and revved the engine to let the glasspacks sing. He put the Bronco into drive and eased out onto the beach. His eyes had adjusted well enough, so he shut off the headlights and drove by his parking lamps.

After the commotion around the fire, Red walked toward the parked trucks. He stood by his own vehicle and watched as the approaching orange glow got closer and closer. The rumbling sound of the vehicle made it seem closer than it was. Red smiled thinking *He said, I would know when it was him.* He ran to get Trixie.

Trixie was sitting around the fire when Red approached trying not to seem too excited. "Trix ... come with me."

"Red, I just sat down. Grab a beer and sit down."

"Trix. Really. I need you. Come on. I can't say anymore."

She didn't want to, but she got up and followed him through the trees. "Red! Where are we going?"

"Shush! And come on."

Red looked but couldn't see any lights. He could still hear the rumble of the engine though. It seemed to be right on top of them.

"What the hell is that?" asked Trixie.

Red said nothing.

The rumble stopped and it got quiet again. Up ahead, Red saw the faint glow of an interior dome light as a door opened. Then it went out the second he heard the door slam.

"Who is it, Red?"

Red said, "Come on." And they walked further down the beach and stopped. Red was looking around. He couldn't see anything. Everything was quiet, still, and dark.

"There, Red," said Trixie pointing. "Right there in front of us."

The hooded man walked toward them and stopped a few feet away. They studied each other for a while.

"Red. Trixie. Is that you?"

Red smiled and said, "It's me, buddy."

They closed in on each other and exchanged hugs and manly pats on the back. Trixie still didn't understand what was going on and said, "Red? Who is it, dammit?"

Trixie watched as the two parted. The hooded one approached her. They were face to face, their features becoming more distinguishable. Nigel said, "Hello, Trixie."

216

The voice was so familiar, but still ... she reached up and pulled his hoodie back. Now she could see better. As her focus improved and she realized what she was seeing, she said, "Oh shit..."

Nigel reached up with one hand and covered her mouth. All he could see was her eyes, and they were the size of cantaloupes. With his other hand, he placed a finger to his smiling lips. Red chuckled as Nigel removed his hand and Trixie attacked him with hugs. All she could say was, "Oh my God! Oh my God! I can't believe this. Oh my God!"

Nigel laughed and said, "Believe it."

They broke from their hug and she said, "Let me look at you." Red continued to chuckle, which gave Trixie reason to pause. She turned to him and said, "You knew. You asshole. You knew all along and never told me." She looked at Nigel and asked, "How long has he known?"

Nigel laughed and threw up his hands and said, "I'm not getting into the middle of this. No way."

"How long dammit?"

"Since yesterday morning. But I told him not to tell anybody."

"Oh, anybody! So, that's who I am these days? Just some old anybody. Well, I guess that puts you in the shit-house too."

"Trixie ... come on," said Nigel. "You know what I mean."

She smiled back and said, "I know. Just giving you a hard time. You sure are a sight for sore eyes. Holy shit! Where's my crackpipe?"

She went to searching her pockets until she pulled out a large contraption with a mouthpiece. She pulled hard on it and exhaled. When the huge cloud of smoke exited her mouth, Nigel looked at Red.

"My Christmas gift," said Red. "She stopped smoking. She's vaping instead."

Nigel looked confused and Red said, "I'll explain later."

After taking a hard hit, Trixie went back in for another hug. When they broke, she went over to Red, who was grinning from ear to ear, and smacked him on the arm, "You're still in the shit-house."

They were walking back toward the fire when Trixie asked, "What time is it?"

It was 2350. *Ten more minutes*.

They were standing amongst the trees when Nigel asked, "She's here, right?"

217

"Yeah," said Red. "But..."

"But what?"

Red said nothing.

"Come on, now. But what?"

"Dammit, Nigel. She brought somebody. I'm sorry. She brought a date."

"Oh."

It got quiet. Then Nigel asked, "Who? Who is it?"

"They're sitting by the fire."

Nigel put the hoodie back over his head and worked his way through what was left of the trees. As he disappeared in the dark, Trixie smacked Red again and said, "You should be ashamed of yourself."

Moments later Nigel reappeared and said, "You're an asshole, Red."

Both Red and Trixie were smirking as Nigel ducked back through the trees for another look. Nigel stood in the shadow of a tree. His hoodie was down just above his eyes. He watched her as she sat by the fire, her date, Luke McKenzie, by her side. She was gorgeous in the light of the fire. He couldn't quite make out the hair color, but it was dark. No doubt, she would be sporting a fresh color for the New Year. That made him smile. He wanted to run to her, but he didn't.

She and Luke were talking when Trixie sat down next to Candice. She wanted a front row seat. All of a sudden Candice looked up and noticed him by the trees. She held a look and offered a friendly smile. He smiled back and was about to step forward into the light when she went back to talking to Luke and Trixie. She didn't recognize him. She was just being friendly. He kept his eyes on her. He loved watching her every move. He paid no attention to anyone else. He never noticed all the folks running around handing out cups of Champagne until someone shoved one in his own hand.

Then Red came out from around the corner with a huge tree and hollered, "Who's ready for a New Year?"

Everybody stood and cheered. Red said, "Who's got the time?"

The hooded figure in the trees yelled, "I do!"

Everyone was looking at the hooded one. He took a couple of steps forward and looked down at his watch, his face not visible. He started to count down. "Here we go folks! Five! ... four! ..."

Red threw the tree into the fire and Trixie reached down and took Candice's hand. Squeezed it tight. Candice looked to find Trixie wearing a shit-eating grin.

"Three! ... two! ... one!"

With all their cups in the air, everyone yelled, "HAPPY NEW YEAR!"

Nigel pulled the hoodie back and watched as everyone was kissing, hugging, and toasting. Nigel saw someone approach from the side and offer a hand. "Happy New Year, friend."

Nigel took the hand and said, "Yes. Happy New Year."

Brian Bowen held Nigel's hand tight while his mouth fell open. The only words he could find were, "Son of a bitch."

"Hello, Brian."

The tree was starting to go good now. Everybody was watching as the flames shot toward the heavens. It was like a floodlight was turned on, and Nigel returned his gaze to Candice. She was looking at him. Nigel was smiling. She covered her mouth and began to cry. She looked at Trixie with asking eyes and Trixie nodded her head and said, "Yes."

When Candice looked back over at Nigel, he was already heading her way. She began to tremble as Brian yelled, "Hey everybody, look. It's Nigel."

Nigel's pace quickened and Candice moved to meet him halfway. They came together in an explosion of passion. They held each other tight, and she kissed him on the mouth and all over his face. Then she stopped to look at him. "I'm not dreaming, right? It ... it really is you?"

Nigel cradled her face with his hands and took her in for a long kiss. She held him tight as the crowd cheered and the flames began to recede to a normal burn.

Brian stepped up next to Red and said, "Happy New Year, brother."

"Happy New Year, Brian."

"So ... I gather you knew about this, huh?"

Red smiled but didn't say anything.

"Look at 'em go at each other ... damn ... they might get freaky and all, right here."

Red said, "Where there's smoke, there's fire."

"Right on! Right on!"

Nigel and Candice came up for air. They realized they were the center of attention, but didn't care. As far as they were concerned, they were the only two people on the beach. She said, "I've missed you so." She paused then said, "I can't believe this. That you are here."

"Me either. It's a long story that can wait." And he kissed her again.

This time she pulled away and shook her head.

"What?" asked Nigel.

She reached up and grabbed his whiskers. "What the hell is this?"

"My new beard. Do you like it?"

"No!"

"Doesn't it make me look ... sexy?"

"Oh, Hell no!"

Nigel smiled. He was home. He looked at the love of his life. He looked at the fire. And he gazed around at all the people. He turned to Candice and said, "I'm the luckiest guy on Earth right now."

"Not with that beard you're not," she said in a matter-of-fact tone.

"So, you really don't like it?"

"I hate it! Why would you grow such a hideous thing? Whatever gave you the idea?"

Nigel smiled and said, "Poor judgement, I guess. I hate it too."

She bit at her bottom lip and said, "We can fix it. I have a razor at the house."

"I thought you'd never ask."

Epilogue

Nigel and Candice were locked away in her house. They were holed up with no intention of coming out until they had to. All the shades had been pulled down tight to keep it dark. Their only glimpses of daylight came when one or the other cracked the front door to pay for the pizzas they had delivered every day.

On the third day, it came time for the noon feeding. Candice walked into the bathroom. Nigel was stretched out in her huge claw-foot tub. An empty box of Mr. Bubbles rested on its side where it had been thrown. He held a large piece of pizza in each hand. She was holding two cold beers. She wiggled her upper body until her robe slipped off the back of her shoulders. His eyes were locked on her body. He spread his legs and draped his feet over each side of the tub to make room. He raised the slices high as she slipped in. Water and bubbles washed over the side. Neither noticed or cared. More water sloshed over as she leaned forward. She kissed him and said, "Bad news."

He kissed her back, then said, "Impossible. There's no such thing anymore." He fed her a bite of pizza.

As she chewed, she nodded her head, smiled, and made a noise that resembled, "Yes ... possible." She washed down her pizza with a sip of beer. Then she held both bottles high in the air. "These are it."

"These are what?"

"The last two beers."

"Oh shit. That's horrible."

"Told you."

Tracy, Candice's part-time barkeep, was more than happy to take all of Candice's shifts at the bar. "Take your time, baby," laughed Tracy. "Get it out of your system. Don't come back until you've had enough."

When Candice came into the bar, Tracy watched as she walked over and climbed up on a bar stool. They exchanged looks and Tracy said, "Why … don't you have a particular glow about you? Couldn't take it anymore, huh?"

Candice's eyes grew wide; she bit her bottom lip and said, "I don't know. I'm not sure I would put it that way. It was good that we both came out into the daylight, for our own sake."

"Too much of a good thing?" asked Tracy.

Candice nodded her head and said, "Can be a dangerous thing."

Everyone around the marina parking lot stopped to watch the big Ford roll in. A full-size Bronco is already an attention-getter, but add glasspacks and you create your own arrival announcement system. Even at idle speed, there was no ignoring the deep, throaty rumble.

He saw her the second he put the Bronco into park. He looked at her through the windshield and shut down the Bronco. The parking lot went back to its quiet existence. He got out and stood by his vehicle to admire her from afar. She looked as good out of the water as she did in.

The letter Nigel wrote to Red contained several requests and a general Power of Attorney in the event he would not be able to return. There would be several affairs that would need attention. Red would need money, so Nigel provided instructions on finding his safe, and the combination needed to get into his little private bank. Red's jaw dropped when he opened the safe and saw all the neat stacks of wrapped hundred-dollar bills.

The laundry list of things that needed to be done wasn't short. His landlord would need to be notified and all his photography gear, computers, and other stuff removed from the premises. Something would need to happen to *Chumbucket*, his center console Key West 1700. His pickup truck would need to be retrieved. It had been left at the airport. Nigel would later learn that Red gave it to Luke McKenzie, which was fine. Luke's old truck was on life support anyway. And, of course, there was *MisChief*, his 32-foot Pearson Vanguard sailboat. Nigel's instructions were simple. *She's family. Take care of her.*

She was in the marina boatyard sitting high and dry in a cradle. He entered the yard and approached her. He walked along her side and let his palm rub her belly. He inspected and scrutinized her bottom with great attention to detail. It isn't very often that Nigel gets to study his boat out of the water, so he took full advantage of the opportunity. He made a few mental notes, but was satisfied with her condition. A fresh coat of bottom paint and a couple other maintenance details and she would be ready to splash.

He looked around the yard until he found an extension ladder. He took it and set it up against the starboard side of the boat. As he was clearing the last rung and stepping onto the deck, a voice called out. "Hey, mister! What do you think you are doing?"

It was a young guy. Nigel didn't know him. He was wearing a clean, marina staff polo-style shirt, white shorts, and boat shoes. The sight of the guy sent Nigel a subliminal message. *It's January and warm enough to wear shorts. Welcome home.*

Nigel ignored him and started to flip the dials on the combination lock. As he set it to 0017, he jerked the lock open.

"Did you hear me mister? Stop what you're doing and come down from there."

"What's your name, son?"

"Trey. Now get off there."

"I won't be long, Trey. Promise. I just want to take a peek down below."

"You can't do that! You're on private property!"

Nigel smiled at the guy, stepped down into the companionway saying, "I'll just be a few minutes."

Nigel heard the guy yell, "I'm going to call the police." Then thought *Yeah, yeah, yeah ... do what you feel you need to do.*

Nigel inspected all the spaces down below. Aside from the air smelling a little musty, everything was as he expected: Perfect. He crawled up into the V-berth and opened the forward hatch to help circulate some air. Then he flopped on his back so he could lie there and see the sky. As he was just closing his eyes, he heard and felt a hard knock on the hull, then a familiar voice, "Okay fella. Outta the boat! Pronto!"

Nigel emerged from the companionway and said, "John, you could at least open the old girl up every now and then and let her breathe."

"Well, I'll be damned," said John Martin, friend and marina Harbor Master. "So, the rumors are true?"

As Nigel climbed down the ladder, Trey said, "I'm confused. Who is that, John?"

"That's Nigel Logan. The boat's skipper."

"But I heard he was in prison. Shit ... for murder."

Before John could say anything, Nigel hopped off the last couple rungs and said, "And who would have said such a thing?"

As Nigel approached them, Trey sized up Logan's large, 230-pound frame and took a couple small, nervous steps backward. Nigel extended his hand to John and they shook. "Hello, John."

John said, "It's good to see you." And it was true. He was happy to see his friend, but, like everyone else, he had so many questions he wanted to ask. Questions he figured would remain unanswered.

Nigel extended a hand towards Trey and said, "Hello, Trey. I'm Nigel Logan."

Trey hesitated, but took his hand nervously.

"Come on now," said Nigel. "Tighten that grip. Let me know you're there."

Trey said nothing, but he squeezed harder and Nigel did the same. "That's better. Always shake a man's hand like that. That soft, limp-wristed grip shit has no meaning."

They released their grip and Trey stood a little taller with a snicker as Nigel addressed John. "She looks good, doesn't she?" They all three turned to better look at *MisChief.*

"She's gorgeous," John said.

"Do you have a slip for me?"

"Your old slip is still vacant."

"Not anymore. Her bottom isn't bad, but we might as well give her a light sanding and some fresh bottom paint."

"Trinidad SR? Same color?" asked John.

"Exactly, and have the guys replace the cutlass bearing and zincs."

"You got it. Come to the office. We'll start the paperwork."

As Nigel was leaving the marina office, a text message came through. *Bong!* He read it as he walked to his Bronco: Hey Romeo. Is it still too soon to disturb you?

Nigel laughed and called, instead of replying. "Hey, Red. I think Candice will carve some time into our busy schedule."

"Good," said Red. "Meet me at the raw bar. Beers and oysters on me."

"Ha!" Nigel laughed. "What strange force of nature has compelled you to want to pick up the tab?"

Red chuckled and said, "I'm still spending your money."

"Oh, shit."

When Nigel got to the raw bar, there were plenty of handshaking, hugs, and good-to-see-ya comments exchanged as he made his way to the bar. He slapped Red on his back and said, "Hey, buddy," as he went straight to the draft station to pull a pint of Coors Light and to grab a slice of lime. When he climbed up on the stool next to Red, Bucky slid a baker's dozen of oysters in front of him. Nigel gazed at them with a grin. There was a time, just a few months ago, when Nigel wondered if he'd ever see such a beautiful sight again. "Thanks, Buck."

Red stuck his hand out and said, "I'm sure glad you came home. Maybe things can get back to normal around here."

"How many people know why I was gone?"

"Everybody. At first there were tons of questions, then Gloria at the salon figured it out, and that was that."

"Hmm ... figures."

Gloria owns a beauty parlor and it's the local hot-bed of gossip and rumor. However, Gloria prides herself on truth and accuracy. Once she heard the whisperings of Nigel being a serial killer, wanted and captured by the FBI, she ran her own investigation and gathered the truth. She was still shocked by what she learned, but it was better than thinking he was some psycho maniac. She made it a priority to dispel all the untruths.

"Now," said Red, "that people are hearing that you're back, the rumors and questions have started all over again."

Nigel smiled, "Small-town America. It doesn't get any better."

Red lowered his voice, and behind a smile said, "Nigel, there is one rumor that you were released because you're a CIA operative. That's one of the reasons why you always pay in cash. The jail time was just a front." Red tilted his head towards the shucking station and shifted his eyes at Bucky.

Nigel gave his favorite shucker a look and caught Bucky staring at him. Bucky quickly moved his head and eyes back to his box of oysters waiting to be shucked. Nigel called out, "Hey, Buck!"

Bucky heard Nigel, but pretended not to, so Nigel called out again, "Buck! I want to ask you something."

Bucky turned to look with an *Oh, you-talk'n-to-me* look. Nigel continued, "Have you seen any guys snooping around lately? Black suit and tie types? Probably wearing dark sunglasses and black wingtips with white socks?"

Bucky put on a worried face and replied, "No, sir. Not around here."

Nigel said, "Good." He scratched his chin for a bit and continued, "Well, if any guys like that come around asking about me, will you give them a special message for me?"

"Sure, Nigel. Whatever you need."

"Tell them ... and you have to use these exact words ... say, 'The white raven is missing his nest.' Can you remember that?"

"Yes, sir."

"Repeat it back to me."

Bucky did and Nigel said, "Perfect! Now when you get a chance, Red and I will take another couple dozen."

Red got up and recharged their beers. When he sat back down Nigel said, "Speaking of somebody that always pays in cash, where is my damn safe?"

Red reached down and pulled up a big canvas bag off the floor. He reached in and pulled out the safe and slid it in front of Nigel. As Nigel was unlocking it, Red said, "Now, there's something I should probably tell you before you..."

Nigel opened the safe and peeked in. His eyes opened wide and he slammed it shut. He turned to deliver a shocked look at Red.

Red said, "That's what I was going to tell you..."

Nigel interrupted, "Where's all my money, Red?"

Nigel opened the safe again and fumbled through what was left of the strapped hundred-dollar bills. He was shaking his head, trying to do the math in his head, but he was having trouble with his mental count.

He looked back at Red and said, "What the hell?"

Red reached into his pocket and handed Nigel an envelope.

"What's this?"

"Just open it," replied Red.

He did and looked over the document. Quick Claim Deed was written in a fancy font across the top. He shook the paper in the air and said, "Red ... I'd really appreciate it if you would stop fucking around and just tell me what this is all about."

"It's the old cottage. The Blown Inn. It's yours now. I bought it ... with your money."

Nigel didn't know if he was happy or mad. "What?"

Red explained, "When I called your landlord in Georgia to break the news to them that you were moving out, they said, 'Oh well,' and that they were planning to put the house on the market when you left anyway."

"Really?"

"Yeah, which was bad timing on their part. I told them the market was still in the shitter, but they didn't believe me. They learned quickly, though, after talking to a few agents. About a month later I called with a low-ball offer of seventy-seven thousand, cash money. They took it."

"Really? Seventy-seven thou?"

"Yeah, but here's the best part. The place didn't appraise, it came in at seventy-one. And that was that."

"You could have told me."

"I did. I wrote you plenty, but until you called me a few days ago, I couldn't understand why my letters were being returned undeliverable."

Nigel said nothing, letting it all sink in.

"Anyway," said Red, "you're a Gulf County taxpayer now. And..."

"And what?" asked Nigel.

"A landlord. You have tenants renting."

Nigel gave Red a look.

"Hell," Red said, "I couldn't let the place just sit there empty. I didn't know you were getting out."

"What kind of tenants are they?"

"So far, so good. A young couple. They both work at the hospital. But..."

"Oh, crap. But what, Red?"

"They're not really happy with your cat, Tom."

Nigel started to laugh. "Tom?"

"Yeah ... I told them the cat was part of the package. It's in the lease, and that it was actually his house, and they should consider themselves as his roommate."

Nigel started to laugh some more.

"It wasn't easy at first. Tom wasn't very happy with them being there, so he shit in their laundry basket a few times the first week or so."

Nigel now had tears in his eyes to match the laughter, but said nothing.

"And the week before Christmas, he brought one of his girlfriends in the house for a little rough sex. It was after midnight, and obviously, the two frisky felines really had a good go of it. The tenants said it sounded like babies being murdered."

Now, Nigel was laughing so hard he could hardly catch his breath. He gasped a couple of times and asked, "And they're staying?"

"Yup. They called to complain. The guy said, 'We can't take it anymore,' but I pointed out that the lease was ironclad, so they better work it out with Tom. I haven't heard from them lately, so I guess they have learned to tolerate each other." Red started to laugh himself and added, "Do you want me to let them out of the lease? Do you want to move back in?"

"Naw. Let them stay. I can stay on the boat or at Candice's."

It was late in the evening on the day after Christmas. The barkeep and his waitresses were working a near-full room. People were drinking away their after-Christmas blues. They were busy, and the carrying on of the customers, coupled with the loud music, made it impossible to hear the backdoor open and the body fall across the boxes then onto the floor. It wasn't until one of the waitresses went to the back storeroom and screamed that the bartender knew there was a problem.

He rushed to the back to find Manchester Lundsford face down on the floor. He turned him over and helped sit him up against the boxes. That's when the bartender and waitress got their first good look at Big Man's face. She let out a short scream and he grimaced as he asked, "Big Man, what happened?"

It hurt to speak clearly, but Manchester grunted with his eyes closed, "Call my doctor and get me a drink, goddammit. Then get me something to eat and a phone."

The bartender took off, and Big Man remained sitting up, resting with his head back against the boxes. When he opened his eyes, the waitress was still standing there staring at him with a hand over her mouth. He shifted his eyes toward her and asked her through his gritted teeth, "What the fuck are you looking at?"

She answered by shaking her head. *Nothing. I'm not looking at anything.*

"Get me a mirror."

She hesitated, and he did his best to yell. "Now, dammit. Get me a damn mirror."

She left him sitting there.

His walk and hitchhike back from the Outer Banks gave him a lot of time to think. *Who had done this to him?* He replayed every moment of the evening in his brain. He tried to remember every word his attacker said, and nothing helped. The only clue he had were the calls from Jimbo's phone. Where had they come from?

There could only be one explanation, but how could that be? The last time he received a call from that phone was after he had sent Jimbo Waters and Willie Bee to Florida to handle Nigel Logan. Something, though, had obviously gone wrong. Terribly wrong. The two have never been heard from again, and when Big Man tried to call Jimbo for a status, the answering voice said, "They're dead. They're all dead. And you're next."

And now, here it is, several months later and he is getting calls from Jimbo's phone. It could only mean one thing.

When she got back with the mirror, Big Man was already sipping his cognac and speaking into the phone. She heard him say, "I don't care if it sounds crazy. Just call someone and find out." After he ended the call and dropped the phone, she handed him the mirror with shaking hands. He snatched it from her and took a long look at himself. Now his own hand was shaking. His right cheek was badly burnt, bruised, and mutilated. The three exit wounds were distinct, the hollow point bullets had done a job on him. He dropped the mirror on the floor and growled as he rubbed his head. He looked up to see the bartender and waitress looking at him. He sent them both a clear message with his eyes and they both vacated the premises.

Big Man was hungry. He tried to eat the sandwich that was brought to him, but it was slow going. It was exhausting to try and eat. Moments later the phone rang.

Soon after, a man carrying a fishing tackle box approached the bar. It was Big Man's doctor. He walked up to the bartender and asked, "Where is he?"

The bartender was about to answer when they both heard a crash and loud bellowing from the back room. They both ran and found Big Man. He had pulled an entire shelf of booze and boxes onto the floor. He was now kicking and slinging boxes and bottles in a rage. The doctor hollered, "Manchester! What is it?"

Big Man turned to face them. Fire and fury shot from his eyes. He was panting and pacing the floor. He picked up an unbroken bottle of cheap brandy and threw it against the wall and yelled, "NIGEL LOGAN!"

###

THANK YOU!

I would like to thank you for purchasing and reading the *Tales from Stool 17* series. If someone shared the book with you, please … thank that person for me. Without a reader, a book is nothing more than a waste of good paper, ink, and effort. You have saved this work from a meaningless existence, and, to that end, I hope you enjoyed it. If so, I would be honored if you would revisit your favorite online retailer and leave an honest review. Honest reviews are so important and serve not only the book, but the development of the author as well.

The next best thing you could do is tell a friend about the *Tales from Stool 17* series. There is nothing better than sharing a story and word-of-mouth endorsements. If you think of someone that might enjoy Nigel's journey, please, spread the word.

And finally, I would love to hear from you. Tell me what you thought about the book. What did you like, or what didn't you like? I'm pretty thick skinned, so don't worry too much about hurting my feelings. Plus, reader comments help me to be a better writer.

Email: mail@kirkjockell.com
Facebook: www.facebook.com/kirk.jockell

www.kirkjockell.com

ABOUT THE AUTHOR

Kirk Jockell claims Port St. Joe as home, but he sleeps most nights in Flowery Branch, Georgia. He keeps a regular job in downtown Atlanta, but is ready to trade it all in for a simpler life on The Forgotten Coast. He is a sailor, avid photographer of boats, and a lover of bourbon, from Jim Beam to any small batch. He loves to fish, throw his cast net for mullet in the surf, and drive his Bronco on the beach. He has recently picked up learning the guitar, but is having a hard time getting past that *one* John Prine song he has learned.

Kirk lives with his lovely wife Joy, a black cat named Stormy, and a head full of dreams and craziness.

Other works by Kirk S. Jockell

Tales from Stool 17; Finding Port St. Joe (book 1)
Tales from Stool 17; Trouble in Tate's Hell (book 2)